Daylight Coming

A Novel By
Sheila Peele-Miller

*Blessings Anita,
enjoy-
Sheila pm*

Daylight Coming

Sheila Peele-Miller

ADIRA BOOKS
P. O. Box 60906
Chicago, Illinois 60660, USA

This book is a work of fiction. Places, events, and situations in this story are purely fictional and any resemblance to actual persons, living or dead, is coincidental.

© 2006 Sheila Peele-Miller
All Rights Reserved.

No part of this book may be reproduced, stored in a retrieval system, or transmitted by any means without the written permission of the author.

ISBN: 0-9771927-3-3 (e-book)
ISBN: 0-9771927-2-5 (paperback)

Library of Congress Control Number: 2006904533

Cover Design: Marion Designs
      www.mariondesigns.com

Book Layout: Shawna A. Grundy
      sag@shawnagrundy.com

Printed in the United States of America

For Benita P. Redmond

Heartbeat props always.

Acknowledgements

Many thanks to everyone who has believed in me and blessed me by sharing in my dreams. For those previously mentioned in **Painted Picture**—you know I'll always love you and will be forever grateful to you. But I also have to give thanks to . . .

The Epiphany Book Club of New Bern, NC /The Evanston Illinois Book Club / Diamonds Book Club in Memphis / The owners and patrons of Mane Concepts (Chicago) and L&E Images (Johnson City, Tennessee) / Dahne Jackson Brown & family / Shonta & LaGala Biggs / Doris Hicks & family / Celeste Lockhart & family / Gloria Hines & family / Jerome Evans & family / Full Circle Books / Jackie Brownlee / Marshall Williams and the Duffest crew / Terrie Ross/ Lydia Michelle Brown/ Latasha Jones/ Edna Redmond-Peele/ Lisa Simms/ Michelle Love/ Wanda & Jessie Brown/ Pat Ford/ Alma Soto/ Curtis & Rhonda Smyles/ Maria Perryman/ Sharon Bryant / Annette Peele / Shelly Collins / the Muhammad, Hartley, Taylor, & Nabih families.

Gevell Wagner, Deanna Michelle Smith, Jacqui Smith, Wanda Hudson, Regina Damon, Nikki Woods, Vickie Simmons, Linda Wilson, Shaye Green, Stormy Steele, Bonita Penn, Sheri Brooks, Dee Brown, Marvin Curtis Reid, Tyren Thomas, Mishawn Purnell O'Neal, Jessica Tilles, and Margie Gosa-Shivers, my author buddies.

Carol Thompson, Pastor Karen Mosby, Nicole Rouse, and Charmaine Parker, my dynamic editors. The staff and management at Ferguson Literary Service, Chicago School Transit, Pierce Elementary School, Brentanno School, Malcolm X College, Tryon Palace & Historic Gardens.

There's more . . . but you'll have to wait until my next book . . . *Lonely Color Blue.*

There is no easy walk to freedom anywhere,
and many of us will have to pass through the valley
of the shadow of death
again and again before we reach
the mountaintop of our desires.

~~Nelson Mandela, 1953

Part One:
In Whom Do We Trust?

1

Standing alone on the marble porch of Holy Hill Baptist Church with its massive white pillars, I leaned against the marble stone, stood up straight, then leaned again, before taking a seat on the steps. My black polyester jumper and white long-sleeved blouse stuck to my skin. And the bacon, eggs, and toast I had eaten for breakfast were long gone, leaving nothing on my stomach except the voice of hunger calling me with angry groans that sounded like I was passing gas. I fanned myself with my Sunday School book as I perspired in the May heat and said good-bye to almost half of the congregation as they rushed past me, anxious to get home to their Sunday dinner. Yet, Mother and a coffee-colored man with a big round face chatted on like food could wait.

Dressed in a navy box-collared dress, she peered up at him with her hand cupped over her eyes as if to prevent the sun from ruining her mocha complexion. No rays touched her, because he was 6'2" with extra wide shoulders. And biceps that formed into king-sized muscles every time he dabbed sweat from his forehead with the pressed white handkerchief he snatched out of the pocket of his starched white shirt.

I was finished with all of the exercises for my next three Sunday School lessons when she finally came over to me. "Let's go," she said. I gathered my things sprawled on the church porch and raced to our white Cadillac, glad to be on our way. She started the car. Instead of putting it into drive, she waited, her eyes on something in the rearview mirror. I turned around to see what she was looking at. A black Grand Prix crept next to us. The big man who had detained her for nearly an hour, rolled his window down and nodded.

He followed us straight to the front door of our two-story house on Madison Street in Evanston, Illinois, a suburb north of Chicago, perched on the banks of Lake Michigan. I was in the pantry getting our best dinner napkins when it dawned on me why he was at our house. And why he constantly stared at me with a gigantic grin while Mother kept talking about my excellent grades and how good I could cook, clean, and do laundry.

Reluctant steps carried me back into the dining room, my black patent leather shoes squeaking on our gleaming hardwood floors. I eased into my usual seat at her right, not letting my eyes move beyond the mashed potatoes, string beans, fresh-baked sweet potatoes, pot roast, and homemade rolls she had gotten up at six in the morning to cook.

Seated in her high-back chair at the end of our mahogany table, adorned with our best silverware and linen place mats, she touched my hand with more affection than I could ever remember experiencing.

"Nicole, aren't you hungry, honey?"

I mumbled, "No, ma'am," uncertain if I heard *honey* come out of her mouth and be addressed to me.

"Jeff, Nicole is very shy and hasn't ever been on a date before," she said to our guest with a smile that could penetrate the heart of the most sinister. He grinned even harder. "Jeff wants to take you on a Sunday drive, Nicole. Isn't that sweet?" It was 1975. I thought Sunday drives had gone out of style along with blue suede shoes.

RudyAnn almost choked. I glanced up at my only sister. She mouthed, "It's about time you got a date."

One-by-one, tears dripped down my cheeks. I tried to brush them away before Mother saw them. She said, "Nicole, I need to see you in the kitchen?" She stood up, smoothing her white-ruffled apron. I dragged behind her. She closed the door and pulled me over to the pantry, out of hearing range.

"I know you're nervous with this being your first date, but Brother Kingston is a man who lives for God. He's in church every Sunday and you know I wouldn't let you go anywhere with anybody I can't trust."

"But Mother . . . " I wouldn't dare call her anything else. "I don't know nothing about this man. Ain't he too old for me?"

"The word is I don't know *anything*. And what have I told you about usin' *ain't*? Jeff is only twenty-five." I thought, *I'm seventeen. RudyAnn is twenty-four. He's closer to her age than mine. And you said she needs to start thinking about marriage.*

"He has an excellent job deliverin' produce. He owns a house right here in Evanston. He grew up in the church and he's a Christian. Which is a lot better than those punks I been seein' you eyeballin'."

Her catching me in the wrong once again wasn't my greatest fear. Being alone with *the big man* squeezed at my empty stomach. More tears I couldn't contain fell from my eyes. *Slap.* Her open hand landed on my cheek with the ferocity of a bee sting. "What is wrong with you? You're actin' like I'm sendin' you off to be executed."

"Mother, I don't wanna go no . . . anywhere with that man," I said, trying to rub the sting away. "Well, too bad. Jeff is out there waitin' for you and I'm not tellin' him you don't wanna go. He's very nice and like I said, he has a good job. And I know his parents."

"But I don't know them. Him, either."

Her back straightened. "Are you gettin' smart with me?"

I said, "No, ma'am," to the pink satin house shoes she had recently bought to match her new silk robe.

"I didn't think so." She snatched me by my arm and pushed me back into the dining room.

Jeff stood up. "Is everything all right?"

"Nicole is just a little nervous but I told her not to worry, because the Lord has sent her a blessing here today. Amen. Yes, he has!"

RudyAnn stood on our front porch straightening the red skintight dress she claimed she wore to morning service at a friend's church. I knew better and I'm sure Mother did, too. Five feet nine, the tallest of us, she had to have weighed at least one hundred-eighty pounds, most of it in her backside. A shade lighter than Mother and me with silky black tresses that hung down her back, she was so tickled she kept putting her hand over her mouth to stifle her laughter. "Bye-bye, Nicole. Have fun."

My shoes felt like they were weighted down with concrete. The pain in my stomach was even worse. Mother said, as she escorted us to Jeff's car, "If it was anybody else, she would have to be home at eight o'clock on a Sunday, but considerin', it's you . . . " She laid her hand on his arm. "She can stay out until ten. But I want her home at ten prompt. She has school tomorrow."

"Yes, ma'am," he said, opening the door of his Grand Prix. He waited patiently for me to get inside. I dropped into the seat, my head hung down to my chest.

Mother stuck her head in the window he had left rolled down. "Quit actin' like you're two years old and be thankful that *somebody* wanna take you somewhere. You hear me?"

"Yes, ma'am," I replied, fighting tears I sensed at that point might get me knocked out cold.

Jeff hopped into his car. "We'll see you later." He started driving, then asked, "So, Nicole, what you wanna do?" I kept my eyes on the familiar houses on each tree-lined street he drove down. "I gotta run by my place to change clothes. That all right with you?"

He was parked in front of his white A-framed house before I could respond. Not that I was capable of doing so. "You wanna come in?"

He got out and opened my door. I couldn't lift my legs or move my feet. He grabbed my hand and pulled me to the front door. The smell of old grease from something fried lingered on the porch along with the detectable stench of a

DAYLIGHT COMING

rotting onion. He peeped inside his mailbox, then snapped it shut. Considering all of the bragging he had done, "I got this and I own that," I thought I was going to be walking into a place fit for a king, not a two-bedroom shanty with dirty yellow walls and a rickety kitchen table surrounded by three lopsided chairs.

"Have a seat," he said, pointing at his dingy beige sofa. I preferred to stand.

Jeff went into his bedroom. He returned wearing a fresh white shirt. "So, Nicole, what do you like to do?" I looked at my feet. "Well, let's go for that ride I promised you."

I dashed out the door. He said, "Slow down," hurrying behind me. He got in on his side of the car, not being as courteous as he was in front of Mother. He turned the radio on. And switched from station-to-station the entire time he drove around Chicago pointing out historical landmarks, like I had never been there before, while I hugged the car door like it was my Lord and savior.

Curfew was met with him walking me up the steps. Mother was waiting on the front porch. "Well, how did things go?"

Jeff nodded. "Perfect. Perfect." He grinned so hard I thought his face was going to crack. I hurried inside even more anxious to get away from him. I wanted to jump into the shower to rid myself of how dirty I felt being in his presence.

Our other so-called dates soon began and ended the same way. Dinner at our house, where he spent most of his time flattering Mother. "Mother Borge, I consider myself so blessed to have met you. Wow, that dress looks great on you. So, how was your day today? Nicole, can I help you with the dishes?" A drive over the city, then back to his house where I dreaded being anywhere near him just like I despised the greasy foods he was always smacking on. And the old movies he loved to watch on his floor-model television, the only thing he owned other than his car and wardrobe that wasn't a century old.

All the while I was with him, I refused to talk unless it was necessary. I yawned constantly and picked over my food, which he always finished. I hoped I would bore him into wanting to date somebody else. Still he insisted upon acting like we were a couple, opening doors for me and walking next to me with his hand in the small of my back. Every time he touched me, I would cringe and try to ease out of his reach.

I was already one of the top seniors in my class and knew I was graduating with honors. But I'd do extra work so I'd have an excuse not to spend time with him. Begging Mother not to force me never worked. She insisted, "Jeff is a good man, Nicole, and you're goin'. I'm not takin' care of you for the rest of your life."

I wanted to throw up every time I thought about him—his big hands; the Dentyne gum he always chewed; the way he always said, "I wanna marry you, Nicole."

Every time the words exited his mouth, I reminded him, "I'm goin' to college to become an architect."

Still he dropped in after five dates and approximately two minutes after Mother had gotten home from her job as assistant to the Director of Community Relations at Northwestern University. Dinner was ready: baked salmon, yellow rice, fresh garden salad, crescent rolls, and an ice-cold pitcher of Lipton tea was in the refrigerator, just like she demanded.

The second the bell chimed throughout the house, something told me, *It's him again.*

Mother answered the door. "Jeff, what a pleasant surprise. Come in."

"I hope I ain't disturbin' you."

"Not at all." Just before he arrived, she had said, "I'm so tired that all I wanna do is lay down and take a nap. So make sure nobody bothers me." "So what do we owe this visit?" she asked.

"Can I talk to you, please? In private."

She stuck her head in the kitchen door. "Nicole, make Jeff a plate, then run my bath. Wake your sister up, too, so she can eat while the food is still hot."

"Yes ma'am," I said, anxious to know what he had to tell her *in private.*

Minutes later, with his belly stuffed and her tub full of hot water with a drop of lavender oil for her exhausted body, she yelled, "Nicole! Nicole, I need to see you downstairs."

DAYLIGHT COMING

I took my time, already dreading whatever it was she was going to make me do. Jeff met me at the bottom of the steps with a red box in his right hand. He reached for me with his left. I shrugged away. Mother cleared her throat.

"Nicole," he said, dropping on one knee. "Will you marry me?"

I flew back up the steps. Mother hurried behind me. "What is wrong with you?" she said, slamming my bedroom door.

I cried into my sunshine-yellow bedspread. "I don't wanna marry him."

"Well, it's not like anybody's beatin' down the door to get to you."

"But I don't wanna get married, Mother. I wanna go to college."

"With what money?"

I sat up, wiping my face. "I'll work, but please, Mother, don't make me marry him. Please!"

"I don't have to, because you're doin' it anyway. Like I said, I'm not takin' care of you for the rest of your life."

Four months out of high school, on a day much warmer than we anticipated for October, I stood face-to-face with Jeff in the sanctuary of our church. It was decorated with silver bells, white roses, and violets, Mother's favorite flowers. I repeated the words Pastor Dorthea, her best friend of thirty years, said and felt myself sinking deeper into the lies I was agreeing to. Like to love and to honor. For better or for worse. I could barely stomach being near Jeff, him holding my hand, or slipping his cheap gold wedding band on my finger.

He pulled me into his arms after we made our oral commitments and jammed his tongue in my mouth. When he was done slobbering, I turned to Mother, trying to wipe away my need to vomit. She had a beam on her face that should have lit up the city.

I thought, *She won't be able to tell me what to do anymore. I can wear heels, miniskirts, and get a haircut, a pedicure and manicure, whenever I like. And come and go as I please.* I felt a twinge of happiness that lasted thirty seconds tops. She was ecstatic during the entire ceremony and even more at the reception. Jesus was given loads of praises for blessing me with a good man, who held on to me most of the evening as if I was going to escape.

Whenever I could slip away from him, I went to the bathroom and sat in a stall, trying to figure out how I could get out of what I'd been dreading ever since he and Mother set a date for our wedding. He met me coming out the door, after my eighth disappearance. "Come on, let's tell everybody goodnight. I'm ready to go home. Ain't you?"

With the car loaded with plates of leftover food and our gifts thrown in the trunk and all over the backseat of his Grand Prix, he raced to his house from the church hall. He jumped out of the car and ran over to my side. He pulled me into his arms, smacked a kiss on my lips, then carried me straight to the bedroom. He dropped me on the bed and unzipped his tuxedo pants.

Jeff's eager hand went up my gown and snatched my panties off. No sooner than they were thrown across the room, he slapped my legs open and started forcing his humongous member inside me. I screamed for mercy. He threw his hand over my mouth and continued prying me open with his merciless friend, humping hard and fast until I thought I was going to be crippled from the worst pain I ever experienced. And he got an orgasm that almost threw his back and my back out at the same time.

He rolled off me when he was done. "Whew, you was tight."

I felt like slime lying on his filthy sheets and hurt so bad I prayed to die. But even death seemed too good for me so I wrapped my arms around myself and sobbed from deep within my soul. He got up from the bed, his limp privates hanging out of his pants. He staggered into the kitchen.

He came back into the room, carrying a bottle of Asti Spumante and two filled martini glasses on a wooden tray. He placed the tray on the nightstand, then sat next to me. "Wanna drink?" I held myself tighter, sniffling and trembling to the point whereas the bed was shaking. He swallowed his glass of wine. "You sure you don't want none? It sho is good."

He gulped down the one he was trying to coerce me into drinking, then rubbed my hip. I pushed his hand off. He pulled me to the center of the bed by my leg. He flipped me on my stomach. I tried desperately to get away from him, but he planted all of his weight on my back, disregarding me begging him to, "Please, stop." Once he was inside me again, he pounded my insides even harder and moaned as he reached his point of pleasure. "Oh, I been wantin' you for a long time. O-o-w you feel good."

As if trying to split me in two during our first session wasn't punishment enough, for three days after Jeff was done exercising his marital rights, I could barely walk, use the bathroom, or sit down. I slept on the couch in my clothes and only went into the bathroom when he wasn't home. But on day four, I heard the putt-putt of his delivery truck as I was throwing out a bucket of mop water in the back. I heard the front door slam.

"Nicole! Nicole, where you at?"

I went into the yard. I turned on the hose and sprayed water into the bucket. He stuck his head out the backdoor. "What'cha doin'?" I splashed the water around, poured it out, then ran more inside. "Come on in. I need to talk to ya."

"I'll be done in a minute."

"Well, I gotta get back to work."

I threw the water out and took tiny steps toward him. He grabbed my hand. I snatched it back. "What?"

"You might as well get used to this."

Jeff wrapped his arm around my waist and hauled me into the bedroom, pleading, "No!" all the way. Once again, he dropped me on the bed. I tried to roll off. But he locked his fingers around my wrists. He took off his boots, pants, and boxers with his free hand.

"You might as well quit fightin' me," he said, positioning his best friend between my legs. After he was done ejaculating like an animal, he bragged, "Now that shoulda made me a son."

2

The most communicating Mother and I ever did was after I married. She called me every day with tidbits on cleaning and cooking as if she did any of that. It was my job from the moment I was old enough to pick up a broom and hold a pot in my hand. I pretended I was interested in what she had to say, while thinking if she had any words to spare, they should have been said on or before my wedding night.

She had no idea I wasn't a virgin and could have told me something. She or RudyAnn. Just like neither told me anything about my period coming. My health teacher, Mrs. Wyndale, had discussed it, but said, "You girls should expect your menstruation to start probably around the age of thirteen."

Mine came when I was twelve. So I was still unprepared. And so ashamed the first time I saw my white cotton underwear stained, I threw them away when I got home from school, because Mother was always insisting, "Nicole, you don't know how to take care of anything. You're so destructive."

My first one was very mild. But with the second one, I bled like I was hemorrhaging. I worried all day if it was obvious, especially during gym class. I was sitting on the toilet after a vigorous forty-five minutes of exercising, waiting for Anna Torry to finish her business, when my makeshift pad fell out of my hand. Although I snatched it up in a hurry, I was still a petrified soul, because not only was she the biggest girl in our sixth-grade class, she also had the biggest mouth.

She threw a box over the stall door. "Girl, that thang you usin' is old. Don't nobody use rags no mo." I sat staring at the Kotex pad, trying to figure out how to secure it so it wouldn't fall out of my panties. "Just use yo safety pins and pin it to your drawers."

But who would have thought that one minor incident would have led us to becoming best friends and that as a married woman, I would need her to help a sista out all over again?

After standing in line at the main branch of the Evanston Post Office for nearly fifteen minutes, I slapped a stamp on an envelope and dropped the check to Jeff's mother in the slot. She had insisted, "Can you bring it to me or put it in the mail 'cause I can't get nobody to take me nowhere."

For the third time in three months, she had called with a need for immediate cash for something wrong with their run-down two-flat on the Westside of Chicago. "I hate to keep buggin' you but we got a bad backup over here. We need five hundred dollars to get our basement rodded out," she had said. Previously, she had needed three hundred to replace the front door somebody's child had kicked in and seven hundred to have the roof patched.

Although her pleas were always to Jeff, "Jeffy" as she called him, it was always me forking over the money. Not because we were close or had the funds to give away but because I knew she was in need, taking care of everybody and their kids. Also just because it's my nature. Too darn compassionate and *no* is something I seldom say. I thought, *This is the last time. These are Jeff's folks. So the next time she wants money, I'm just gonna have to . . .*

I thought myself into the path of a black BMW. The driver blasted the horn as I stepped off the curb. The person raced into park. The door flew open.

"Nicole. Nicole Borge!" the woman yelled. I stared at the unfamiliar face with a rich pecan complexion as she exited her ride. "Girl, how the hell are you?" She looked like she should have been on a runway in her pink shantung heels and matching suit. But not by her speech.

DAYLIGHT COMING

"I'm okay." *But who the heck are you?*

"Girl, are you going to keep standing there looking at me like I'm crazy or are you going to give me a hug like we haven't seen each other in years?" She pulled me into her arms and for some reason I wanted to hold on to her. She let me go. "I know you can't be still trying to figure out who I am." She threw her hand over her heart. "It's Anna."

"Anna Torry?"

"Duh-h-h!" We had gone to school together from the fourth grade through our senior year and she had been my best friend, but didn't look like herself.

"Girl, where in the world have you been?"

"Right here in Evanston." The surprised look on my face made her elaborate. "After graduation, I hung around here for a minute. Got tired of doing nothing, then went to college in Champaign. I lived there for six years. Got married and moved to Kansas City. Been there ever since."

"So how long have you been back in Evanston?"

"A year and a half."

"Why didn't you . . ."

"Call you? I did. But the minute I said who I was, Mrs. Borge said, 'Nicole is a married woman and don't have time for so-called friends, past or present.' You and I haven't seen each other since high school graduation. Almost twenty years have gone by and she was still being her ornery self, so I assumed I would see you when I see you!"

Mother never cared for anyone I liked but treated Anna the worst, because she came from a family of prostitutes and never had an inkling who her father was. I was happy to see my old friend, just as I was when we were kids, and I had to sneak to spend time with her.

I listened to her talk, still fascinated by what she had to say. "Nicole, you won't believe how blessed my life has been since I moved out of mama's house, paid my way through college, and quit my nasty habits of too many men and much more weed." I desired her kind of peace.

Yet, I found it hard to believe that cigarette and weed smoking, butt kicking, cursing, which she still did like a sailor,

Anna, was wearing a business suit, owned three condos on the lake, and a string of apartment buildings and houses. Her chubbiness had evolved into a size nine, perfect for her 5'9" frame. All of her acne was gone. Her front teeth had been repaired and straightened. She was also happily married.

"Ver-doe-lachk?" I asked when she told me her last name. "You married a white guy?" I considered how pro-black she had been.

She laughed. "He's not white. He's German. That's different."

"How?"

"Because I said so."

She treated me to lunch at Sammy's, the most popular African-American restaurant in Evanston. We reminisced over the days gone by as we enjoyed our steaks. I clung to every word she said, admiring how far she had come. The one who people thought would be the most likely *not* to succeed was a real estate developer and a manager at Third Trust Bank.

Just like she knew about the streets when we were kids and how to make a quick buck, Anna knew even more about becoming your own boss, even somewhat convincing me, "Property management isn't a hard business to get into, Nicole. You just have to be willing to invest your money. Pay close attention to what you're doing and most of all, listen to me."

"I don't know, Anna. The only kind of work I've ever done has been in a factory."

"And?"

"But you work at a bank. You went to college. The only place I went was from Mother's to marriage."

"It doesn't matter. Because when I bought my first piece of property, I did it on a whim. To be honest, I really didn't know what I was doing, because I went from being a liberal arts major to an accounting major, then enrolled in a dental program, then went back to accounting."

"But you still went to college."

"Would you just listen? I used to couldn't get you to say five words." We laughed. "The first piece of property I bought was in Kansas City. It was a piece of junk. Half of it was burned up; the other half was water damaged like you wouldn't believe. I found some guys to work for me for cheap, drew out what I wanted them to do, and gave them a deadline."

"But— "

"Nicole, you'll never know what you can do if you don't try."

I sipped down half of my iced raspberry tea, then twirled the straw in the glass. "My pension is the only money I have and when my unemployment runs out . . . "

After working for nineteen years at General Electric, they announced they were closing and moving to Alabama. I had been trying for three months to find another job as a distribution clerk but had had no luck.

"Do I hear doubt in your voice? Do you honestly think I would lead you down a path to bankruptcy?" I smiled at her sense of humor. "All jokes aside. I know this is a gamble for you, but if you play your cards right . . . I know people. I know the market and I know I can coach you through this."

"Takin' my money. Buyin' a junk house. Fixin' it up. Then sellin' it."

"People do it every day."

"Maybe, but—"

"Come on, Nicole, get with the program. It's 1995, the year of the woman!"

After forty hours or more of thinking about what she had said, "You can do this, Nicole, people are going to always need a place to stay," I met her at her office in downtown Evanston. As I entered her suite, Anna finished a call and hung up. "Have a seat." She pointed at a burgundy leather chair ornamented with brass studs. Several paintings depicting African-American life were on the walls, and frosted glass vases sat on marble stands. She tossed a cup in the leather basket next to her cherrywood desk.

"You want some coffee? Tea? A pop?"

"No, thank you."

"I just got off the telephone with my friend. You know, the one I told you about who does the seminars. He says he still has room for a few more people."

"People for what?'

"The two-day class on property management at the Palmer House in Chicago. I've only been telling you about it for two days."

"When is it?"

"Next week. And there's a conference on managing a business coming up at the O'Hare Hilton."

"Anna, I—"

"Don't tell me you can't do it, Nicole, because I know you can. Remember how I used to get stuck doing biology in ninth grade?" I nodded because science was not her best subject. "And you used to tutor me during lunch and you would always say, 'You can do this, Anna. Just focus and listen to me.' "

I smiled. "Yeah."

"Well, now the tables have turned. You *can* do this, Nicole."

A part of me wanted to believe her, but a part of me also worried, *if I do this and things happen for me as she believes, what am I gonna do about Jeff? I already can't put my purse down around him.*

"Uh-um." Anna cleared her throat. "Could you pay attention?"

"I'm listenin'."

"What did I say?" I shrugged my shoulders. "We have to do something about your appearance."

"Excuse me."

"Honey, you have to look the part."

"Meanin'?"

"Just meet me at Marshall Field's at the Old Orchard Mall at five o'clock. I have three afternoon appointments. So if I'm a little late, wait for me." She laughed, picking up the telephone to make another call. "I can't believe you're still dressing like you did in high school."

I glanced down at my navy jumper, white turtleneck, tights, and navy loafers. *What's wrong with the way I dress*

Anna waltzed into Field's department store like she owned the place. I received a few, "Can I help you please?" But the salespeople practically ran up to her, eager to assist the lady wearing a white embroidered suit with the matching pumps and pearl necklace. A long trip from blue jeans with holes in the knees, lopsided dresses, run-over shoes and socks flopping around her feet.

From aisle to aisle, she pointed at several items she felt I should have. Just looking at the price of a Coach briefcase that she said, "This is you, Nicole. Sleek, sexy and sophisticated," made me hyperventilate. I couldn't fathom lugging around anything so expensive when a K-mart backpack would have been fine.

Yet Anna insisted, "It's not like you don't deserve it. So live a little."

Her living-a-little consisted of brand name everything: a BMW, Jaguar, and Toyota 4-Runner. She loved steak, caviar, and French food. I was a Burger King and Wendy's woman. It tickled her to see how conservative I was.

I argued with her about buying a fifteen-dollar box of Uniball pens when the Bic brand was twelve for eighty-nine cents. "It won't hurt you to start doing something for yourself," she said. "Hell. You worked hard for every dime you have, so why not enjoy some of it? I'm not saying spend it down to the last penny, but treat yourself sometimes, Nicole. Because if you don't and you die tomorrow, who do you think will be enjoying it? Big time!"

3

Anna parked her 4-Runner in the driveway of a red brick house in the heart of a block where young black men, sporting down coats and sagging jeans, slipped their hands in slowly moving cars, then stuffed their pockets with crumpled dollars. It was the worst neighborhood on the southeast end of Evanston.

She said, "This baby is gonna make you a nice piece of cash. It's a four-bedroom ranch. The family who owns this place. They have f—, let's just say they have messed it up. Big time! It's also getting ready to go into foreclosure. But look around you. Gangbangers and dope dealers own these streets. But, trust me. There's four or five more houses for sale over here and if families who care about their property start buying these places, this riff-raff will be outta here and home values are guaranteed to go up."

I nodded. *This place looks like it ought to be condemned. The shutters are broken. The bay window is cracked. The garage door is tilted. She must think I'm crazy.*

Anna rolled her window down. She inhaled the November air. "I know these people. Nice couple, but he's out of work. She had to take a cut in her salary and they're eager to sell. Remember what I told you to say."

We rehearsed my approach twice, her quizzing me like a college professor. I really didn't want to gamble on such a raggedy place. But the adrenaline that flowed through my body as I convinced the couple why they should, "Sell your house to me. I pay top dollar. And if you need help relocatin',

DAYLIGHT COMING

I know plenty people who can assist you with that as well," was like none I had ever experienced.

Approximately two months after my first attempt to purchase property, the keys were in my anxious hands. Anna had introduced me to a friend of her family, Mark Knowles, a week before closing. She said, "He helped my uncle redo my auntie's kitchen and it is gorgeous. You just have to see it."

Impressed with the walnut cabinets and granite countertops, I agreed to hire him. Standing at the front door of my house, after he called me to let me know it was ready, I smiled to myself. *I did it. I really did it!* I kicked the snow off my boots, dying to see the oak kitchen cabinets I had bought on sale at Menard's. My mouth flew open and I threw my hand across my chest as I stared at them, hung according to plan—but at an angle.

I went into the dining room next. Mark was supposed to have removed the flowered wallpaper and painted the walls light rose. Every flower, leaf, and rip was visible through the thin layer of latex he had slapped on and dripped on the oak floor, which was supposed to have been sanded, buffed, and polished. They were polished only with a thick coat of a muddy-looking varnish that stuck to the soles of my boots.

I pried myself out of the goo and marched to the main bath. The new toilet was installed as agreed, but the porcelain fixture was just as lopsided as the kitchen cabinets. And the vanity was just as crooked as the toilet. I called Mark, who was out back under the hood of his truck. He dropped his screwdriver back into his bucket of tools and took his time coming inside, not bothering to kick any of the snow off his shoes.

"What's up?" I led him from room to room, pointing out every wrong thing I could find. "You get what you pay for, Sista. Because I could make a helluva lot more than what you payin' me in the white neighborhoods. And they would appreciate my hard work."

"That's still no excuse for all of these defects. I can't sell nobody something I wouldn't live in."

"So what you sayin'?"

"That you won't get the rest of your money until you fix everything I pointed out. We had a deal."

"And I did my part."

"No, you half-assed everything. None of the stuff you were supposed to do is done right and I ain't payin' you another dime until you take care of it!"

I walked away, leaving him standing in the master bedroom. He followed me into the kitchen. "Like I said, unless you fix this stuff, you won't get nothin' else from me."

Six-four and maybe a good two hundred-fifty pounds, Mark leaned over in my face, something Jeff often did when we argued. "You can keep the rest of your money, bitch. And while you at it, buy your bony ass something to eat." He brushed past me, knocking a can of white paint on the floor. It sloshed all over the lower cabinets and splattered the legs of my new black wool slacks.

I ran behind him. "You come back here." But he left me steaming. I cleaned up as much of the mess as I could with some paper towels and rags he had left behind. I then headed to the convenience store blocks away from the house to call Anna.

The minute I said her name, she said, "Nicole, what the hell did you curse Mark out for? Need I remind you that he did give you a fair price and—"

"Before you jump on my case, you need to come over here and see this for yourself."

I returned to the house and paced all over, finding more defects: windows painted and stuck, doors hung uneven, among other things, as I waited for her. She knocked on the door and walked in, immaculate as usual in a chocolate wool pantsuit. "Show me everything you have a problem with."

She grabbed a notepad out of her leather purse and jotted down what I wasn't satisfied with and things I had missed. None of the closets were painted nor had Mark refinished any

DAYLIGHT COMING

of the floors in them. He had also replaced all of the broken windowpanes throughout the house with plexiglass.

"I can't believe he thinks you ought to pay him for this shit. It's bad enough I recommended his sorry ass. Come on, because he's not getting away with this," she said.

I hurried out the door behind her. She drove around until we found him coming out of a liquor store near the Evanston-Chicago border. She threw her 4-Runner into park, jumped out of it and straight into his face. She snapped on him so tough he begged me for the keys. But once a bridge is burned with me, I'm very skeptical about allowing it to be crossed again.

Although I no longer trusted him, I agreed, mainly because of Anna's insistence, to let him finish the job. He promised he would show up the following morning at eight sharp. I barely slept that night and left home at seven just to see if he was going to honor his word. I drove over to McDonalds for a cup of coffee, then rushed to my house. The trip took less than twenty minutes.

Mark was not there. I decided to take advantage of it to see if I could find anything else he needed to take care of. I unlocked the door to another shocker. What was left of the materials I had bought was gone. The Formica kitchen countertop was bashed in several places and the cabinets were sliced, with chunks of the oak facing missing. Eyeing the damage, I felt Mark's guilt down in my bones. The police were on another case by the time he showed up.

"Sorry I'm late but I went to a friend's bachelor party last night and I overslept." I told him what had happened.

"So I guess I'm finished here until you find some more money for more material. Or get yourself another contractor."

I went home, fell on my bed, and stared at the ceiling until Anna buzzing the doorbell nonstop forced me up from my place of misery. I opened the door hurt and angry. "So what happened with Mark?" she asked.

I thought, *As if you don't know.* Still I told her the story, trying to refrain from snapping on her.

"Nicole, I am so sorry he screwed you like he did. I had no idea he was so lowdown. But I'll pay whatever it costs to have it done the right way. It's the least I can do."

I cut my eyes at her like, *yeah right.* I started to close the door. She braced her hand against it and stepped inside. "I know damn well you don't think I had something to do with the shit Mark pulled?"

I folded my arms across my chest. "How dare you when all I've tried to do is help you make money! Why would I do you like that when I can make more money in six months than you and Jeff can make in a year? Put together. Besides, if that's the kind of person you think I am, I can take my friendship elsewhere!" She marched back out the door and down the steps.

"Anna, I'm sorry."

"I didn't hear you. Say it again," she said with her back to me.

"I apologize. I'm sorry. "

She walked back over to me and grabbed me with a big hug. "You better be. Because I was about to invite your bony ass outside."

I laughed. "I'm bigger than you are."

She pinched my arm. "Since when?"

I thought about her proposal to foot the rest of the bill for what needed to be done to my purchase as I said good-bye to her. It didn't feel right accepting her offer. So I told her, "I'll think about it," just to get her away from the house before Jeff came home.

It just didn't sit right with me. But that was minute compared to having to spend another evening listening to him whine about his day as a truck driver for Locking Produce, watching him swallow his dinner in gulps, then flop on the couch for a nap. Snoring loud enough to crack the walls and farting louder. I went back inside to make myself a cup of green tea. I hoped it would soothe my anxiety before he walked though the door. He stormed inside the house a second after I took my first sip.

DAYLIGHT COMING

"NICOLE!" His lunchbox whirled through the air, hit the back door, then crashed on the kitchen floor. I dropped the cup on the table and ran into the living room.

"Jeff, what the—"

"What the hell is this?"

He waved the Truth-In-Lending statement I had signed three months prior in the air. It had been in the glove compartment of my car, which I was positive was locked. He rushed over to me, put the papers before my eyes, then snatched them back. "How in the hell are you gonna buy a damn house without my permission?"

"I don't need your damn permission," I said, trying to sound confident. "Now gimme my papers."

He held them over my head. "Where the hell did you get that kinda money?" He thought about it, then said, "How in the hell are you gonna take our savings—"

"Our savings? There ain't never been no *ours* around here."

"How can you be so irresponsible? We damn near in the hole. How much did you get anyway?"

"Maybe you're in the hole! But I ain't. Because I don't spend all of my money on ass. I save mine when I can keep your hands off of it!"

"Really? Well, we'll just see about that."

Jeff marched to his bedroom. We had been married for less than six months when I decided I'd never sleep in the same room with him again. I rushed behind him, trying to reach the telephone before him. He pushed me aside and hit speed dial and the loudspeaker almost at the same time.

"Hello," Mother said.

"Mother Borge, you won't believe what Nicole did." He whined the rest of the story while looking over the papers, although they didn't prove a thing since it was only an estimate of proposed costs.

"Nicole, this is the most idiotic thing you have ever done," Mother said. "Why on earth would you even consider buyin' a house? Like you already don't have one! And without consultin' your husband! Sometimes I don't think you have the sense the good Lord gave you."

Jeff nodded, his balding head in dire need of a haircut. "I tell her that all the time. But she don't listen to me. She never has. And another thing, why would she buy a house unless she plannin' on leavin' me? The least she coulda done was tell me she didn't wanna be married no more and not leave me here stuck with all this debt we in."

Jeff and I were married three months when I got my first job. And Mother had made it very clear to both of us, "He's head of the household, Nicole, and responsible for all of your finances."

I just couldn't foresee her meaning every time I needed or wanted anything outside of what he said I could have, we couldn't afford it. Yet, if it was something he wanted, Jeff would swear, "I wouldn't buy it if I didn't need it." Like vibrant designer suits, shoes, jewelry. And a 1976 Mercury Marquis right off the assembly line, while the '69 Chevy Nova he bought me from a junkyard owner had more rust than body, leaked oil and backfired all the way to work.

After he bought me the Nova, I did get an increase in my allowance. It went from twenty-five dollars every other week to thirty to cover my gas costs, which he would sometimes take back if I didn't hide it or hurry up and spend it. He would confiscate the rest of my paycheck and say, "It goes towards your share of the bills, Nicole." Which we didn't have that many. "And our savings." Which I never saw or had access to.

He did the same thing with the money and checks dropped in our wishing well during our wedding reception. He stood over me watching as I opened each card and filled out the thank-you notes. Once I was done and he was certain I hadn't stuffed a twenty in my bra, he said, "Let me get that so I can deposit it in our account." I put all one-thousand four-hundred dollars in his hands and never saw *our* money again.

After two years of him meeting me every payday at noon, taking my check right out of my hand, I decided *not anymore*. I believe if we hadn't been standing in the parking lot of GE, he would have beaten it out of me.

I folded my arms defiantly across my chest. "I work too hard for my money to keep givin' it to you to waste. Because we ain't got no decent furniture. I'm wearin' the cheapest stuff money can buy. And we ain't got that many bills, which you can't never seem to pay on time. So where's my money goin', other than on your back? You wanna walk around lookin' like a pimp, then use your check to buy your damn clothes. And pay your damn hookers."

He stopped contributing anything to the household. At all. But he was still startled by my all-new boldness, justified by his refusal to honor the vows we took. For the umpteenth time, I had demanded to know, "Jeff, who is . . . " This time it was *Kathy K* scribbled on a McDonald's receipt he left on his dresser.

"I don't know."

"Then why is her name and number with your things?"

"Nicole, don't start with me, because I don't know who Kathy or whatever you say her name is." He mumbled, "Every day I have to go through this shit with you."

"Excuse me."

"You heard me. I'm tired of you bein' so jealous."

Dressed in a pair of bright-blue pants with a blue multi-colored shirt and bright-blue patent-leather shoes some desperate salesman talked him into buying, I said, "You ain't worth my jealousy lookin' like a damn peacock. I just don't like the way you're always throwin' your whores in my face. The least you could do is pretend you have a wife and have your affairs in another town. But you gotta do it right here in Evanston where everybody knows who we are and everywhere I go somebody is laughin' at me."

"That's *your* insecurity."

I thought, *This black bastard*. But before giving him the pleasure of continuing to think he meant anything to me, I snatched his underwear out of the clothesbasket, threw them in his drawer, and slammed it shut.

"Boo-hoo, look at the baby. Gonna run and lock herself up in the bathroom because she can't stand the truth. She's jealous of me and she knows it."

I charged at him. "I ain't jealous of your black ass!"

"Quit lyin'," he said, poking me between my eyes. I kicked his shin. He back-handed me. I flew across the bed. I soared from off the backside like a rocket. He held me at bay with his hand wrapped around my neck.

"Little Nicole wants to fi-ight. Nicole wants to fi-ight. She don't know how to act, because she's too busy actin' like a baby."

He threw his gigantic hand over my face, pushing me away from him. I stumbled back until I landed between the bed and the nightstand. He rushed into the bathroom, laughing like it was hilarious. I dashed behind him. He slammed the door in my face. I kicked it like I was trying to tear it down. He snatched it open, grabbed my arm, and tossed me outside like I was the garbage.

I took my spare keys out of the mailbox and jumped into my Nova, bent on leaving him for good. After an hour of riding around with nowhere to go, I stopped at the neighborhood convenience store to buy Band-aids for my wounds.

Mother, in her red plaid pajamas and pink hair-rollers, was standing on the porch when I returned home. Before I could get out of my car, she said, "Nicole, you should be ashamed of yourself out here runnin' the streets this time of the night." I cut my eyes at Jeff. He smirked.

"Mother Borge, I knew Nicole was mad at me, because I was goin' to a gospel concert on the Westside. I even asked her to go with me. But I didn't know she was gonna sneak out of the house after I left."

"Jeff, you need to quit lyin' because—"

"Shut up!" Mother snapped.

"But, Mother, look at my—"

"Didn't I tell you to shut your mouth? Now Jeff, go ahead and finish tellin' me what happened."

"Mother Borge, she didn't have a scratch on her when I last saw her. I swear to you I ain't laid a hand on Nicole."

DAYLIGHT COMING

Mother grabbed my cheeks with her nails. "There's no tellin' how she got those things."

"But Mother, he . . . "

She squeezed them tighter. "Apologize to Jeff for worryin' him like you do." I stared at her as if she was going to take back her demand. "Apologize. Now!"

I mumbled, "I'm sorry."

"Say it louder. I'm sure you weren't talkin' this low when you were out in the streets doin' who knows what."

Jeff added, "With who knows who."

"I apologize, Jeff." She let me go and I left them standing on our front lawn talking about how I was going to hell if I didn't change my wicked ways.

4

I knew Jeff wasn't going to return my Truth-In-Lending-Statement so I decided to let him keep it. I really didn't have a choice. An ache of what he could do with my information, if he started snooping around, set in my temples. It also made my stomach queasy, although Anna had said, "Nicole, you don't need his permission to invest a dime of your money. It's your severance pay and those are your bonds. You gave GE almost twenty years of your life. So it's your hard-earned money to do whatever you want with it." She also had added, "But you do need for your husband to sign off on it waiving his rights to your purchase."

I thought about her advice even more as I drove downtown Evanston to check out a couple of the boutiques she frequented. The nervous ache in the pit of my stomach seemed to become even more intense, but I continued circling blocks looking for a place to park. I cruised around until I saw a white Benz pulling out of a spot near the Holiday Inn. As I got out of my car, the doorman, an older gentleman, toffee with a close cut, broad shoulders, and a heartwarming smile, made me stop and stare.

He nodded. "Good evenin'," then went to assist two senior citizens getting out of a Yellow Cab.

Two hours later, after spending money like I was born into it, I returned to my car with more items than I intended to buy. He caught me gazing again. Where I knew him from and how handsome he was stayed with me the entire time I was trying on summer dresses and slipping my feet into sandals with names I couldn't pronounce. And before running into Anna at the post office, wouldn't have dreamed of buying.

Not that I was thinking about us in any kind of a relationship. He came over to help me with my bags.

"Good evenin' again," he said with that same knock-out smile.

"Do I know you?"

"You might. What's your name?"

"Nicole Kingston. Well, it was Borge, before I got married." I surprised myself by how relaxed I was with him since I'm never that informal with anybody.

"You Leola and Walter's daughter?"

"Yes," I said, surprised he knew them.

"So how is Leola?"

I smiled. "She's still Leola."

Isaac Mackey had been clocked out for ten minutes. He was also three weeks released from prison, sent there for manslaughter. I vaguely remembered the story, but knew it had something to do with him and another man's wife. I also remembered he had once been a skilled craftsman and his eight-room bachelor pad had been the envy of his block. Following his arrest, somebody burned it to the ground.

The arson made the front page of the *Evanston Review* along with a big photograph of him the police had taken holding up the sign with his jail numbers. The stern look on his face was what I recalled most, because it was the same look my deceased father had in his and Mother's wedding picture.

He said, "It's good to see you all grown up and takin' good care of yourself, Nicole."

"I try."

"So, what do you do for a livin'?"

"I was workin' at GE out in Northbrook. But they relocated to Alabama. Now I'm lookin' for a job."

"That's too bad."

"Yeah. But it'll be okay, I guess."

"Why do you say that?"

"Because I just bought this house and I'm in the process of havin' it rehabbed to sell." I sighed. "If I could just find somebody who's dependable, knows what they're doin', and not tryin' to take me for everything I got."

We looked at each other at the same time, Isaac smelling the sawdust and me seeing the price doubling on my four-bedroom ranch. "What kind of work does the house need?"

I told him my entire story from being reunited with Anna to my encounter with Mark. He listened attentively, then said, "I can come by and take a look at it. Maybe I can help."

"You don't mind?"

"Not at all. I only work part-time here. And after I clock out, I really don't have nothing else to do."

"Well, if you wanna work for me, I have to tell you, I really can't pay you that much. At least not right now."

"That's a bridge we can cross when we get to it. I don't have to be at work tomorrow until noon. Want me to stop by in the morning?"

No sooner than Mother heard I had befriended Isaac Mackey, she hit somebody else's roof. "Nicole, what in the world is wrong with you hangin' around that man? Didn't he just get out of prison? And need I remind you that you are a married woman. You know sometimes I think you don't even try to use your brain! You're such a imbecile."

One of the faithful reporters of our church called her at work eager to tell Isaac and I were at Home Depot. Somebody else, whom I hadn't seen, had stopped Jeff while he was on one of his routes, even more anxious to tell we were riding in my car with the windows down and the music blasting. Jeff came home midday almost on the verge of going into cardiac arrest. "I heard you screwin' that jailbird. Somebody said you and him be together everyday. How dare you be courtin' him right in my face? And embarassin' me like that." I thought, *how dare you?*

DAYLIGHT COMING

Before we married, I didn't know anything about Jeff, except the women in our church adored the black man with the alto voice who could sing the hell out of a hymn. He could also talk the panties off a nun. Being that he was not only eight years older but more experienced than me, he had a sexual appetite I didn't know how to or want to satisfy. But there is such a thing called discretion. Just about every affair he had, it was like he and whomever he was dealing with at the moment, liked throwing it in my face.

For example, Sharon Stovall. I congratulated her for being pregnant a week before her and Jeff's son, Russell, was born. This was in October 1977. She was in the church bathroom with her three sisters. They stopped talking when I came in. Noticing the bulge under her robe and her steady rubbing on it, I offered her my best wishes. I knew Pastor must have not known she was pregnant and still single or she would have been kicked out of the choir with the quickness.

"Thank you, Nicole," she said, smiling like we were best friends. Two months after Russell Kingston Stovall was born, she had him baptized at Holy Hill. Of course Jeff got a bad case of diarrhea and couldn't attend church, sending me there without a clue as to what was going on. After service, I went over to Mother, looking at her with, *so what do you think about your precious Jeff now*, written all over my face.

She said before a syllable exited my mouth, "Nicole, everybody is entitled to a mistake. Just forgive him and move on. Please! I don't have time for your snivelin' today."

She got into her Cadillac and left me standing on the sidewalk while all of Holy Hill whispered about how much Russell resembled Jeff. I quit going to Sunday School soon after, because suddenly, Sharon started bringing Russell to class with her claiming, "I just can't stand to leave my baby in the nursery."

Her little bubble was burst nine months later, in July 1978, when Sophia Chadwick became pregnant. Sophia didn't have a problem flaunting her stuff and announcing she was having twins. She and Jeff had been dating off and on for some years before he spotted me and just had to have me. Sophia was a big girl, pretty, and she knew it. Honey complexion, hair always perfect and was one of the best-dressed women in the church other than Mother and RudyAnn. When she found out Jeff was Russell's father, she called him every day—several times a day. A couple of times she even stopped by our house, asking like I was the maid, "Is Jeff here?"

Suspecting, but not positive because, just like RudyAnn, she was always testifying to what the Lord had done for her and shouting all over the place, I asked, "Jeff, why is Sophia Chadwick callin' here so much? And how come she keeps stoppin' by and leavin' notes for you to call her?"

"Church business."

I'm sure the good Lord thoroughly disagreed. Because not only was Jeff seeing Sharon, he was also kicking it with Sophia who thought she was the only one—other than me. That's why he came home early from work one day with a busted lip, scratches on his neck and arms, and his shirt damn near tore off, swearing he got into a fight at a gas station with two white boys. Of course, he was the only witness.

Sophia was the boldest of all of his women. To make it known Jeff was the father of her twins, first she staged this act, crying nonstop, saying she wanted to rededicate her life to Christ while we were having Tuesday night Bible study.

Our teacher said, "I understand your need, Sister Sophia, but can't we do this after class? God knows your heart and He knows your intentions."

But Sophia kept pressing. So she called her to the front of the class. She had Sophia repeat a prayer of repentance. After saying, "Amen, thank you, Jesus," Sophia went into a testimony about how she was having an affair with a married man and how ashamed she was to be pregnant by him. All eyes fell on me.

To get the attention back on her, the girl hit the floor. Passed right out, trembling, shaking, and kicking her heels up like she was having a Holy Ghost seizure. Everybody in the room surrounded her while still looking at me. I politely picked up my possessions and walked out the door straight to my car, holding my head high, yet wanting to go postal. Before I reached our block once again, I said a prayer pleading with God to bless me to refrain from killing Jeff and to remove me from the hell I was in.

I sat in my Nova for some minutes trying to conjure up the energy to open the car door and go inside, since I knew in spite of my prayers, the moment Jeff said a word to me, it was on. We had been married for almost three years and every time I turned around he was with somebody new. In my face! He met me at the door in his boxers and hard enough to chop some serious wood.

My thoughts zoomed in on the hammer I kept under the sofa, the screwdriver under the pillow, and the lamp I deliberately kept unplugged. I said, "Sophia's the one who's havin' your babies so take your ass back over there and get some from her. Because unless you plan on dyin', you better not ever touch me again."

"Nicole, if you were takin' care of my needs..."

"Damn you and your needs, Jeff, because for all I care, you can go to hell."

He pointed his finger in my face. "Don't you be cursin' at me!"

I slapped it away. "Fuck you."

He grabbed my lips, twisting them. I clawed at his arms and hands until he bent my arm behind my back, forcing me on the floor with his knee in my back and my face in the carpet. He held me down, reached on the coffee table for the phone, and dialed Mother's number.

"Mother Borge, Nicole is over here actin' up again. She just got home from Bible study. Can you believe her? And wanna fight. And I ain't done nothin' to her. I was in here readin' my Bible, tryin' to meditate on the Word so that I can be a good deacon to the church, and she just came home fussin' and cussin' about who knows what. Scratchin' up my arms and hands. You should see them. I can't go to work like this."

All the while he was lying, I damned his soul and called him everything, *but* a child of God. He laid the telephone next to me and stuck the earpiece to my ear.

Mother said, "Nicole, cut it out! I don't know what's wrong with you, but we're gonna fix it right now."

She chanted, "Oh-h-h bless her, Lord. Bless her, Jesus. Remove . . . " He hit the mute button, then stuck his hand up my skirt.

I started squirming violently, trying to get away from him. He said, "Yeah, Nicole, that's how I like it. Keep on movin' like that." He took my panties off with the one hand he wasn't using to hold me hostage and kissed down the side of my face, chanting, "Amen, Mother. Thank you, Jesus." He sucked on my ear. "Thank you, Father."

When he had my panties down to my ankles, he slid them off with his foot. He brought me up to where he wanted me to be. With a little maneuvering, he rammed his erection in as far as it would go. My scream began in my belly and raced to my throat, but like he always did whenever he was torturing me, he threw his hand over my mouth and held it so tight I could hardly breathe, let alone cry out in agony, even though Mother wouldn't have been able to hear me. She never had anyway.

He humped hard and fast, mumbling, "Bless her Father. Bless her Father," the entire time was trying to knock my liver up to my lungs. He reached a climax that made him groan, then slump over. We dropped to the floor. My face slammed into the carpet, dampened by my tears.

"Got-damn," he replied. He reached over my head and took the phone off mute. Mother was finishing her prayer. He said, "Thank you, Mother Borge. Thank you."

She said, "Nicole, you behave yourself now. Because as I'm always tellin' you, Jeff is a good man. And in order to be a good wife, you have to first believe in God and second, obey your husband." The husband who was lying on my back, moaning in my ear, "That was good, Nicole. Damn that was good."

"Did you say something, Jeff?" Mother asked.

He froze, then said, "No. No-o-o, Mother Borge, just that you have been such a blessin' to us tonight." He threw his pelvis against me in a quick hump. "Right, Nicole."

DAYLIGHT COMING

"Praise the Lord," she said. "Well, I'll talk to you later. I gotta get up early in the morning."

Three years later, he fathered another child by another Holy Hill member who later married our church custodian. With so many of his brats running around and me trying to keep my spiritual composure, I endured watching her, Sharon, and Sophia take turns pushing their babies in the aisles for the congregation to see. I mostly sat in the back, trying to stay focused on the Sunday message, but it was becoming harder.

Jeff didn't make it any easier because everywhere we went, if he wasn't grinning in some woman's face, she was grinning in his. He was also giving our number out right and left, claiming he was doing so in the name of the Lord. Tired of his crap, I snatched my wedding rings off one night and threw them in his face.

He insisted, "It don't make me no difference." But the moment we sat down for Sunday dinner, he said, "Mother Borge, have you noticed that Nicole ain't been wearin' her weddin' rings lately?" I cut him an evil glare, wondering how I could slit his throat and get away with it.

"Nicole, where are your rings?"

"Considerin' Jeff has chosen not to honor our marriage by makin' not one—but *four* babies . . ." His head dropped as though if he could have found a hole, he would have dived in it. "I decided there's no use in me wearin' 'em. Since *married* don't seem to mean nothin' to him. Not that it ever did."

Mother said, "Nicole, let me see you in the kitchen." I tried ignoring her angry eyes. She shouted, "Now!"

She couldn't wait to close the kitchen door behind us. "I know you wasn't tryin' to get smart with me, because you still aren't too old that I won't smack the taste outta your mouth."

I thought, *just try it*. Then my conscience reminded me I was supposed to honor her and that disobedient children were an insult and grief to their parents.

"Nicole, I'm gonna tell you this once more since you don't have sense enough to see it! Jeff is a good man. You hear me, a good man. A God-fearin' man. He has made a mistake or two, but evidently you aren't doin' something right yourself or none of this woulda happened. A man has needs, and a wife is obligated to meet those needs or he will stray. So while you're pointin' the finger at him, just think of what you coulda done to rectify the situation."

She walked away, leaving me wanting to hurt somebody—anybody. But I walked out the back door and stomped home, all twenty blocks, oblivious to it being ten degrees outside. I removed the key from the mailbox and let myself in. The telephone rang as I was taking off my snow-filled loafers.

"Jeff, this is me. You know you were supposed to take the twins out today and buy their Christmas presents. So where in the hell are you?" Sophia yelled into the answering machine.

She was just that obnoxious and was always finding something sarcastic to say whenever I was in her presence, as if I was the one who had screwed her husband. I tried my damnedest to ignore her. But the Tuesday afternoon following her call, I was stopping by Madonna's, the women's dress boutique she and Mother always shopped at. She was getting into her white Cougar when I pulled up. Instead of going about her business, she and her friend Karla, another one of Holy Hill's tramps, got back out of the car.

I opened my door. Sophia said, "Karla, I forgot to tell you that Jeff spent all day with me and the boys yesterday. We had so much fun. He even took us to Marshall Field's and bought us everything we wanted."

I knew she was lying, because Jeff was home in bed with a bad case of the flu and whining about how bad he felt—as if I was supposed to show him an ounce of sympathy. Plus he was too cheap to splurge on anybody, but himself.

"He really knows what I like."

"If he knew, then why didn't he marry you?" I said, as I was coming around to the passenger side to remove the black suit I was returning for Mother.

"Because he felt sorry for your bony ass," she said, working her head and shoulders at the same time. "Because everybody knows Mother Borge paid him to marry you. Because you couldn't get a man no other way. You can't have children and you scared of sex. He told me all about you."

DAYLIGHT COMING

He just failed to mention my temper, because I beat her ass all over the parking lot. And never had another problem with her. Even though Mother called me and talked about me like I was somebody else's child, I was still proud of what I had done. Because I considered myself fighting for my honor—too naïve to see that she was the least of my problems.

5

Rumors about Isaac and me sailed through Evanston so fast, he suggested, "Maybe you should find somebody else to do the work you need, because I don't wanna cause you no problems."

I liked being around him, watching him work. He taught me things I didn't have a clue about, like how to strip wallpaper with extremely hot water and extra thick rubber gloves, sand down walls in need of spackling, and use a paintbrush and roller properly. I was so infatuated by his skills and persona that I asked him to be my guest at church.

I was upstairs getting extra envelopes for tithing when he parked his battered green truck in our main lot. I rushed downstairs just as he entered the vestibule. Mouths dropped and people stopped to stare. And I'm sure everybody seated turned around when he walked into the sanctuary.

Spotting a semi-vacant pew, Isaac said, "Pardon me," to Brother and Sister Thomas. They turned toward him in unison, then grabbed their belongings and found a seat on the far side of the church even though they sat in the same spot every Sunday. I hurried to his side.

"Good mornin', Isaac. Welcome to Holy Hill."

"Mornin', Nicole."

He removed his tweed blazer and laid it on the pew in front of him. "You don't think they're gonna lynch us for me bein' here, do you?"

I laughed and joined our choir in singing "Blessed Assurance." At the closing of the hymn, Pastor Dorthea grabbed the microphone. She was a small woman, but had a powerful voice.

"This song ought to make y'all wanna greet somebody in Jesus' name. Just turn to your neighbor and give them a good old-fashioned hug. Then find somebody you ain't seen in a long time. That you ain't spoke to in a long time. And show them the God in you." Nobody came our way. Not even Jeff. But he made sure he wrapped his arms around everyone who crossed his path. Especially the women.

Mother couldn't concentrate on the morning message for looking over her shoulder at me. It also seemed Pastor Dorthea preached her entire sermon on lost values, staring at me.

I met Anna and her husband, Roger, at Marcello's for their delicious veal parmesan, topped with aged mozzarella cheese, and potatoes wedges sautéed in garlic juice after church, to avoid what I knew was coming.

When Mother finally reached me, by way of the telephone, she said, "How dare you miss Sunday dinner, knowin' it's something we do as a family every week?" Like I wanted to be there so she and Jeff could take turns kicking me in my behind. "And didn't I tell you to stay away from that disgustin' creature?"

"Mother, Isaac is nothin' like the man who went to jail twenty years ago."

"You would say that because you're too naïve to know any better. He's lookin' for a free ride, Nicole. Just look at him. Havin' the nerve to park that beat-up, who knows if there is a model for the trap he was drivin', right in front of the church. I'm so glad that today wasn't Friends and Family day."

"I thought every Sunday was supposed to be friends and family day?"

"And that's supposed to mean?" I dropped a few of my things into the washing machine as if I hadn't heard her question. "That's what I thought."

Four weeks after Isaac finished renovating my first purchase, I was at another closing. We celebrated at Dominic Salgado's along with Anna. My treat. After dessert, fried vanilla ice cream, I announced, "I've finally come up with a name for my business."

"So let's hear it," Anna said.

"NCS Management Company."

She nodded. "And that stands for?"

"Nicole's Management Company."

She laughed. "Sounds fine to me."

"So what do you think, Isaac?"

He said, "If you like it. I love it." We laughed.

"I have another surprise." I slipped him the envelope that had been conveniently lying in my lap throughout dinner. He looked at me as if to say, *What's this?*

"Open it."

He peeped at the check, then slid it back to me. "I can't take this much money from you."

"Isaac, you've been workin' for me for pennies. I wouldn't have made that much on the house if it wasn't for you."

"But this is . . . ten thousand dollars is entirely too much."

"Do you value my friendship?"

"You know I do."

"Then take the money, please. It's the least I can do."

Our next project, a partially burned farmhouse, was two stories with a double garage, rotting at the foundation. It had been struck by lightning while the couple who owned it was at their summer home in Fort Lauderdale. They had called Anna, eager to sell. I was dying to see what Isaac was going to do with it, since the minute we drove up to it, I saw creativity in his eyes.

With help from three of his friends from back-in-the-day, we had the house and garage completely remodeled in less than six months. I made even more of a profit than I did off my first purchase. Two back-to-back lucrative deals put me in a higher tax bracket. It also added more controversy to my life.

Jeff started to cry even more about me keeping secrets from him and wasting money. And Mother began accusing me of being selfish, irresponsible, and throwing in the word greedy, which I have never been. Their comments became harsher after I treated myself to an Acura Legend. Black, loaded with everything. A 1996 model, sizzling off the lot.

I pulled up in front of our house and got out of my new toy just as Jeff was parking his 1995 Lincoln Town Car, his eighth brand-new ride since we married. Until I bought the Honda, I rode around in any trap I could afford. He ran over to me.

"Where you keep gettin' all this money? You ain't worked in damn near a year. And I know you ain't gettin' it from that jailbird! I'm tired of you bein' stuck-up under him all the damn time. "

I had my Legend for two weeks before Mother got a chance to turn her nose up at it. Busy staking out my next property, I had very little time for her degrading conversations. So she left her dirty messages on my answering machine.

"Nicole, you should be shamed of yourself, runnin' around with that man the way you do. You're just disgustin'. Deplorable. And you're about to drive your husband insane."

Jeff's sanity was my least concern, because I could hang wallpaper, paint a room, and tear a wall out like a pro, then go home, shower, put on a suit, and meet a mortgage banker or property owner with finesse. But . . . issues with my family would not go away. They just kept festering like nasty sores.

Not one to ask me for anything, RudyAnn just took whatever she wanted or demanded it, knowing Mother was going to make me fork it over. Too pretty to work, Mother took care of her and her family, considering her husband, Lennox, couldn't keep a job staring out of a window. He's the only person I know who will start a new position on Monday and call in on Tuesday. Yet, every job he lost was always *the white man's* fault.

His problem was RudyAnn. He was so terrified that some other man was going to look her way that it was sad, even though she had long ago lost her hourglass shape. High-yellow with curly-brown hair, he had cruised up to our church door in a shiny red Mustang, strutting his stuff in a dark-gray tailored suit and claiming to be an ordained minister. He not only captured the eye of many of the women in Holy Hill's congregation, but Mother's and RudyAnn's as well. The car and the suit turned out to be his best friend's who was in the hospital. He was enrolled in a bible institute majoring in Theology and was so broke he had to borrow money from Mother to get a hotel room on their wedding night.

Having scorned her with his deceit, it was his ability to rock the church that got him back in good standing with Mother. He could preach for five minutes and wigs would be flying off. People would be passing out all over the place and many ran to the altar for their souls to be saved. RudyAnn led the pack, laying her holy hands on the many sinners begging to be healed from their illnesses, have their broken finances mended or be spared from the fires of hell. Like she was purer—as they say—as the driven snow. Only the Lord knows how many were doing the driving.

RudyAnn was born from Mother's first marriage to her high school sweetheart. He died from a stroke four years after she was born. Looking a lot like him, she was Mother's favorite. But she had enough hips for two more people. Had them ever since I could remember. It was the only imperfection Mother could find about her even though she had been slinging her stuff ever since she was thirteen. Or probably earlier than that, because if it wore boxers or briefs, her panties were guaranteed to come down until she met this guy named Ricardo "Silk" Williams a week before her twenty-first birthday.

Silk was from a community south of Evanston, called Rogers Park, which is the far north side of Chicago. He was so cool I swear butter melted in his presence. They met on a Friday morning while we were supposed to be buying groceries. Come Friday night, he was creeping in her bedroom.

Mother slept on the first floor in the front of our house. Our rooms were upstairs. Many a night, guys were lined up for a *RudyAnn Special*. Sometimes she would have two in her room and one waiting, or one in her room with two waiting. But once she beheld Silk's light brown eyes and got a taste of his sweet and creamy chocolate, her goods were off limits to everybody else unless he said so. They made so much noise I didn't see how Mother couldn't have heard her screeching like a cat in heat or him moaning where he wanted it and how he wanted it. It made me tingly inside, but not enough for him to be tipping into my bedroom.

But as nature would have it, I was coming out of the bathroom just before sunrise. Silk was coming out of RudyAnn's room. He grinned when he saw me. I tried to make a dash for my bedroom. But he caught me inches away from my door. He dragged me back inside the bathroom with his hand over my mouth.

"Calm down, beautiful."

"Let me go," I murmured, trying to get away from him.

"Only if you promise not to scream."

I nodded. He eased up on his grip. I tried to run over to the door. He wrapped his long arms around me and scooped me closer to him.

"Let me go, Silk," I said, breathing hard and trying to avoid his hardness against my thigh.

"Okay, but you gotta calm down."

"And you're gonna let me go."

"Only if you promise not to run."

"And you're gonna let me go."

He spun me around in his arms, his erection smack dab against my pelvis. I stuck my butt out to avoid it. He wrapped his hand around his stiffness. "You want some of this. Your sister be beggin' for it every night. You wanna taste it, too, with your fine little self." I shook my head. "Yes, you do." He unzipped his pants. "Touch it." He rubbed it against my leg. "Touch it. See how hard it is for you. Just take it in your hands and . . . " He rubbed it with gentle strokes, while licking his lips. I pushed him away from me with all of my might and made another attempt to reach the door. He stumbled back, then caught himself and me with one swift motion. He wrapped his leg around mine, trying to force me to the floor.

"I'm gonna tell my mama if you don't leave me alone."

He stopped trying to lay me down, but stuck his hand between my legs. "Let me make you feel good. Please, beautiful. Let me get some."

"You better get outta here or I'm tellin' my mama and you know she'll call the police on you."

He may have thought he was super smooth, but I knew he wasn't stupid enough to catch a case for attempted rape of a fourteen-year-old. He opened the door, peeped out, then pimped across the hall. He stuck his head in RudyAnn's door.

"Y'all through?"

Two guys came out, giving him a high-five and some dollars. He mouthed me a kiss, then left down the back steps.

RudyAnn's door opened again. She came out with her hair all over her head and wrapped up in her pink sheet, wet in spots. "What the hell you lookin' at?"

I had nothing to say. I just went back to my room wondering how she could call herself saved messing around with so many guys. I was even more curious if sex was that good that you needed that many men at once.

RudyAnn pulled in behind me after I parked in front of my most recent purchase. From the sale of my second house, I put down a hefty deposit on an apartment building at the corners of Dempster and Maple. It had four two-bedroom, one-bath rentals with a two-car garage and laundry room in the basement. The exterior was in fine shape, but the inside! When I say those people should have been ashamed of themselves, it's an understatement. Getting rid of them was worse. They were family, each having Section 8 and determined not to go anywhere until they found something to accommodate the twenty of them.

Three months after I closed, they were still living there—rent free, taking seven months longer than Isaac anticipated before the apartments were even close to being finished. Cabinet and closet doors had to be replaced. All of the toilets were either cracked or backed up. There were holes in some of the walls the size of humans. And their six Rottweilers had scratched out chunks of sheetrock in the basement and had crapped all over the place.

Isaac was standing in the doorway smoking a Newport when RudyAnn walked up to my car as if I had done her wrong. I eyeballed her even harder, wondering how in the hell she had found me.

"I need rent money."

"You can't say good mornin' before you start beggin'."

"Mother said she ain't got it, so get it from you."

For Mother to have called me stupid or asinine as many times as she had when I had told her, "Isaac and I have gone into business together," it became very convenient for her to dump her prized child's woes off on me. I just shook my head as RudyAnn stood tapping her foot on the sidewalk with her hands on her disfigured hips. I snatched my checkbook out of my glove compartment.

"We ain't got groceries, either, so you might as well add two hundred extra for food."

I stopped writing the date. "Well, you might as well get a damn job. Because this is the third month you've come to me with your hand out. It's also my last time givin' you a check. It ain't my responsibility to take care of your family."

"You got cash or what? Like I said, we need food."

I wrote the check for her rent only, then went into my ashtray. Before I could offer her the only twenty I had, she took it out of my hand.

"Thanks for nothin'," she said, twisting back to the Cadillac DeVille Mother had just given her. Every couple of years when Mother bought a new car, the old one would go to her, although RudyAnn never had money for gas, insurance, or maintenance.

I got out of my car to tell her about her ungrateful self. To my surprise she had her two teenage sons, Limmell and LJ, with her. Most of the time when she was out, she was alone. I calmed myself and started walking to the car to say hello to them and to see why there weren't in school, considering it was Tuesday. She threw the Cadillac in drive and sped off.

"Just in case you're wonderin'," I said to Isaac, "that was my big sister and her sons." We watched RudyAnn racing down the street.

He nodded. "So, why you never told me you were a aunt?"

"I don't know. I guess it's because I don't get to see my nephews that much, even though they live right here in Evanston."

"And why's that?"

"My sister and I don't get along. At all."

"But that shouldn't keep you from spendin' time with your nephews."

"You got a point, as far as they're concerned, but . . ."

"They're still your family, right?"

"Yeah."

"Then maybe you should start spendin' some time with them."

"That's true. But why are you so adamant about it?"

"Just a thought," he said. "Ready to start workin'?"

I made an attempt to rekindle my relationship with my nephews during a Saturday evening invitation to dinner and the movies. Coming out of the house, both boys at fifteen and sixteen, getting taller and even more handsome, appeared to be happy, but a bit thin for their close to six-foot frames. We went out to eat first. As I paid for the food, Limmell picked up the tray. Black marks identical to the many I had were on his lower arms. I let him enjoy his meal, then took his hands into mine. I slid back the sleeves of his sweatshirt.

"Limmell, what happened to you?"

He snatched away. LJ said, "We were playin' and he fell on one of RudyAnn's rose bushes."

"When did RudyAnn ever plant a rose bush or anything else?"

LJ hung his head. "Can I get another burger?"

DAYLIGHT COMING

Both boys had just downed a double Whopper, a cheeseburger, a large order of fries, and a large pop, going back three times for refills. "Wow, when is the last time you two ate?" The way their faces dropped made me suspicious. But I changed the subject. "So, what have you guys been doin'? How's school?"

LJ answered for both. "We just be at the crib, chillin'. Both of us are maxin' all of our subjects."

"Why didn't you call me and tell me so I could give you a couple of dollars for all of those A's you're gettin'?"

"Because RudyAnn says you ain't got time for us. You're too busy in your own world."

"That's not true. All you guys gotta do is pick up the phone and we can do something. I wanna start spendin' more time with you. Remember how much fun we used to have? We can still hang out unless you've outgrown your favorite auntie."

They tried to smile, but I knew by the look in their eyes they were in pain. I just never would have imagined how much.

6

Out of all the purchases I made none required as much manual labor as the one I dubbed the Dempster/Maple building, named by the street corners it sat on. Isaac and I worked around the clock trying to get it up to par. It wasn't only because anything vacant doesn't bring in any money, but I got tired of working on it, anxious to move on to something else. Every day it was something.

We had just finished pulling up carpet in the hall on the second floor. I was dead tired, zooming down Dodge Avenue near Evanston High School, anxious to take a hot shower and crawl into my bed. I spotted LJ and Limmell walking down the block ahead of a group of black boys and a husky white boy with cornrows, or maybe he was very light complexioned. He pushed Limmell hard enough to make him stumble but not fall.

I swerved into park, anxious to see what was going to happen next, not wanting to react too quickly, just in case my nephew decided to kick his behind. He and LJ just kept walking while the boy talked smack in both of their faces, the black boys cheering him on. I grabbed my umbrella off the backseat as I hurried out of my car. Three of the boys taunting them, I recognized from church.

"What the hell is your problem?" I asked.

They eased back. The white boy grabbed Limmell in the collar, spit in his face, then pimp-smacked him to the ground. I leaped into attack, wailing on him with my umbrella like a thing from the wild. A school security guard and a male parent passing by had to pull me away from him.

The security guard said, "Ma'am, calm down."

DAYLIGHT COMING

"What the hell do you mean 'calm down'? That bastard spit in my nephew's face."

The parent said, "That's what he gets because he always 'round here messin' with somebody," in my favor.

"True dat," the security guard replied, looking uncertain if he wanted to turn me loose. "But, ma'am, you can't be jumpin' on kids like that. Lucky for you he a dropout and not supposed to be over here because you could be arrested."

"He's the one who should be arrested!"

"We can call the police, but it's up to you to press charges."

The rest of the kids had scattered, but the boy was pacing back and forth, stopping to rub his wounds. The security guard walked over to him. He shouted, "You see what that bitch did!" He wiped blood from his nose with the back of his hand.

The security guard said, "Watch your mouth, boy! Because that's what you get. Now get outta here!"

"LJ and Limmell, get in the car," I ordered. "And if that bastard ever puts his hands on you again, just let me know. Because he sure as hell won't live to tell about it!" He kept walking without looking back.

I dropped them off down the street from their house. Still shaken, they pleaded with me not to mention what had happened.

"Why don't you want RudyAnn or Lennox to know? He should be arrested."

"Please don't tell," they said in unison and got out of my car.

More determined than ever to find out what exactly was going on with them, I hired them to work for me after school. I later learned from the security guard what happened wasn't the first time. He also said they were always being joked about their outdated clothes, and sometimes they smelled.

One thing about my sister, if RudyAnn doesn't do anything else, she will wash her behind. I never smelled Lennox, either. So why would their boys have a reputation for stinking? I decided to make it a part of my daily routine to check on them and to pick them up in the same area they were attacked in, mainly so others could see I was there, ready for whatever they were going to bring their way. Whether they were kids or not.

Limmell saw me waiting for them for the third consecutive school day. He rushed to beat his big brother to the front seat. He dove inside my car.

"Hey-y-y, Nikki."

"Limmell, don't you have deodorant at home?" I said, letting down my window.

His smiled disappeared. He peered over his shoulder at LJ, who replied, "Naw, we don't."

"Why not? Y'all put your windows down."

"Because we ain't got no money."

"I just paid you Friday. Today is Monday. How could you be broke so soon? Woo-oo, Limmell, you're musty enough to be hosed down."

LJ spoke up once again. "We had to help out RudyAnn and Lennox."

"With what? I'm payin' their rent and every time I turn around if she ain't beggin' from me. She's hittin' up your grandmother."

Limmell had his frightened-about-to-cry look just like he did anytime we discussed RudyAnn and Lennox. I sighed, feeling bad about my reaction. "LJ, how much of your money did you give them?"

He turned his head toward the window. "All of it."

"Why the hell did you give them all of your money?"

"Because Lennox said if we man enough to work, we ought to be man enough to pay rent. So we gotta give him two hundred dollars a week." I was only paying them twenty dollars a day to help out with the small stuff.

"That's all your money! I swear him and RudyAnn are some greedy bastards. It's bad enough they leech off your grandmother and me. But they ain't gettin' no more of your money."

Both boys pleaded with me to leave it alone, tears flowing from Limmell's eyes like a waterfall. LJ said through the fear he was trying to conceal, "Lennox said he better not find out we been tellin' you our family business—so please, Nikki, don't say nothin'. Please."

DAYLIGHT COMING

I bought them a bag of personal items before we did anything else. I also made Limmell shower at my house before he started work. The minute I dropped them off at home Lennox met them at the door and took their bags out of their hands. Through the mini-blinds in their living room, I watched him going through their stuff. Satisfied with getting the best of what they had, he bumped Limmell out of his way and went upstairs.

The only time LJ and Limmell ever really had any fun was when they were with me. In their younger years, we spent many afternoons on the playground and attending special events in the Chicagoland area. The Annual Bud Billiken Parade was our favorite. The boys were nine and ten when we attended our last one. RudyAnn invited herself and Lennox. So I knew the day was going to be a disaster, the moment she said, "We're going, too. Boys, y'all get in the backseat." I always let them ride up front with me.

Crowded like always, we lucked up on a spot on Martin Luther King Drive and 35th Street. As usual she was the one Lennox focused all of his attention on and pushed in front of everybody else. Seeing the look of disappointment in the boys' eyes every time he kissed her cheek or pointed something out to her, I said, "Y'all hungry?" The boys nodded. "Okay, then let's go get us some hotdogs."

Lennox said, "Bring us one, too." He handed me a five-dollar bill like it was supposed to fill him and RudyAnn up the way they ate. I glanced at the crumbled bill and said to LJ and Limmell, "Come on."

The hotdog line was long and locating RudyAnn and Lennox was almost impossible. We finally wandered up on them with his arms wrapped around her waist and her eyeballing every man walking by.

"Where's our change?" she said, taking more than her share of hotdogs out of my hand.

"What change? Lennox only gave me five—"

"No, he gave you a fifty."

"RudyAnn, he gave me a five-dollar bill. Didn't you, Lennox?"

He opened his mouth like he wanted to say something, but couldn't get the words out. She got in my face. "Don't make me have to kick your ass out here! Now, gimme my husband's money." It shocked me. Because she would pop the crap out of me quick. Sometimes I would get bold enough to hit her back, but I was never any competition because RudyAnn could downright brawl. She had to, because she was always getting caught with somebody's boyfriend or husband. Still Mother would always insist, "Women are just jealous of her."

I had recently gotten paid, so I knew she must have seen how much money I had when I stopped for gas. She snatched my purse out of my hand. I snatched it back, knowing the dollars I had belonged to the light company. That's why I wasn't buying any souvenirs for LJ and Limmell.

Once we got back to Evanston, she jumped out of my car. I dashed behind her, knowing the lie she was going to tell. Mother's eyes blazed murder the entire time she swore up and down I had pocketed her husband's change, both of them knowing Lennox didn't have a job. Neither did she. They were living with Mother. So where would he have gotten a fifty-dollar bill? Unless he had stolen it!

Mother walked toward me as I attempted to tell her what she knew was the truth. She ripped my purse off my shoulder, took all of the money I had, then threw it at me. "Now take your thievin' behind home." I tried to catch my purse, but it fell on the floor. I picked it up and marched to the front door, too pissed to say anything more.

She told the boys, as I opened it to leave, "Now, you boys know what a thief looks like. Make sure you don't grow up to be like her."

"That's right," RudyAnn added.

I cried all way home, more concerned with what Limmell and LJ would now think of me, as opposed to how I was going to pay the light bill. Jeff was on his way out the door as I was on my way in. Sensing something was wrong by my refusal to look his way, he suggested, "Keep your ass home sometimes and you won't have to worry about your mama hurting your feelings."

Hurt feelings were mild compared to what I went through as a child. Because if the Department of Children and Family Services had gotten wind of how precise she was with an extension cord, holier than thou, good Mother Borge would have caught a serious case. Because when she was on my behind, she showed no mercy.

Feeling sorry for my nephews and considering it to be my duty since I was their only aunt, I bought them the latest fashions, fed them every night before I took them home, plus gave them extra money so they could eat all they wanted at school. It only made Lennox demand more of them.

When LJ told me of his all-new request, I said, "He must be outta his damn mind to charge you three hundred dollars a week rent. I ain't givin' you a raise for his greedy ass! He ought to get a damn job." He relayed the message—somewhat. Lennox and RudyAnn made a Jeff move on me.

"Nicole," Mother barked over the waves of my new cell phone, "what gives you the right to work those boys like you do and not give them anything?"

"I pay them twenty dollars a day and RudyAnn and Lennox take every penny they make."

"Have you seen them take every penny they make?"

"No."

"Then in a court of law you have no case."

"But they— "

"You're just startin' some more of your mess by flashin' your little change around."

"Excuse me."

"I didn't stutter."

I mumbled, "I'm so sick of this shit."

"Nicole, did you just curse me?" Mother repeated herself, adding, "I knew it was gonna come down to this because once you start keepin' company with filth, you start waddlin' in filth. Ever since you started hangin' around that Torry girl." Meaning Anna. "And Isaac Mackey. That old pervert. Everything I ever tried to teach you has been a joke. Just look at yourself.

"Most of the time wearin' faded jeans and men shirts with paint all over your body. You hardly come to church anymore and you're lyin' to your husband around the clock about what you're up to. You're a embarrassment, Nicole! Not only to me, but Jeff as well. As hard as he works and as good as he's been to you, you gallivantin' around with that jailbird like he's your pimp and you're his whore!"

Having gotten her punch in for the day, she slammed the telephone down. I hung up my cell and gave the cashier in Ace Hardware two twenty-dollar bills for the boxes of three-inch nails and drywall screws Isaac had told me to pick up. I was doing all I could to keep from running in the store's bathroom and crying my eyes out. Because no matter how tough I tried to be, I could never win a battle with Mother, because she could break a sister down.

7

I didn't give LJ and Limmell their weekly pay with the raise Lennox told them they had better ask for. Instead, I gave them half their salary and a receipt for what I had deposited in a joint savings account I opened for them. Although excited, they were still a bit nervous, uncertain how RudyAnn and Lennox would react.

She rang my doorbell, holding her finger on the buzzer.

I snatched the door open. "What?"

"I want the rest of my boys' money, that's what."

"And I ain't givin' it to you, because you and your poor-excuse for a husband ought to get off your royal asses and get a damn job. Who the hell do you think you are that we're supposed to feed y'all and put a roof over your heads? LJ and Limmell work hard for their money and I ain't givin' you a damn thang!" I looked at Lennox, having the nerve to be wearing a black suit and a silk tie as if he was coming from a real job. "And you call yourself a preacher and a man. I thought the Bible said you're supposed to feed your children, not the other way around."

His face turned bright pink. He stepped behind RudyAnn. She tried staring me down, but saw I wasn't going to budge from my decision. "Come on, Lenny, before I have to beat her ass."

Back in the day, she would have. But I wasn't the same little girl she used to slap around. "Ain't nothin' between you and me but air."

She eyeballed me up and down, then walked away. Jeff was getting out of his Lincoln. She said, "You need to talk to your wife, because she about to make me hurt her."

I urged, "Bring it on!" She turned around and gave me the finger.

Come Monday morning, LJ called me on my cell phone from the payphone at school. "Why you had to do that, Nikki? Now you done messed up everything."

"What do you mean?" He hung up.

I left Isaac sanding floors, raced home, and took a shower. I changed into a linen pantsuit, and headed for Evanston Township High School. LJ came into the office with the pain of Lennox mistreating him so obvious on his face I wanted to run over to their house with a check in my hand. Limmell came into the room next. Head hanging low, his jaw slightly swollen. I ushered them out of hearing range of the clerk at the front desk.

I examined Limmell's face. "What happened to you?"

"Nothin'," he replied, staring over my head, his eyes glistening with tears. LJ wouldn't look at me.

"Boys, I am so sorry for what I've done. I had no idea Lennox was gonna start back beatin' on you. But I promise I'll make it up to you."

LJ snapped, "How, when he said we can't come around you no more? And now he's threatenin' to put us out if we don't find another job."

"What?"

Limmell said in a barely audible voice, "Because he says we're too much trouble."

"You guys are no trouble. You guys are the best. And I . . ." I almost choked. "I love you so much. And I'm gonna help you find another job."

"When?" LJ asked.

"Soon, but in the meantime, I'm gonna take the rest of your money to RudyAnn as soon as I leave from here. I'll say I feel bad for openin' up a account for you without talkin' to them first." I opened my purse and took out fifty dollars. "So here's a little something. Just put it up somewhere."

LJ kept his hands in his pockets." He always finds our money. We can't hide nothin' from him. Because he says if it comes in his house, then it belongs to him."

"Ain't there some place he don't check?"

"No."

Limmell said, "Yeah, it is."

"Where?" LJ asked.

"Our Bibles. He looks through our school stuff and drawers, but he never checks our Bibles."

"So hide the money in there."

LJ refused it. Limmell took it out of my hand. He slipped it into his pocket. It was painful looking into their eyes knowing what Lennox was doing to them, so I did what I felt I had to do.

Later in the evening, I said, after rehearsing my approach several times, "Jeff, Lennox ain't treatin' LJ and Limmell right. They have scars all over their bodies and if he gets mad at one or the other, he won't let them eat, so I'm lettin' them move in here."

"No, in the hell they ain't because I ain't takin' on Lennox's mess."

"They ain't mess. They're my nephews."

"Have you ever thought about what *your nephews* might be doin' to make Lennox act the way he do?"

"What could they be doing so bad that they can't eat dinner? And lately if I didn't buy clothes for them, they wouldn't get any. You see how him and RudyAnn dress."

"That's their problem, because they ain't comin' here."

"How can you be so insensitive? They've got scars, Jeff. All over their bodies where he beats them."

"How do you know?"

"Haven't you noticed that even in the summertime LJ and Limmell have on long sleeves and pants? It's because they're scarred. Real bad." *Worse than the ones I have.*

Jeff was so adamant about LJ and Limmell not living in *his damn house* I let it rest. He couldn't wait to carry the bone, though. He left for work at five forty-five. Mother called me at six.

"Nicole, I can not believe you would stoop so low as to spread lies like that about Lennox. Have you ever seen him raise a hand to hit either one of those boys?" That was how she always addressed LJ and Limmell—*those boys*—as if they weren't a part of our family.

"Have you? Well, I don't know what scheme you're workin' on, but this foolishness stops right now. Because they don't look like they're starvin' to me and you know Lennox has been in and out of jobs. So quite naturally he can't afford to buy for them every time they grow out of something. Common sense should tell you that. But you're too busy tryin' to get something started."

Although taught at a very young age what went on in *our* family, stayed in *our* family, I still took it to another source. After seeing a "Help Wanted" sign, I said to the manager at the McDonald's I frequented, "I have two nephews. Both are well behaved, smart, and eager to work."

"Tell them to come in and fill out an application. And we'll see what happens," the manager said.

Both boys were hired on the same day they interviewed. It put them somewhat back in the good graces of Lennox, especially since he could drop by every payday, have them sign their checks over to him, and spend every penny of their earnings. I still made sure they had pocket money and would purchase clothes for them, being sure to remove the tags, because Lennox and RudyAnn would try to take their things back to the store if I didn't and exchange it for something for themselves.

They worked as many hours as they could. Yet Lennox would still act the fool if their checks were anything less than what he thought they should be, even after he started to earn a decent salary himself at Underwriters Laboratories. It was hard as heck to get hired there. I had tried myself, many times. But Lennox worked three weeks, then insisted he got a calling from God who told him to quit and trust in Him. Had he stayed on, he would have been making forty grand a year. So if he got a calling from God to quit a position that put food on their table and kept a roof over their heads, I *am* the Immaculate One.

His holy revelation put them right back where they started. He demanded more hours for LJ and Limmell at McDonald's. The manager finally told him, "I have more people on my staff than your sons." He got indignant with her. So she let both boys go.

With their family in even more of a financial bind, RudyAnn hinted about them moving back in with Mother. They had only been gone for a year. She quickly broke out her checkbook, catching them up on everything. But like always, it was my fault.

As more of my time was being spent with Isaac, I came to rely on him so much that whenever Anna gave me a scoop on anything, I wouldn't make a decision without him. The minute she told me the address of a mega-sized house soon to go on the market, with a price I could afford, I begged him to put the lid back on the varnish he had just opened and dragged him to see it.

He said, "Is this what you want?" as we sat in the unpaved driveway.

"Yes?"

"Then make her an offer. You don't need me to tell you that."

"Can't you see me ownin' it?"

"I appreciate you valuin' what I think, but you're a big girl."

"But what do you think?"

What I liked most about the Tudor were the five enormous bedrooms, even if it did only have a bath and a half. The frame and roof were in topnotch condition, but the house needed rewiring, pipes replaced, and insulation in the basement, which was prone to flood. And all of the walls still had wallpaper from when it was built in the 1920s.

The owner, a widow for five years, lived there alone. Her neighbor, a real estate agent, had brought his best friend and his wife to visit her with an insulting purchase offer that she refused. He then started calling her repeatedly and leaving messages in her mailbox or taped to her front door, demanding she clean her property, and trim her trees, because her leaves were blowing in his yard. He also complained there was a foul odor coming from her overgrown garden. When it became obvious she wasn't going to be bullied, he called the city of Evanston with a three-page list of complaints about her. True enough, there were a number of violations inside the house alone, but she was determined he wasn't going to force her out.

Anna's mother had met her at the doctor's office and the worried homeowner had told her about her distressing situation. Anna's mother suggested she allow Anna to help her. Being the realist she was, Anna set out a list of the woman's options. She could remodel by refinancing, but the interest would have been sky-high because of her age. She could dip into the monies her husband had left her, which was getting low, focusing on major repairs only. Or she could sell and move into a private residence for active seniors.

She asked Anna to give her three days to think about it, but called her the next day anxious to meet the young lady Anna knew who would value her house and not let her neighbor get his hands on it. Yet while I was basking in the joy of buying my dream house, Lennox was still giving Limmell and LJ hell.

With RudyAnn's permission, I was going to take them Easter shopping, with the condition I buy her these four suits she had seen while she was at the Evergreen Plaza on the Southside. She would barter for anything she could get before letting them spend time with me.

At eight thirty-five a.m., Limmell called. LJ always spoke for them so something told me it was more to his story than, "We gotta cut grass today. We forgot."

"Okay . . . but are you sure everything is alright? If something's up, you know you can tell me."

"We're fine. But, I gotta go now." He whispered, "I love you. Bye."

DAYLIGHT COMING

I knew if I went over there after he called and Lennox found out, they would be in even more trouble, so I decided to leave it alone. The telephone rang twenty minutes later.

"Nikki, you gotta come over. Please, Nikki. Please! It's Limmell!" LJ screamed.

I grabbed my purse from under my bed and drove like a maniac to their townhouse.

LJ met me at the front door. "You gotta help us, Nikki. You gotta help us. Lennox is gonna kill us if he finds out Limmell broke a chair."

"What?"

"He broke a chair. What are we gonna do?"

"Did he try to kill y'all? What is goin' on?"

He pointed upstairs. I bolted up the steps. The door to Limmell's room was open. An ancient chair with padded seating from a kitchen set Mother had given RudyAnn was lying in the middle of the floor with a broken leg. A sheet was on the floor next to it. And Limmell was crouched in a nearby corner in his boxers, sobbing and rocking back and forth.

I ran over to him. "Limmell." He looked up at me. His face was wet with snot and tears. "I'm sorry, Nikki" he said, his voice a decimal above a whisper.

"Are you all right? What happened? You tried to kill yourself?"

He put his head down. I gasped. "Oh, my God." Whelps of all sizes were all over his upper torso.

LJ said, "What are we gonna do?"

I pulled out my cell phone. "I'm sick of this."

Limmell grabbed my pant leg. "Please don't call the police, Nikki. Lennox will kill us. He already said if we told you or anybody our family business, we would end up in a body bag."

"If I call the police, they'll protect you."

"Lennox said there ain't a place we can hide from him. So please, Nikki. I don't wanna die."

"Then why in the hell did you try to kill yourself?"

He moaned something about not knowing what to do and he was tired of being worthless. I sat on the floor next to him and grabbed him in my arms. He cried out in pain.

"What are we gonna do about the chair?" LJ asked.

"Damn the chair. We need to get your brother to a hospital."

"Do you know what Lennox would do to me?" Limmell sobbed.

"It can't be no worse than what he's already done."

LJ said, "I'll take care of him. I always do. Don't I, Limmell?"

"I'm sorry I got you in trouble this mornin', LJ."

"What happened this mornin'?"

"Lennox started beatin' me with his belt for not polishin' his shoes. I forgot. I really did. LJ tried to stop him and Lennox punched him in his face."

I thought his jaw looked sunk in when he opened the door, but he deliberately kept it turned away from me. I felt myself about to break down, but said, "That sorry-ass bastard. I'm sick of the way he treats you, and RudyAnn just lets him get away with it. But this ceases right now."

LJ asked, "What are you gonna do?"

"Move y'all in with me and Jeff."

"Lennox won't let you. He says he'll kill you if you try to interfere in our business. Didn't he, LJ?" LJ nodded.

"Do you think I'm afraid of Lennox, with his punk ass? And it's time I let him know. Get your stuff!"

As much as I begged them, LJ and Limmell would not leave. So I had no other choice but to page Isaac after I took care of Limmell's wounds. Isaac came over and fixed the chair, not leaving a hint it was ever broken. Thankful for the favor and making him promise never to mention it, he said, "I'll take this thing back downstairs. Nicole, I just need you to show me where to put it." He picked it up and started out the door.

"I'll show you," LJ said, glancing at Limmell, who was a bit more calmed, but still obviously in pain and frightened.

"I'll do it. I need to see Isaac out anyway," I replied.

DAYLIGHT COMING

I followed him down the steps. "You know I ain't one to be in your business," he said, keeping his voice low, "but this chair is the least of their problems."

"I'm aware of that. And you heard me begging them to leave. But what can I do? If I call the police and they don't admit that their father has been abusing them, and he finds out, he'll probably kill them for sure." I started to cry. "I wanna help them, but they won't let me. They're too scared."

He shook his head. "When do you expect your sister back?"

"Most of the time, they're in church all day on Sundays and since it's so close to Easter, I'm sure it'll be late tonight before they come home."

"This wood-glue should be dry soon. Y'all just need to open the windows to let the smell out."

"Isaac, thank you so very much."

"Not a problem. I just wish there was more I could do to help."

I went back upstairs after he left and begged LJ and Limmell until I was in tears to leave with me. They still refused, too traumatized to believe I could save them from the wrath of their father.

Lennox didn't give Limmell hardly anytime to heal from the wounds he had already inflicted on him, because he attacked Limmell in their backyard two days later. A neighbor called the police and Limmell was rushed to the hospital. LJ called me on my cell phone while I was picking up a few items from the grocery store. I left my cart in the middle of the isle and rushed to be by his side. Mother was sitting in the waiting room, reading the Evanston Review when I ran into the ER.

"Where's Limmell?" I asked, trying to refrain from going ballistic.

"Where do you think?" she replied, her eyes still on the newspaper.

"See, I told you that Lennox has been beating on LJ and Limmell."

"He was just frustrated, because he's been out of work for a while now and he was at his boilin' point. You know how hardheaded those boys can be and they're so lazy."

"Mother, their house wouldn't get cleaned or dinner wouldn't get cooked if it wasn't for them. Besides, what could Limmell have done so bad to make Lennox beat him up like that? He was fightin' him like he was fightin' a man."

"Were you there? Did you see it?"

"I didn't have to. Because LJ told me."

"I'm sure he did."

"Mother, your son-in-law just sent your grandson to the hospital. Or does that concern you?"

"What concerns me is your meddlin'."

"I'm *meddlin'* when I see my nephews being mistreated and try to help them. If it had been me and my children, you would've had me arrested. But since it's RudyAnn, it's all a big mistake. Well, explain the scars all over their bodies. Did they just pop up there all by themselves?"

She folded the paper, laid it on the coffee table in front of her, and went to the bathroom.

Neither Limmell or LJ would talk about what had happened the day Lennox sent Limmell to the ER with a dislocated shoulder, so Limmell's case was dropped for lack of evidence. Lennox told Mother, "They can't come back here." So I moved them in with us. But Jeff was so nasty to them, I asked Anna, "Can you rent me one of your studio apartments until my house is ready?"

"Girl, I couldn't take your money! Besides, why put them in a studio when I have a two-bedroom available as we speak. But..." she said, pinching my arm as she always did whenever she wanted to make a point, "The next time something like that is going down, don't wait until something tragic happens. You should've let me know from the get-go and I would've moved them in with me if it was necessary." She even provided most of their furniture and made them promise if they saw Lennox on their block, they would call the police. Or her.

Hearing the news of her sixteen- and seventeen-year-old sons being set up in a cozy apartment near Northwestern

DAYLIGHT COMING

University, RudyAnn rang my cell phone. "Nicole," she said, "How could you get them their own place and we about to be evicted? Lenny said they can come back here and you can use the money you spending on them to help us out."

"As far as I'm concerned you and *Lenny* can go to hell, because I wouldn't give either one of you a drop of piss if you were dyin' and I was your last chance to live."

Mother called me two minutes after I hung up on her. "Nicole, you should be ashamed of yourself."

My thoughts were, *yeah, yeah, yeah* as she quoted the Bible about family and changing my evil ways. I put the phone down to take a sip from my bottle of water. When she realized I was no longer there, she hung up.

I skipped church the following Sunday and went to my house, eager for Isaac to add the final touches so I could move in. It took him a year to install everything I wanted: marble floors, ceramic-tile walls in the baths and kitchen, a granite countertop, a wet bar constructed from block glass in the basement, two gas fireplaces, and an open deck with built-in flower boxes and a gas range, among many other things. But still! A house is never a home where there is no love or happiness.

8

We were four months into rehabbing my dream house before Jeff had an inkling I was on my way out of our bogus marriage. He was at Mother's taking the garbage out, something he hadn't done since we married, when the guy who Mother always paid to wash her car congratulated him on our big-ass house on Sheridan Road. He had spotted me in the front yard some weeks earlier weeding out the flowerbed when he stopped by to be nosey. Jeff came home, eyes so red, I could have sworn he was crying.

"How dare you?" he screamed. "Where you keep gettin' all this money? We can't afford to move on Sheridan Road!"

"What the hell do you mean by *we*? Because I ain't your mother and I ain't obligated to put a roof over your head and feed your big ass, too. So when you get paid again, instead of buyin' ass and runnin' over to Mother's tryin' to impress her, you better send American Capital some money because I've written my last check for this place."

He stood staring at me like cutting my throat was weighing heavy on his mind.

"And yes, you heard me right. I ain't payin' another dime for *your* mortgage. And I refuse to pay anybody else," mostly the neighborhood drifters and alcoholics, "to do another thing around here." Besides, Jeff had never put my name on his mortgage or acted like he cared whether the house stood or fell unless he was around Mother or trying to get some money out of me. The house was almost paid for anyway.

"You're always braggin' about being the man of the house. Well, man! Your free ride is over unless you plan on bein' homeless. Because like I said, you ain't movin' in *my* damn house!"

"It ain't like our marriage is workin' no way. You too busy listenin' to Anna with her crazy ass and being stuck up under Mackey. I can't tell you nothin'. You only listen to him. So go be with him. We ain't slept in the same bed in damn near twenty years no way."

"If it had of been up to me, we never would have."

Herb Kent was jamming on the radio in our kitchen window as I busied myself in the backyard, trying to make some sense out of the junk Jeff kept finding on his route and was always throwing there. He had made friends with these two guys from Charleston, South Carolina who lived two houses over from us and spent plenty of time with them.

Although we had been married for four months and were what some would still call newlyweds, I didn't go too many places with Jeff unless it was necessary or if I got tired of him begging. So whenever he visited them I stayed at home, except the one time we went to one of their birthday parties. I was back home in less than ten minutes because everybody—men included—were half-naked. And there was every bit of fifty of us jammed inside their four-room box.

I glanced in the direction of the house after Jeff's laugher rang throughout the neighborhood. He and one of the guys were standing in the alley talking to Sallie Parker, one of our deacons' wives. I watched them for a few seconds, Jeff doing most of the conversing while the guy grinned as if he was in awe as to what Jeff was jabbering about. Soon Sallie sped off. He came home.

"What you gettin' ready to do?"

I had a bottle of Windex and some old newspapers in my hands and was headed out the front door. "Wash the windows."

"Why don't you forget all this work and go do something for yourself. I know you be tired of stayin' in the house all the time."

"But I don't have no money. Then I gotta take a bath. And change clothes."

"You look fine as is."

I had on a long khaki skirt, a red bandana tied around my head and a T-shirt. "No, I better finish this."

He took the cleaning supplies out of my hand. He threw them in the lawn chair on the porch. "I can handle it." He reached into his pocket. "Just go and have yourself some fun for a change and stay as long as you like. And take my car."

"I can't because I got work to do."

He kept prodding. I eventually said, "Okay," but refused his latter invitation. I was on my way to my favorite mall, blasting the music on my radio and bobbing my head to Parliament's "Tear the Roof off the Sucker," when wifely intuition said, *Hold up. How come Jeff wanted to get me out of the house so bad? And since when has he ever volunteered to clean anything other than his plate? And how come he gave me fifty dollars to buy myself something when he just complained yesterday about me spendin' five dollars of my money on some new glasses? And how come he kept insistin' I take my time and shop as long as I like?*

I pulled over, checked for oncoming traffic, then made a U-turn. I ran red lights and raced down side streets, swearing, "He better not have that bitch in my house." I couldn't get home fast enough and shouldn't have been surprised to find Sallie Parker with her heels locked around Jeff's neck. And him trying to knock her uterus out.

He said, "Damn girl, you got some good stuff! Damn, it's good!" And was humping so hard the headboard was slamming into the wall.

I snatched my loafer off and slapped him upside the head with it. His eyes popped open, but he kept grinding as deep inside of her as he could, his butt bouncing up and down like a basketball. I hit him over and over again, each time harder than the previous. He pounded inside her even faster and finished handling his business like he didn't feel anything beyond being inside of this woman. Once he finished emptying his juices, he rolled off her. He jumped to his feet while she was still clawing at him, begging, "Hurt me. Hurt me."

I screamed, "Jeff, you no-good bastard!" And she was a triflin' ass whore. "What the hell do you think you're doin' in my house?"

"Honey, if you were handlin' your business like you supposed to, he wouldn't of invited me in *yo* house."

I leaped at her. Jeff caught me mid-air. I slapped him. He grabbed my hands. "Nicole, just calm down."

I kicked him. "You calm down. You sorry ass-dog. And you ..." I tried even harder to get my hands on Sallie.

She said, as she was rolling off the bed, "Sweetheart, I don't know why you so mad at me, because I wasn't screwin' your husband. He was screwin' me. You saw who was on top."

Stunned, I presume, Jeff let me go. I ran up on Sallie swinging like a major leaguer. She knocked me down like a professional boxer. I popped right back up. But every time I got near her, she sent me sailing back across the room while Jeff, with his punk ass, just watched as I kept going back for more, which is the kind of fighter RudyAnn had taught me to be.

She always said, "Nikki, don't ever give up in a fight. If you gotta take something and bust 'em in the head or dig their eyes out. You go for what you know." I guess she figured her kicking my behind was enough.

So the last time Sallie slammed me into the dresser, I picked up a family-sized jar of Bergamot hair grease and threw it at her like I was trying to strike her out. It broke in her face and cut her under her left eye. She lunged at me like a bloodthirsty animal. Jeff grabbed her locking his arms in folds of her stomach. But he could barely contain her. Once he thought he had convinced her to "just calm down and let's talk about this," she knocked him out of her way and turned my size-five behind every way but loose.

After he managed to wrestle her out of the room he came back for her clothes, lips twitching to keep from smiling. My face was scratched pretty badly. My nose was bleeding. I had knots in my head. I was bruised everywhere, but was more furious than in pain. He escorted her out the door, then went into the bathroom, whistling "Don't Ask My Neighbor."

I barreled into the kitchen, seizing the one thing I thought would do the most damage. An aluminum frying pan. Like one ass kicking in one day wasn't enough. I snatched the shower curtain back and tried to beat him into a coma. Jeff tried to fight back, but crashed on the tub floor and got tangled in the plastic curtain. When he finally managed to crawl out, I was confined to bed for a week.

Although our holy wedlock got less than holy every year, I still kept our drama to myself, lying about my injuries. But I wouldn't be honest if I didn't admit lots of times I drew first blood. Jeff would do something I would consider disrespectful and I would snap. Yet, for the sake of being in Mother's good grace, I still prayed to God to love him through me, just like I had heard Pastor Dorthea preach so many times.

Pastor said, with fury in her voice and her eyes roaming over the congregation, "If you in the flesh can't love somebody—you might even think you hate them—just get on your knees and ask the Lord—to love that person through you. Don't you dare condemn yourselves to hell for hatin'! Because the Lord can fix all of your situations. All of your aches and your pains. Your dreams and your ambitions. And the Lord says. Listen to me good. How can you love me—whom thou has never seen, but hate your brother who you see every day?"

Jeff never made it easy for me to even like him. The many comments from Mother, such as, "He's a blessin' to you, Nicole," didn't help, either.

In the first few weeks of our marriage he would ask me to do things for him, then he started demanding, "Nicole, make me a plate." I would fix it. "Go get me the salt." I would bring it to him and sit down to eat. "Get me the pepper." Then he would need another helping or a refill of whatever he was drinking.

The pitcher would be in front of him. He would tilt his glass at me, then clear his throat until I filled it. And every night before bed, he would stand over me, not caring what I was doing. "Go turn the sheets back." If I didn't do what he said, he would take it straight to Mother just so he could hear her say, "He's head of the household, Nicole. It's your duty to do what your husband says. When he says it!"

Mother's hand in my life was another thing I had planned to leave behind as I hopped out of bed at five a.m. on the day I had scheduled to move into my dream house. I reached under my bed, pulling out the boxes I had bought from the U-Haul store for my personal things, because Jeff was welcome to have everything else. Three were missing. I jumped to my feet. I rushed toward the front door, hoping I had left them in the trunk of my car, but positive I hadn't. I heard the screeching sound of tape being ripped. I knocked Jeff's bedroom door open.

"What the hell are you doin'?"

"I'm packin'. What do it look like?"

"I thought you said you're stayin' here."

"When? Because if you think you gonna buy a big fancy house and leave me here in this dump, you must be outta your damn mind?"

I threw my finger up, waving it inches from his nose. "First of all, this is your dump. You made it that when you quit contributin' to the household and started spendin' your check on hookers and tryin' to buy my mother's love."

"Excuse me."

"And not once did you offer to give me anything on the house or to paint a room after you found out I bought it. I did it all by myself just like I've been holdin' us down for years, because you think you can take your paycheck and do whatever you want. But I've got news for you. You ain't movin' in my damn house!"

I should have saved my breath, because he rode up and down Sheridan Road until he spotted the movers I had hired unloading all of the new furnishings I had in storage. I was unpacking a plastic container filled with the sculptures I had been collecting when he marched inside, followed by Mother and RudyAnn.

Now beautiful is beautiful and I don't like to brag, but when I say my house was laid out . . . I'm talking floors gleaming, a chef's kitchen with stainless steel appliances, plush white carpet in the living and family rooms and white leather furniture—a dream come true for a girl who took her severance pay and bought and sold property until she could afford the house she truly wanted and did it with a lot of feet in her behind every step of the way.

Although I was pissed to the max when I saw them, I still expected Mother to say, "Wow, this is beautiful, Nicole." But she just said, "Where's the bathroom? I can use it, can't I?"

I led her down the hall and pointed to the guest bathroom, decorated with turquoise and ecru accessories. And directly across from the sunken family room with mahogany beams in the vaulted ceiling. She walked past me, turning sideways so she wouldn't have to touch me. "I guess you *really* think you're something now," she said and slammed the door.

I went back into the living room, shaking my head with wonder. Jeff was on his way upstairs. RudyAnn was headed for the kitchen, probably to the refrigerator. I caught up with him just as he stuck his head in the master suite, already set up with my ten-piece black Italian bedroom group.

"What are you doin' here?" I said, trying to keep him from going any further. He bumped me out of his way and walked over to the bathroom. Isaac had turned the adjoining room into a full bath with a double walk-in closet, double vanity, black marble tiles with chrome fixtures, and a black clawfoot tub with a separate shower. Jeff peeped inside, nodding his head in approval.

"You ain't welcome here, Jeff. I demand you leave now!"

He threw his hands on his hips. "Put me out!"

9

After soaking in a tub of ginger-scented sea salt and mango bubblebath for an hour, I painted my nails and toes Midnight Copper, then stretched across my bed, breathing in the smell of new all around me. Jeff slithered into my bedroom, wearing an ankle-length white robe, white silk boxers, white shower shoes, and reeking of a flower and spice cologne. He carried the same ugly wood tray he had on our wedding, only this time he was trying to romance me with a bottle of unknown champagne, cheese squares, and Saltine crackers.

I sat up. "What do you want? And haven't you ever heard of knockin'?"

He glanced down at his peace offering, then back up at me. "I just wanna talk to you."

"About?"

"Can't we christen our house like a husband and wife should?"

"Jeff, this ain't *your* house. Not today. Not tomorrow. Not ever. You didn't put shit on this place, so I'm just lettin' you live here until I can figure out how to get rid of your ass!"

"But, Nicole . . . " He walked toward me. I threw my hand up. His head dropped like a wounded child. "Can't we just try?"

"No! Especially when you come paradin' in my room talkin' about *our* new house. This ain't *your* house. And there damn sho won't be no christenin' because I'm lettin' you know, put one finger on me and I'll cut your damn throat."

As big as my dream house was and as easy as I could get lost upstairs in my luxurious bedroom, Jeff being there took all of the fun out of having it. He would come home with flowers and leave boxes of candy on my bed even though I told him every day, "Stay outta my damn room." He even started walking around in an open robe with his boxers and coming in early from work.

"Nicole, is there something I can help you with? Want me to run you some bath water? Wash your hair?"

"I don't want you to do a damn thang except stay the hell outta my way."

Him trying to add a little spice to our hopeless marriage was just as nauseating as me having to look at him strutting around my house as if he belonged there. Eating up everything I brought home, as usual. One tamale. It would be gone. A Snickers bar. It would disappear. I couldn't even leave half a pop in the fridge or he would suck that up, too. I also couldn't focus when he was around, trying to flatter me with his pretentious charm. But, as the old saying goes, "a leopard can't change its spots."

As things started to look up for me at NCS Management, and because I had an excellent reputation for being reasonable with my rent and for paying a fair price for property, people started calling me constantly or seeking me out through Isaac. The day after his parole ended, he quit working for the hotel and set up a small office in the two-bedroom house he rented.

With Mackey Builders, Isaac and a few of the neighborhood derelicts he was trying to help, rehabbing all over the place, the same church folks who had once turned their noses up at him were anxious to hire him for their remodeling needs. Especially single women. But the problem with most people is they want a lot of something for a little of nothing. Isaac had set prices. A lot of the folks, the same ones who treated him like he was a serpent, wanted discounts, because they went way back. I especially resented him having anything to do with anybody from Holy Hill.

"Isaac, why do you bother yourself with those people?"

"Because I don't take everything personal like you do."

"They're the ones who's supposed to be so saved and sanctified. And always tryin' to get over on somebody, lyin', sayin' they ain't got no money. But look at how they dress and what they drive."

"If they're lyin', that's between them and God. Either way, *Mother*, you know I get half up front and the rest when the job is near completion. Now can we get back to what we're doin'?"

He and two of his employees had just finished remodeling the first-floor unit of a three-flat I had bought. They were moving my black-lacquer desk and file cabinet, copier, fax machine, and computer into my new office. Content with the China-white glazed walls, black and white symmetrical borders, and black mini-blinds, I said, "So I guess now all I gotta do is figure out what I'm gonna do with the bedroom in the back?"

One of the guys said, "I could easily answer that."

Isaac cut his eyes at him. He ducked outside to get the box of copy paper I had left on the back porch, laughing at his insinuation. Isaac shook his head.

"Gettin' back to what we were discussin', why not set up a bedroom or get a daybed or a nice sofa, because you look like you ain't been gettin' no sleep."

He was right regarding me and sleep. Every night for two weeks straight, I dreamed about Limmell falling into a hole and me not being able to reach him. I woke up with him remaining on my mind until the early morning. He and LJ, a junior and senior in high school, were still living in Anna's building. They were getting excellent grades and were working at Dominick's grocery store.

I asked them several times about moving in with me, but living the life of bachelors was more appealing, so I quit bugging them. I also quit fussing over them as much, because I thought since they were out of Lennox's house, things were much better. But what is *better*?

With my computer booted up and a hot cup of Blue Mountain coffee in hand, I sat back looking over the latest property for sale in Evanston. The telephone rang. I glanced at the Caller ID, then answered the call.

"He's dead, Nikki. He's dead."

I shot out of my seat. "Who, LJ? Who's dead?"

"Nikki, he's dead. Oh God. I can't believe it."

"Who?"

"Oh God, he's dead. I can't believe it!"

I slammed the telephone down, grabbed my keys out of my drawer, and raced to my Legend at top speed. Isaac was stopping by for a couple of sheets of drywall, because whenever there was a sale on the material we used most, we would stock up and store it in my garage. I zoomed past him. He grabbed my arm to find out what was happening.

When Isaac and I got to LJ and Limmell's apartment, a fire truck, ambulance, and several policemen were there. Water was all over the place. And a white sheet covered a body stretched out on the beige carpet. I dived past the crowd, snatching it back. I gasped, trying to call Limmell's name to tell him to get up, but somebody threw the sheet back over him as I sank to the floor.

Isaac helped me over to the couch where LJ was on his knees. His clothes were soaked and his face was buried in his hands. We grabbed each other at the same time.

"What happened to him, LJ?"

"Why did he have to do it, Nikki? I told him everything was gonna be alright and that Lennox couldn't hurt him no more, but he was so scared."

"What did Lennox do?"

"I don't know. But Limmell called me at work and he was cryin' sayin' he couldn't take it no more and that Lennox was right. He wasn't worth the air he breathed. I tried to tell him

Lennox was wrong, but he said . . ." LJ's head fell into his hands again. "He said Lennox was right. Then he said he loved me . . . and he hoped I would forgive him."

LJ and I bawled together while Isaac held us both. RudyAnn rushed in, her hair looking like a bad wig. She screamed, "Oh my God!" when the police told her they suspected Limmell James had cut his wrists. She also just happened to fall into the arms of the best-looking officer in the room.

LJ and Limmell's neighbor across the hall cried with us while telling us how Lennox had come banging on their door. She said, "I knew Limmell was home even though he didn't let him in. He came here last week, too, cursing Limmell through the door and kicking it, saying, 'You're gonna burn in hell because you're a faggy and God hates fags.'"

She continued, tear after tear falling from her eyes. Her hands trembled as she attempted to wipe them away. "He was a good kid and such a gentleman. He always said, 'Yes, ma'am' and 'No ma'am.' Would help me with my groceries and washed my car. He was so sweet. How could that man have treated him like that?"

10

Making the arrangements for Limmell's funeral was just as heart-wrenching as seeing him carried out of the apartment he had come to love without any chances of ever living in it again. Or fulfilling any of his dreams—especially the one he had of going to college alongside his big brother and one day teaching his favorite subject, Black history. I cried myself to sleep whenever I could, and woke up in the morning doing the same thing. I couldn't help it, especially when I saw anything or anyone in Carolina blue. A die-hard Tarheel fan, Limmell loved it even though Lennox called it a faggy color. Mother almost jumped out of her skin when she saw it was what I chose to bury him in.

"They didn't have anything black in his size?" she asked, ogling the double-breasted suit as if I had misplaced my mind.

LJ said, "My brother never had anything his way in his life. So I think he deserves to have it in his death. You did the right thing, Nikki. I don't care what none of these people say."

At the wake, the second Lennox walked in the church door with his mother, whom he had conveniently been staying with, LJ pounced on him like a tiger, pounding him with his fists. Isaac, Jeff, and one of our deacons pulled him off Lennox, but LJ broke away from them. He stomped Lennox about the head and face. They tried to restrain him again, but the rage he had pinned up inside made him more difficult to hold on to.

"I'm gonna kill him!" LJ cried. "I'm gonna kill him!"

Mother said to Pastor Dorthea, "Look at him, carryin' on just like them," meaning LJ's father's side of the family. The Williamses. Her and Lennox's reason for treating him and

Limmell like they had been the one who brought shame upon the family and not RudyAnn.

It took Isaac, Anna, and I the longest time to calm him down so the services could get underway. Anna and I held on to him with all of our might when we walked back into the sanctuary, me silently praying the funeral would soon be over.

While LJ and I were writing the obituary, he insisted he wanted Adam, one of Holy Hill's young choir members, to sing "It's So Hard to Say Good-bye to Yesterday." The boy sang the words *"how can I say good-bye?"* LJ snatched away from us and stormed out of the church. We ran behind him.

Jeff followed us to the corner we were huddled in. He laid his hand on my shoulder. "Nicole and LJ, it's gonna be all right. Just give it time."

I pushed his hand away. "Get away from me!" Trying to be supportive in front of Mother and Pastor, he didn't bat an eye when I said, "LJ is comin' to live with me."

He said, "I agree, because he'll never be able to go back there after what happened." But he kept asking when we were alone, "How long is he gonna be with us?"

The day after Limmell was laid to rest in a sunny spot in Lake View Memorial Gardens Jeff came to my bedroom. He took his usual stance in my doorway.

"You found someplace for that boy to go?"

"If anybody's gettin' out, it'll be you."

He stomped back to his room. I got up to make dinner, since I couldn't remember the last time I had seen LJ eat anything. We were barely able to digest our baked potatoes loaded with butter, sour cream, cheddar cheese, and Jalapeno peppers. Jeff gobbled up four. I kissed LJ good-night, then dragged myself back upstairs to my bedroom with a twelve-ounce glass of Long Island Iced Tea after doing the dishes.

LJ came upstairs and said, "I'll see you, later, Nikki."

"Where you goin'?"

"Out."

"Okay, but don't be gone too long."

He threw on his black-hooded sweatshirt, laced his white Nike gym shoes, and rushed out the door. I woke up at seven in the morning. His bed hadn't been slept in. With no numbers to call, I threw on a pair of jeans and a sweater and drove around looking for him. Three days I searched for him, calling the police repeatedly. I called so much I could hear whomever sigh when I said, "I'm callin' because my nephew still ain't come home."

Jeff finally said, "Nicole, he's with his girlfriend," after finding me in the study at my PC, crying like it was the end of the world.

I leaped out of my chair. "What the hell do you mean *his girlfriend*?"

"He just didn't want you to know. And I think that's the best place for him."

"Why wouldn't he want me to know? What did you say to him?"

LJ had moved in with Bethany, a girl he had known for only six months. She was a petite girl with big round eyes, dark lashes, and the face of an angel. But she was also sixteen with a nine-month-old son and two months' pregnant, claiming it was his. I tried to make him move back in with me, pointing out how she wasn't right for him and how he wasn't thinking.

He said, "You see how your husband be trippin' with me. Complainin' about every little thing I do. Watchin' me like I'm gonna steal something. I can't live like that. He'll mess around and say the wrong thing and I'll end up havin' to kill him. Because nobody will ever treat me like Lennox did again. And live to tell about it."

Unaware that him being with me was what was keeping me sane, I didn't argue with him. I just tried to lose my troubles in searching for more property to buy. It didn't help, because I couldn't focus on anything. And I was dog-tired. I hated to go to bed at night and once I did, hated even more to get up in the morning. I stayed in my room around the clock singling out everybody who had ever done anything bad to Limmell and LJ.

Lennox had to be rushed to the ER for severe chest pains and was diagnosed as having a nervous breakdown two hours after the funeral. I thought, *Good enough for him. I hope he dies there*. RudyAnn decided it would be best for her to move in with Mother. I said, "I hope they burn up." LJ was worse than me.

Although I didn't want him to know, some Good Samaritan had told him who his father really was and introduced him to his other family, the Williamses, known throughout Evanston for being nothing but a bunch of thieves and hustlers. Silk, who I felt was more RudyAnn's pimp as opposed to her boyfriend, had been killed in a car accident in Houston when LJ was five and Limmell was four. Even after she married, RudyAnn would still sex anybody he told her to and would leave with him and be gone for days while Lennox stayed at home with the boys.

The Williams, having heard through the Evanston grapevine many times, LJ and Limmell were his, welcomed his remaining son into the family without hesitation. LJ started spending time with them, staying out all times of the night, drinking, and cursing like he was born to do it. His change in attitude caused problems for him and Bethany, who thought she had found herself the ideal man. They started having heated arguments every day. Her mother was one of those weak, let-her-child-do-what-she-wanted parents, but would call 9-1-1 if she couldn't make them behave. The police finally got tired of going over there and LJ's flip mouth.

Bethany called me late one night crying. "They arrestin' LJ!"

"What?"

"They put handcuffs on him," she bawled. "But I started it, Nikki. He made me so mad I slapped him. I didn't mean it, but he called me nasty." If LJ didn't clean up, the place did look like crap and he wasn't used to living like that.

She said, "It's all my fault. He walked away from me. But I threw a ashtray at him and it hit him in the back. Then he tried to leave the house, but I started scratchin' and kickin' him. All he did was push me out of his way so he could leave."

It was still a serious offense, because she was pregnant. I tried to tell LJ this after the police released him into my care without pressing charges.

He said, "You need to mind your damn business, because I'm grown. And I don't need you, Leola, RudyAnn, none of y'all. Y'all wasn't there to prevent my brother from killing himself."

He hurt me to my soul and made me want to cry, "Why LJ? Why turn on me? I love you." But he was glaring at me with so much rage on his face I had to walk away.

"That's right. Walk away. Fuck you too, then!"

I turned around and punched him in his jaw. "How dare you talk to me like that?" I slapped him. I kicked him.

He grabbed my hands, tears in his eyes. "Nikki, I . . . " I snatched away from him and ran to my car, my vision blurred by my tears and in so much agony I could barely breathe. I opened the door and fell inside, crying for my nephews—wanting to touch Limmell—to hold him and tell him how much I loved him. And to let LJ know how sorry I was for letting them down.

When I could finally think beyond my pain, I drove home. Jeff met me coming in the door. "Nicole, where you been? Why won't you let me help see you through this?"

I went upstairs and crawled into my bed, so overwhelmed I held myself, writhing in pain. Then I jumped up. I slapped my perfumes off the dresser and kicked over the ottoman in front of the chair in the corner.

Jeff knocked on the door. "Nicole, are you all right? Did you break something?"

I threw one pillow after another at the locked door, snatched my covers off the bed, and punched the mattress until I was too tired to hit anymore. Still I couldn't shake my sorrow.

Just as any great friend would, Anna decided to stop by to see how I was doing after too many of her calls went to my voice mail. I'm sure she was surprised that Jeff let her in, but not as shocked as she was to find me lying on the floor, after she picked the lock, with a picture of Limmell wrapped in my arms. It was one of the several trips she made to my house to talk me out of my distress, but my misery wouldn't budge. It was like a drug—a monkey on my back—that just wouldn't go away.

Finally, she couldn't take watching me drowning in my distress any longer. "You're giving the devil exactly what he wants, Nicole." I felt another outburst coming. My head dropped even further. She propped it back up.

"You're giving up on yourself and you look like crap," she continued. "It's been I don't know how many weeks since you been in this room. And I love you, girl. But you ain't gonna keep stressing me out. I know Limmell is gone and you loved him more than life. He loved you, too. But right now I know he's looking down on you from heaven, embarrassed as hell. Because your shit is matted to your head. And you look like that girl from *The Exorcist*."

I laughed. She laughed. Then we cried. She said, "That's right. Get it out of your system. Let it all out. Then get up and take a damn bath, because you stink!"

I stuck my nose down my T-shirt. I jumped up from the floor and ran to the bathroom to shower and wash my hair. Anna twisted it into a bun once I was done, then rushed me out the door to our favorite salon, Tramina's. She treated me to a massage, herbal wrap, pedicure, and manicure, and had my hair re-washed and my ends clipped.

Following her advice for me to do something special for me, I treated myself to a flaming red Volvo. I chose a new car because Limmell had rode in the front seat of my Legend too often for me to continue to drive it. LJ didn't have that problem so I gave the Legend to him. He came to visit me during my black days, but I refused to look at him. Not because I was dwelling on what he had said. As much as it felt like he had stomped on my heart, I knew he didn't mean a word of it regarding me. I didn't mean to hit him either, because I had never touched him like that in my life. He just looked so much like Limmell I couldn't stand being near him. I explained my reason to him.

"That's okay, Nikki. And I'm sorry I cursed you. I love you more than anybody else in the world. You've done more for me than anybody, and I almost messed up everything between us being stupid and disrespectful. But I'm glad you forgave me and you're okay. Getting your ride is cool, too."

"It's the least I could do since I missed your graduation."

"I wasn't gonna walk without you being there. But Anna said if I didn't, as hard as you worked to make sure I made it through high school, she would kick my . . . you know. She made me go to my prom, too. Grandma Williams bought our stuff and Anna rented me and Bethany a limo. I didn't want to do that, either. But everybody insisted. Man, I wish Limmell coulda been there."

11

In my opinion RudyAnn didn't appear to grieve after her performance at Limmell's funeral, because the whole while Lennox was hospitalized she and this basketball player she used to screw during high school started back seeing each other. Hearing I was back in my right mind, probably from Jeff, she called me.

"Nicole," she said, sounding like she was my boss. "How much do you have left from the policy you had on Limmell?"

"Hello to you, too."

"Just answer the question. How much do you have left from the policy you had on my son?"

"If you must know, I never had one."

"Quit lyin', because I know you don't think I believe you got that much money."

"I could care less what you believe."

"Just bring me the rest of his money."

"Like I said, there ain't no money! Me and Anna paid for his funeral considering you and your sorry-ass husband never had a job long enough to buy any insurance. Or anything else."

"Look, chick! You can't have a policy on my child and cash it in, buyin' yourself a new car without givin' me nothin'. I can't keep stayin' here with Mother for free."

"It ain't never seemed to bother you before."

"You know what . . . you are one greedy-ass ho!"

"Ho? Who in the hell are you to call anybody a whore with your low-down funky ass?"

By the time I finished telling her about the sluttish stuff she used to do and was still doing, for the first time in her life, RudyAnn was speechless. I finished our conversation with a bit of sisterly advice. "From this day on, chick, you had better stay the hell away from me. Because I don't owe you money from Limmell. I owe you an ass-kickin' *for* Limmell!"

Satisfied with having made my point, I decided I had a business to run. I had my eyes on three graystones on Chicago's Southside that I knew were going to bring me a healthy sum once I bought, rehabbed, and sold them. They had three massive bedrooms each, walk-in closets, two full baths, a huge kitchen and even larger dining room with a built-in hutch and a spacious enclosed porch. I had been negotiating with the owner, stubborn Jeremiah Thomas, when everything around me went berserk. I had met him through my mail lady. He was her uncle and wanted to sell them so he could move back to Atlanta, but wanted to keep the property in the family, so to speak.

He initially wanted $450,000 per building, which was extremely high for the neighborhood they were in. Although they weren't far from the downtown area, derelicts and dilapidated dwellings made up the entire block, not even considering the amount of work they required. I initially insulted him by offering three-fifty for all of them, so I had to kiss his butt big-time to get him to even talk to me again. I made an afternoon appointment to meet him at the Soul Queen restaurant on the Southside.

Since he was anxious to sell, so he wouldn't have to spend another winter in the city, I told myself, *We won't say good-bye until we agree on a price.* Isaac had already checked the buildings out, drawn up a floor plan and estimated how much it would cost for what I wanted him to do. I was on my way to our meeting when a drop of rain fell, followed by a billion more. I turned my wipers on. They didn't budge. I clicked them off, then tried them again. I called Anna.

"Quit tripping, Nicole. Just call the dealership. If they need to keep your car, you can borrow one of mine. Or you can get a loaner. It's not like they don't have them."

DAYLIGHT COMING

I sat on the street, three blocks from my house, for almost twenty minutes waiting for the rain to subside. When I decided I could see good enough to drive to the city of Lake Forest where I had bought my Volvo, I pulled into the Demetri Autoplex Car Care Center with much attitude.

Gus, the shop manager, whom I was told I needed to see, met me with a broad smile on his leathery face. Before I could snap on him or anybody else for being inconvenienced, the epitome of every woman's fantasy came walking toward us. I'm talking a deep shade of mahogany, waves in his faded-cut, 6' even, and a body like "Whoa!" I could barely argue my point for eyeballing him in his blue Phat Farm jeans with the matching button-down shirt. And if him looking like he should be mine wasn't enough, he was wearing a citrus cologne that made my toes curl. I had to keep looking down at my feet and will them to straighten back up.

"You wanna check it out?" Gus said, tossing him the keys. He got into my car. He flipped the wiper switch on, then popped the hood, while I was hearing Salt-n-Pepa rapping the song, "Shoop." Especially the part where they said something about the brotha being packed and stacked. Especially in the back. I was so mesmerized by how heaven must have been missing an angel I didn't hear a word he said until he came and stood next to me.

"Try it now."

I flipped my wipers on. *Damn! Why the hell did these things have to work?* Because I could have hung around the shop all day with my eyes on every move he made. I said, "Thank you," and threw my purse on the seat on the passenger side, humiliated by how awed I was by this gorgeous black specimen, considering after meeting Jeff I had given up on all men.

"Nikki, you don't remember me, do you?"

He called me Nikki. Nobody calls me that but LJ and Limmell. Oh my Lord! He called me Nikki! "How do you . . ." I asked, my heart pounding like I was being stalked.

"As many times as I was at your house, why wouldn't I?"

"Are you a friend of my . . . my sister?" *Please don't tell me you screwed RudyAnn.* Even though he looked way too young for her, but with her, one would never know.

He smiled. "No." *Thank you, Jesus!*

He took his leather wallet out of his back pocket. He opened it to a Polaroid picture we had taken together at Great America Amusement Park. He was sixteen, in baggy jean shorts and a Chicago Bears T-shirt. I was twenty-eight, wearing a plain-white blouse and a red skirt, just as skinny as he was. Even back then, Alex was taller than me. I looked into the eyes I spent many days and nights longing to see, with my hand across my heart. I screamed out his name, then threw my arms around him, hugging him tight, and oh-so glad to see my long-lost friend.

The retiring shop manager said, "I been here for thirty years now and no customer has ever been this grateful to me. Especially one this purty."

I let Alex go, laughing, yet crying so hard he had to go get me tissue. The other technicians gathered around us, curious to know the story behind me being hostile as hell one minute and all over their new boss the next. "I knew him when he was a kid." I laughed and wiped away my joyful tears.

Our audience thought I was joking, because they thought I was still in my twenties. I wished I was as I watched Alex telling a trainee how to read some kind of gadget built especially for foreign cars. And man, was he looking good enough to devour in those jeans. We met, the following day, at Kamari's, a Greek restaurant, down the street from his job and known for its tantalizing seafood dishes.

I had been so anxious about seeing him again, I could barely sleep or focus during my meeting to buy the graystones. He had only been back in Illinois for three months having decided to stay after the death of his grandfather. Having run away from home in his senior year, he went to Atlanta, and from there to Florida. From Miami Beach to Jacksonville to Orlando. He enrolled in high school, graduated with honors, then paid his way through trade school, becoming a certified mechanic. He always had a calling, because even as a teenager he could fix cars just as good as the alley experts. He could also mend a broken heart and patch up a crushed self-esteem. Somewhat.

As a husband, the best thing Jeff ever did for me was to introduce me to Alex. This was seven years into the thing we called marriage. Jeff brought him home with him to shovel the snow piled on our front porch and sidewalk. I immediately became concerned about him, because it was zero below and obvious his worn corduroys and windbreaker weren't doing anything to protect him from the cold. I fixed him a bowl of homemade beef soup, toasted him some garlic bread, and made him a large cup of hot chocolate. He gobbled his food up in swallows, then glanced down at his bowl when he was done, too embarrassed to ask for more.

Alex, thirteen and in the eighth grade, lived with his alcoholic mother, Roxanne, in a small brick house two streets east of ours. Jeff, having met him pumping gas and washing windows at the station not far from us, was impressed with his knowledge of motor vehicles. He invited him to do other jobs around our house: changing the oil and other fluids in his car, washing it, and keeping our grass cut once the weather broke. Things Jeff was too lazy to do. It provided pocket change for Alex, which should have been a lot more than the five dollars Jeff would give him as if he was doing him a favor.

Once we became friends, I gave Alex money whenever I could and made sure every time he came to our house he ate. I even bought him his first set of clippers, because his hair was always a nappy mess. He taught himself how to groom it with licensed perfection and learned how to give a heck of a shave, which he did for Jeff for free since Jeff never paid him anything more than the usual.

During our first summer, after getting to know one another, we spent a number of weekends hanging out at Navy Pier in downtown Chicago and went to a couple of Cubs games. He also liked going to the beach. I would sit on the shore reading or trying not to think about my problems while he swam a couple of laps. Strangers would see us together laughing about something hilarious he had said and would ask, "Are you his big sister?"

He would always say, "No, she's my mother," even though I didn't look old enough to have a teen-age son. Before they got the chance to ask any more questions, he would grab my hand. "Come on, mama, let's do such and such." Like playing video games, foos ball, pool, or pinball, his favorite pastime. He wasn't as outgoing around Jeff, who insisted, "Something is wrong with that boy. He don't like to do nothin' people his age do."

In Jeff's presence, Alex was very soft-spoken, but we had chemistry from the moment we said, "Pleased to meet you."

He picked up on things quickly, so we decided he would become an accountant. We had planned for him to start City College in the fall, me promising to help him with his expenses before he disappeared. We even talked about him getting an apartment nearby and how I was going to drop in to help him with his studies. Even back then, he knew a lot about responsibilities and money. He loved to share his dreams of prosperity with me.

"Nikki, one day, I'm gonna be rich."

"I never wanna be rich, Alex, just happy."

"You will, one day. I promise."

When I found out he had run away, I was grieved for I don't know how long. It was the kind of pain I could easily associate with mothers—except mine—whose children are abducted. This was four years after we met. I was waiting for him to come over when his mother knocked on our door. "Where the hell is my son?" she demanded to know. Because all of his belongings were gone.

Jeff and I had been arguing on and off for two days. Every time he looked at me, he found something to nag at me about and every time he said my name I would snap. Having finished his fried chicken, snow peas, and mashed potatoes, he burped his way back to his room to get ready for a night out with one of his many girlfriends. I returned to the kitchen. Our back doorbell rang as I was washing the dishes.

"Hey, Nikki. What's up?"

"How you doin', Alex? Come on in. You hungry?"

"Naw, I just ate." He cupped his hands around his mouth. He blew into them.

"Have a seat."

Jeff stomped out of his room. He brushed past him as if he didn't know we had company, considering how loud our bell was. He wrapped his fist in the collar of my blouse.

"Where the hell is my wallet, Nicole, and I don't wanna hear you don't know."

I slapped his hand. "I don't know! And I don't care. Now get your hands off me!"

He leaned over in my face. "Gimme my wallet, Nicole."

"I ain't got it!"

He let me go and threw his mitt-sized paw over my face, making my neck snap. My wet hand landed on his cheek. He slapped me almost to my knees. Alex dashed between us and pushed Jeff away from me. Jeff stumbled back like a mighty tree. The house shook when he landed on his behind.

He jumped to his feet. "Boy!" He grabbed Alex by the back of his corduroy jacket, opened the back door and slung him out on the porch. Alex fell on one knee, sprang to his feet, and rushed back inside. I jumped in front of him.

"Alex, go home."

He swung around me. Jeff grabbed his face, then looked down at his hand. Blood ran down his chin from his busted lip. He hurried over to the drawer where we kept the things we didn't know where else to put. He snatched out a rusty pistol he had found on one of his delivery routes.

"You think you man enough to handle me?" He aimed it at Alex's chest. "Well, let's see how good you can take a bullet."

Alex pushed me to the side. I grabbed him by his rail-thin arm and jumped in front of him again.

"Please, Alex, go home."

"But he hit you, Nikki," he said, trying to get his hands on Jeff. I pushed Alex back out the door and slammed it in Jeff's face. Jeff bammed on it with his fists. "Nicole, open this damn door!" Then he kicked it with all of his might. "That boy don't know who he messin' with." He shook the knob. "Open this damn door!"

I said, "Alex, please. Go—"

"But—"

"Go! Get outta here. Now!"

Hurt sprang in his eyes. He shook his head and raced down the porch steps, fleeing down the alley into the night. I let the doorknob go. Like something reaching out of the abyss, Jeff snatched me inside. He slapped me upside my head.

"What the hell is your problem? You my wife and . . ." I pushed him away from me and ran over to the drawer where we kept our knives. He dashed behind me and slammed his body into mine. "You gonna try and kill me over him?" He knocked the butcher knife out of my hand. "That piece of trash? That raggedy-ass boy? You screwin' him? That's what you been doin' while I'm workin'?"

"Get away from me, Jeff." I tried to kick him, but he had me pinned against the kitchen counter so tight my foot could barely move. The more I tried to free myself, the more stimulating it became to him. He grinded his erection against my leg.

"That's what you like, Nicole. A little boy." He grabbed my ponytail, snatched my head back, and licked down my throat. "That's what turns you on. Little boys." Jeff threw me on the floor. "Well, I'm gonna teach you what a real man is supposed to do with a whore like you."

Part Two:
According To Whose Rules!

12

Following my reunion with Alex, we met for lunch, dinner and breakfast to listen to music, or take a walk in the park, inseparable like old times. Jeff heard through the Evanston grapevine I had a new boyfriend. I would be driving my car, look in my rearview mirror, and his delivery truck would be right behind me. Next thing I knew, he was off work for a week. He claimed to be on vacation. I was aware he had three weeks a year and hadn't used any of his time. But by week number four, I called Locking Produce.

I asked to leave him a message, knowing he was still laid up in bed. The switchboard operator transferred me to Human Resources. The woman said, "I'm sorry, but Mr. Kingston retired five weeks ago."

I was livid, but Jeff being Jeff had an excellent excuse. "You know I told you my doctor said I got high blood pressure. And I been tellin' you for years now that ridin' in that truck all day is bad for my knees and keeps givin' me hemorrhoids."

"You ain't told me a damn thang! I don't know who you think is gonna take care of you, because I ain't. So you can either find another job or get out!"

"Why? So you can move whoever you messin' around with up in here? I hate to disappoint you, but I ain't goin' nowhere."

"Well, you're gonna be hungry as hell, because I ain't feedin' you!"

"I don't need you to feed me."

"You didn't need me to put a roof over your head either, but I see I'm the one who's been footin' all the bills for the past twenty years."

"That's all I ever hear from you. But as long as you takin' care of me, then you won't be able to spend none of my money on your boyfriend."

"Jeff, I'm tellin' you this for the last time. What I earn belongs to me! I don't ask for none of your money, so you ain't gettin' no more of mine."

"We'll see."

Between Alex, LJ, and work—Jeff's jealous escapades, trying to follow me around, searching my bedroom, making frequent trips to my office, checking my mail, and stealing my cell phone—became the last thing on my mind. LJ was getting ready to start his first semester at Northwestern University, destined to become a P.E. Teacher. And for the first time he was happy. Bethany still had some growing up to do, but she loved him and he loved her. He was such a handsome young man, just like his father, and the girls loved him. Even the ones who once shunned him had started trying to sling their stuff his way.

"LJ, don't let yourself get caught up," I advised, after he informed me that a former classmate just wouldn't leave him alone.

"Ain't you one to talk?"

"Pardon."

"Yeah, I heard."

"Heard what? Well, to set the record straight, I'm not havin' a affair. This guy is just a friend. That's it! We've known each other for a long time."

"Then how come I ain't never seen him."

I stopped throwing away the receipts in my wallet I didn't need. "He's been away." I shook my head and opened my desk drawer.

"So, who is he?"

"You don't know him."

"Try me."

"His name is Alex."

"The only Alex I remember is the picture you had of that skinny boy with the big Afro who used to wash y'all cars."

"You remember that?"

"Yeah." I started laughing, because Alex was a stick back in the day. "That's him? Oo-oo-w, Nikki, you nasty. You old enough to be his mother."

"Like I said. We're just friends. And I'm only twelve years older than him, thank you."

"Does the bear know?"

"There's nothin' to know."

"You say that now. But just wait until Alex gets you between the sheets."

"Excuse me."

"I hear he's got a body like LL."

"See, that's why I don't like you."

"Auntie done roped her a stallion. You go, girl."

"Bye, LJ. And you better keep me posted on your grades, because I ain't uppin' a dime if you got anything below a three-point-five."

Since we had become best friends, he told me all of his business, although sometimes I had to put my fingers in my ears. I enjoyed our conversations, which almost came to an end after Alex and I were reunited. The same with Anna. She insisted, "Girl, you do your thang."

Even Isaac noticed the change in me. He asked, as I stood watching him load mortar in the back of his truck, "So what's been goin' on with you?" Like he hadn't heard.

"I've been really busy lately."

He nodded. I missed being around him, because he was so skilled with his hands that he amazed me and he was always eager to teach me something. But I ached any time I was away from Alex. I knew what was happening, called myself stupid for even considering it, and decided to lay low.

Alex called my office. "Nikki, why you cancel lunch with me three days in a row? And tell me the truth."

"I've just been very busy."

"Well, I miss you. Lunch don't seem the same without you. So can we hook up?"

I finished jotting down the items I needed from Office Depot and rushed out the door on my way to Demetri Autoplex. Alex met me getting out of my car and showed me how glad he was to see me with a broad smile and a kiss on my cheek.

"So how you been?" I asked, trying to refrain from grinning like a damn fool.

"I would be better if you returned my calls."

"Sorry."

"So what's been up with you?"

If only you knew. Thirty minutes before he had called, Jeff had come to my office and stood over me like he was my master and I was his slave. I sighed. "Jeff, what do you want now?"

"You might as well quit fightin' me, Nicole, because this place right here is *our* business."

"Since when?"

"Since I retired from my job." Which just happened to be approximately two weeks after he found out I had an office. "Because it's time I started makin' some financial decisions around here."

"So you just got up this mornin' and threw on this lemon-lime Don Juan suit, with your matchin' snakeskin shoes, and decided to barge in here thinkin' I'm just gonna let you. You don't even know what kind of business I'm runnin'!"

"Well, I think it's about time I got my fair share of some of this money you makin'. Ridin' around in a new Volvo and buyin' up clothes every day like they goin' outta style."

"If you were so damn concerned about makin' money, you should've never quit your job, because NCS is my business. So if you wanna be CEO of a company, start your own. Now bye!"

"Say all you wanna say but as the law states, what's yours is mine."

"The only thing of mine that will ever become yours, is my fist upside your head if you don't get the hell outta my office."

"I guess you think you tough now since you sleepin' around. And I'm gonna find out who he is." He shook his fist at me. "And when I do!"

"Jeff, get outta my office."

"This business is just as much mine as it is yours. Just as long as you got my last name. So you might as well get used to me bein' around."

He dropped in the black leather chair across from my desk and picked up a small pile of envelopes I was planning to toss in the black metal basket in the corner. I seized them out of his hand.

"Bye, Jeff."

He cut his eyes at me with his arms folded across his chest. I grabbed the cup of Starbucks coffee I had bought, which he never gave me a chance to finish off my desk. I tossed it in his lap.

He jumped up. "You stupid . . . " He brushed himself off, then spoke in a calmer tone. "I ain't gonna argue with you today, Nicole, in spite of the childish things you do. I ain't gonna fight with you, either, because we're partners."

"You are not and never will be my partner. So please! I'm beggin' you. Get the hell outta my office before I hit you with something other than coffee!"

He headed out the door. "See, I'm tryin' to be reasonable with you. But you wanna act up. Either way, this is a family business and I *will* be back."

He returned the next day and the next, destroying the solace I found at my place of business. It took hardly any time before I was ready to hire a hit man to knock him off, especially when he started snatching up my telephone on the first ring, talking to whoever called like he was my boss. Leaving crumbs all over my desk. And like he did at home, pissing all over the damn toilet and leaving the lid up.

Frustrated and not seeing any way to rid myself of him, I avoided going to my office at all. Bad move. A very bad one. Because the lock on the back door mysteriously broke. Still I should have known he was up to more than helping me out. Nor did he want to really spend any time with me. The first thing I suspect he did, in my absence, was to go through my file cabinet for anything he could find, although the majority of my pertinent information was kept in a safety deposit box in the bank where Anna worked.

Still my Social Security number was on various documents in my locked files. I also had an American Express card for large purchases, which I always paid within a week or two of using it, and one Visa, even though I never had a need for credit cards. Jeff applied for three Visas and one MasterCard in my name with complimentary cards for himself.

By the time I picked up the first bill, laying in the alley behind my office, he had maxed out two of them. I had to have credit alerts filled out with all three of the major reporting agencies and warn my bank not to handle any transactions from him regarding me or my business. I then had all of my mail switched to a P. O. box so I could be the first one to get my hands on whatever was addressed to me, because he would swipe my mail in a heartbeat. The more he hurt for money, the worse he became.

"Mrs. Kingston," one of my tenants said on the other line, "we had another theft last night."

"What?"

"Once again they took all the money out of the washers and dryers. I still can't figure out for the life of me how these people keep gettin' in here unless they have a key." Sandi Crawford, a freelance writer, was always home during the day while everyone else was at work. "There's never any forced entry or noise. It's so scary. And we know it's no one who lives here."

"So you still haven't seen anybody unusual?"

"Like I told your husband this mornin' . . . "

"My husband?"

"Yes."

"How do you know him?"

"He dropped in some days ago to introduce himself."

"I wasn't aware."

"I thought it was unusual myself, but he knows Ralph on the first floor. He had Ralph escortin' him over the buildin' and introducin' us. Last Friday to be exact."

I called Jeff on his new cell phone. "Jeff, what were you doin' at my buildin' introducin'—"

"What are you talkin' about?" he said, smacking on whatever he was eating.

"I got a call from one of my tenants and—"

"Well, it wasn't me, whatever she's talkin' about."

"How do you know it was a she?"

"He or she, it wasn't me. So it must've been your boyfriend."

I got a bill from Ace Hardware, two weeks later, proving it wasn't. I went looking for Jeff after I snapped on the manager at Ace.

I asked the man, "How are you gonna let somebody just walk in here, make copies of some keys, then put it on my bill? Check my account! The only name I have authorized to get anything is Isaac Mackey. So how in the hell did I get billed for something I didn't authorize?"

"We didn't know, Mrs. Kingston. He showed us his driver's license and since you do have the same last name and home address—I wasn't gonna approve it at first, but he said he's been lettin' you handle things, but now since he's retired from his other job, he's takin' over. He said he had to get those keys made because you had no idea where you put the extra ring."

The set Jeff had swiped was in the kitchen cabinet on the top shelf all the way in the back. He had to have been doing some serious snooping to have found them. Still I should have been grateful to find out, even if it did cost me a whole lot more to have Isaac change all of the locks plus have those keys duplicated. Those I left in his care. I then had to mail certified reminders to my tenants so they wouldn't forget rent was to be given to no one but me and mailed only to my P. O. Box.

With his good thing spoiled, Jeff took his good-for-nothing keys over to Mother's. He had already lied to her saying Locking was closing and had cut back on their employees. I brought her attention to the *Chicago Tribune* ad, which said they were hiring.

She said, "From what I hear you're havin' a affair with some young boy. So who are you to accuse anybody of doin' anything?"

Locking approved Jeff getting his pension six months after his early retirement, but he lost a large portion of it in penalties. Instead of putting away some of his dollars for hard times, he put a down payment on a used Benz, then blew the rest on who knows what. His money ran out in two months. He sold his house next, which had been vacant since we moved. I tried to tell him he could have rented it out or had it rehabbed and sold for a higher price, but Jeff didn't want to hear anything I had to say unless it was what he wanted to hear. Which was me paying Isaac to remodel it and him making one hundred percent profit off it after it was sold.

With the monies he did make off his place, he surprisingly paid the Benz off, wasting what was left on daily shopping sprees. Then he got the bright idea to have business cards printed with our names on them and started passing them out like they were government cheese. He would ride around, look at property for sale, put on a big show of interest, then tell the seller, "Just talk to my assistant." People started calling me around the clock with junk property with jacked-up prices, some begging me to take it off their hands.

The stress of the mess he was starting to make out of my small company became so obvious on my face Anna suggested, "Just hire somebody to kill him. Because I would, especially for a man like Alex."

"I keep tellin' you we're only friends. That's it."

"Girl, please. If I had a choice between him and Jeff, Jeff would be batting a thousand if I let him lick my toilet."

"Girl, you are too funny."

"I'm serious. Why waste your time if Jeff's not who you want? Or better yet, why are you allowing him to live in your house? It's not like he can pay for anything, considering he can't get unemployment because he quit his job. So he's just taking up valuable space and blockin' big time!" He was doing a lot more than that.

13

After inspecting every nook and cranny of a four-bedroom bungalow on the southern end of Evanston Anna was considering buying, she decided we should stop by one of the many boutiques she frequented. And I ended up with three pantsuits I really didn't need. A Fed Ex package addressed to Jeff in care of NCS Management Company was hanging out of the mailbox when I stopped by my house to drop them off. I ran my stuff upstairs to my room, tearing it open as I jogged back down the steps. My blood rushed to my head and I had to sit down to keep from falling on my face.

"I can't believe he did that. I can't believe it!" is all I could think to say as I stared at the documents he had signed. My cell phone ringing snapped me out of shock. Assuming it was Anna insisting I hurry up, I answered the call, my mind somewhere between lockdown and unbelief.

"What's up, beautiful?"

"I really can't talk right now, Alex."

"Why not? What's wrong?"

I shook my head as if he could see me. "Something just came up and . . . "

"Why don't you come over here? I'll take you out to lunch and we can talk about it."

"For what? Why would you even wanna spend time with someone with so much drama goin' on in their life?"

"Because I love you like that." *What did you say?* "Hello, you still there?"

I clicked him off and called Anna, knowing she was going to either ring my doorbell or call me to see what was taking me so long. Because she had already said, "Girl, I'm hungry as hell," three times.

"Anna, why don't you go ahead and get something to eat. I need to clean this place and there's a few things I need to take care of."

"Things like what, Nicole? What's going on?"

"Nothin'."

"You don't sound like you did a few minutes ago. So what's wrong?"

"I just wanna clean my house."

She said, "Okay," sounding like she didn't quite believe me. "If you would hire a maid, you wouldn't have to worry about it. Like I keep telling you, I have the best cleaning woman in the world."

I hurried her off the telephone and dialed Jeff's number. "Jeff, how can you be so damn stupid as to sign a damn lease . . . " He hung up on me.

I called him nonstop for hours. He refused to answer each time, then tried to sneak in the house once the calls ceased. I was sitting on the steps, waiting for him, when he opened the door with his shoes in his hands. I jumped up and ran over to him.

"Jeff, how could you be so damn stupid as to sign this fuckin' lease? " I swung at him with the papers. He threw his arms up, blocking me. "How could you be so fuckin' ignorant? You're always doin' something stupid. Makin' me have to pay out unnecessary money. But not this time." I threw the papers in his face. "You signed the damn lease. So you pay the damn rent!"

He picked them up. "That's the key. You always talkin' *I*. I need someplace to run my business."

"What damn business?"

"Nicole, NCS is just as much mine as it is yours. Like I keep tellin' you. You're my wife. And as they say, what's mine is yours and vice versa. And since we are expandin' . . . "

"First of all, *we* ain't expandin'. Second. *We*—meanin' you and I—ain't doin' shit. And third—if you could just use your common sense for just once—need to ask yourself—why in the hell would anybody sign a lease to pay nine hundred-fifty dollars a month for a office in downtown Evanston, when they can keep their office on their own property and not a pay a damn thing?"

"You're just jealous that I'm finally makin' a name for myself. Sure enough I got some things to learn, but you're just jealous because you thought you were the only one who knew how to go out and make some business deals and some money. But I fooled you, didn't I?"

"If you're makin' so much money, the light bill is due and so is the gas and water. And when is the last time you contributed anything on the mortgage? If you can't pay your bills at home, how in the hell are you gonna manage property or an office? Because it's a helluva lot more to it than clown suits and monkey shoes." But talking to him was like talking to a baboon's ass.

After avoiding Alex's calls for two days, he found me at six in the morning coming out of one of my buildings with a hand full of dirty paper towels and a bottle of Windex.

"Good mornin', beautiful."

We stared into each other's eyes as he walked over to me, looking like the black jeans and pullover shirt he was wearing were designed with him in mind. His sandalwood cologne reached me before he did and gave me chills. "How did you know . . ."

"I felt your presence. Need help?" he asked. He walked me to my car. I popped the trunk. He pulled the vacuum cleaner out and sat it on the sidewalk.

"So you wanna talk about it?"

"No. How've you been?"

"Worried about you. Nikki, why don't you let me help you?"

"With what?"

"Any and everything you're goin' through."

"I don't think you have that much time."

DAYLIGHT COMING

He laughed. "I'll make time."

With tax season approaching once again, I found myself spending lots of hours in my office, getting my paperwork together, making sure everything was accounted for. As if my being extra busy was his cue to see how much more he could aggravate the hell out of me, Jeff snatched up my office phone while I was in the bathroom talking to my accountant on my cell phone. I opened the door to catch him jotting something down.

"Jeff, who was that?"

"Wrong number," he replied, stuffing a piece of paper into his pants pocket as he rushed out the front door.

"Well, what were you writin' down?" I looked at the Caller ID. No number was listed, but I knew for a fact the telephone had rung. I ran behind him.

"You deleted my call, didn't you? I don't know what you're up to, but it better not have a damn thang to do with me or any of my business."

He got into his car, burning rubber on the asphalt. I rushed back inside to call Alex, just to be sure it wasn't him. Then I sat tapping my fingers on my desk, wondering who it could have been for Jeff to erase the number and run off like he did. Although I was highly agitated not knowing what he was up to, I still had work to do and taxes to be filed. I dived back into my paperwork. My office line rang some forty minutes later.

"Who the hell do you think you are?" my tenant, Amanda Powell, screamed in my ear. "Do you know what invasion of privacy is? I've been a renter in this city for over twenty years and not once has anyone I've rented from had the audacity to come into my house while I'm away from home! My mother is a very sick woman, Mrs. Kingston. So how dare your husband talk his way into my house and sit down and have tea and cookies with her. You don't have any damn food at home?"

"Amanda, what are you talkin' about?"

"You people don't know shit about me or my mother. But I will tell you this, I'm suin' your ass for everything you own." She slammed the telephone down.

Amanda, a civil rights attorney, lived with her mother and 19-year-old daughter in my condominium on Lake Shore Drive. Her mother, an Alzheimer's patient, telephoned often with concerns about their building, which were all imagined because of her illness. I called Amanda back and had to beg her to explain what was happening. I couldn't believe Jeff would be so low-down as to coax the address out of her mother, then go to their condo.

While he was being entertained, Amanda's daughter dropped in between her college classes to check on her grandmother. Of course she was petrified to see him sitting in their living room as if he belonged there, then introduce himself as their landlord. She went into her bedroom, and called Amanda, who called the police on her way home.

I hurried over there, stepping off the elevator just as the police were escorting Jeff out of her front door in handcuffs. Amanda was all in his face, poking him in the head with her finger while her neighbors stood in the hallway gaping. They were just as shocked as I was that the mild-mannered woman could snap like that. I couldn't even look at Jeff for fear I would grab one of the police officers' guns and blow his damn head off. I identified him as being my husband, while continuing to look everywhere but at him.

After he was put in the elevator along with three policemen, the officer in charge said, "Well, what was he doin' here, ma'am?"

"I don't have a clue. He is retired as he told you, but NCS is my business and he's not my partner, but he's tryin' to be. So from time to time, he drops by some of my buildings to introduce himself."

The officer looked at me like, *Say what?*

"Some people don't mind, but . . . "

The officer gave me a severe scolding regarding me and Jeff needing to get our stuff together, "before somebody comes home and blows his head off for being where he ain't supposed to be." I never felt so much like a idiot before in my life. And if that wasn't bad enough, Amanda's mother had a full-blown temper tantrum afterwards. She thought Jeff was her dead son and Amanda was his ex-wife who was being mean to him for no reason. Amanda cursed me for twenty minutes straight after she got her mother calmed. I just sat there listening until I could get a word in.

I never had to beg anyone for their forgiveness like I had to beg her, although she had every right in the world to be pissed. But for a minute I thought she was going to try to kick my behind. To compensate her for her distress, I agreed to have a new alarm installed in her condo. Plus she wanted her daughter's room painted and new carpet installed before the end of the month. She also asked for a reduction in her monthly parking fee.

She insisted, "I don't want your husband anywhere near me or my family ever again."

"He won't be. And like I keep tellin' you, I am so sorry. He's just been . . . " I sighed. "He just wants to be in the business, but don't have a clue what the hell he's doing. But like I said, I apologize."

"And I do, too, for *some* of the things I said. But please! Keep your damn husband away from us because next time I'm pressin' every charge I possibly can against him. If I didn't like you like I do, he would be in jail right now!"

We hugged and I ran to the elevator, so enraged I couldn't wait to find Jeff. He knew I would be looking for him and I knew he had to eat. I rode around Evanston until I saw his Benz parked around the corner from the Pine Yard Inn, a well-known Chinese restaurant. He and the young girl he claimed to have hired to be his secretary almost choked when I walked in the door.

"I need to see you outside," I said. The minute he stepped onto the sidewalk, I slapped him so hard some of his food flew out of his mouth. "How could you be so damn stupid?"

"What is it now, Nicole?" he asked, rubbing his cheek. "What did I do this time?"

"Don't try and play innocent with me. What the hell were you doin'—".

"Why didn't you tell me you own a condo? That you been havin' it for some months now. What are you pullin' in? Let's see. Three-bedrooms, a bath and a half. You charge a grand, two, fifteen hundred?"

"That's none of your damn business."

"It is in a court of law."

My heart skipped a beat. Still I asked, "What do you mean?"

"You can sneak and buy as much property as you want, but I'm still gonna get half of everything you own. So divorce me. And watch me milk your ass dry."

I wanted to kick him so bad my left foot started twitching. He laughed, then went back inside to finish his meal. I walked over to his car and scratched *"ASSHOLE"* on the hood with my keys, that being about as much revenge as I could seek.

Just as I snatched my car door open, my cell phone rang. I ignored it, but the caller hung up, ringing me right back. "Hello!" I snapped.

"If you didn't wanna have lunch with me, all you had to do was say so."

I slapped myself on my forehead. "Alex, I'm sorry. I—"

"What's goin' on, beautiful?"

"I can't talk about it right now. So let me call you later."

"Nikki, why won't you talk to me now? Let me see you through it. Can't you see I'm here for you?"

"Alex, I . . . " I sniffed to stifle my cry. Still my tears rolled down my cheeks.

"Look, things are slow around here today and my guys can handle whatever. Why don't you meet me at any restaurant you choose. My treat. And we can talk about it."

I whispered, "I can't. Things are just . . . "

"They're what?"

"Nothin'."

"I don't like you bein' this upset. Where are you?"

"Downtown Evanston."

"Just gimme a location and I'm on my way!"

"You know I can't do that."

"But I can't let you go on like this. When you hurt, I hurt. And I know it has a lot to do with me. I'm clockin' out so why don't you meet me at my house?"

"I can't."

"Yes, you can and we're gonna talk. Today. So I'll know how I can help you. You're still my girl, right?"

"Yeah."

"And I'm still your boy, right?"

Not anymore, you're too fine of a man. "Yes."

"It's twelve forty-five. You should be pullin' in my driveway by one fifteen."

I should have followed my intuition and stayed home.

14

All the way to Alex's house, a cute brick bungalow with a big bay window and manicured lawn, I told myself, *Nikki, you ain't got no business at this man's house. You ain't got no business spendin' time with him at all.* I started chewing my thumbnail, something I often do when I'm upset. By the time I parked in his driveway, I had to use both hands to take the key out of the ignition.

He came to the door, wearing a pair of black Joe Boxer lounging pants and no shirt. My eyes zeroed in on the cuts in his arms, then his abs of steel as he walked over to my car. He opened my door, offering his hand. His grip was strong, yet gentle, although his hands were kind of rough. A tingle shot up my spine. I glanced up at him wondering if he noticed the way my body shivered at his touch.

"What took you so long?" He glanced at his pager. "It's two-fifteen. Where'd you go?"

I had showered and curled my hair, even though I had pulled it back into my usual ponytail, and changed from my jean skirt into a red tie-front knit dress with a sash belt and red-leather sandals with a 2-inch heel. I had taken inventory of myself in the five-foot mirror in my bedroom and thought for a second the way the dress hugged my hips and the deep V flaunted my small breasts, I looked damn good. But those thoughts only came and went.

Alex said, "You look beautiful," confirming what my shattered ego had dismissed.

I followed him inside, so entranced by the sensual fragrance of his ocean-breeze cologne that I could have stood in his

DAYLIGHT COMING

shadow and breathed him in. All day long. I loved his house the moment I saw it, the handmade pillows on all of his chairs, clear vases with sand and dried plants in them and statues of lions, elephants, and tigers, carved from wood or ivory. Colorful paintings by Synthia Saint James were in his kitchen. Pictures by Jacob Lawrence were in his hallway and an intriguing painting of a black man draped in a white-hooded robe, titled, *"Night in Day,"* by Thomas Blackshear hung on his living room wall. I envied him being able to surround himself with anything he wanted. I had tried it, but whatever Jeff didn't break, he pawned.

I'm talking costly vases, crystal glasses, wall hangings, dishes, things I knew would increase in value. He even knocked over a grandfather clock made of brass and beveled glass, which took a year to go on sale. Anna swore it was country as hell, but I had to have it. One night, after Alex and I started hanging out, I was coming in from dinner with him. Jeff was standing at the foot of the steps with the broom and dustpan in his hands.

He said, "I know what you thinkin', but it wasn't my fault. I swear. I don't know how this thing fell over."

I sat on Alex's sofa. He went into the kitchen and came out. He handed me an ice-cold bottle of Dasani water, our favorite brand.

"You feelin' better?"

"Somewhat."

"You wanna talk about it?"

"I just wanna sit here and relax, because it has been a l-o-n-g mornin'."

"I see it in your eyes."

"Well, stop lookin' in them and get me something to eat. I'm starvin'."

Food was the last thing on my mind. I stared at the ripples in his abdomen. I got that tingly feeling again. I dismissed it and got up from the couch, not intending to be so close to him. He grabbed my hand with a smile and led me into the kitchen. I ate my baked tilapia, steamed zucchini, wild rice, and fresh sourdough bread while taking girlish glances at him. I wondered as he chewed his food what it would be like to kiss him. We never said good-bye unless he gave me a peck on my nose, forehead, or cheek, but I wanted to press my lips against his. I wanted to feel his tongue inside my mouth. I got those tingles again.

"Why do you keep lookin' at me?" he asked after catching me staring at him for the umpteenth time. "You think I put something in your food?"

"You might've."

He laughed. "I guess you'll just have to wait and see." I smiled. "You know, I enjoy havin' you here."

"Thank you."

"Not necessary. I love your company, your smile. The way you look in that red dress. You do that for me?"

"I just bought it and hadn't had a chance to wear it yet."

I was semi-lying. No, I'd never worn the dress, but I'd had it for a year. Knowing his favorite color by the roses he always gave me whether it be leaving them on my windshield or bringing them with him whenever we had lunch, I pulled out everything red I owned until I decided what to wear.

"You done? Want something else?"

"What's for dessert?"

He dropped the food left on both plates in the disposal. "What would you like?"

Alex knew no matter what I ate or how full I was, I had to have something with sugar. He rinsed our plates off, put them in the dishwasher, then opened the refrigerator door just enough for me to see a Baker's Square box.

"Is that for me?"

"Of course." He pulled the box out of the refrigerator and cut me a gigantic slice of strawberry cheesecake.

"I can't eat all of this in one sittin'."

"Who says you gotta eat it all right now?"

He finished tidying up the kitchen, while I enjoyed every bite of my treat. "You sure you don't want me to help?" I asked, licking my spoon.

"You're my guest. So just chill. I do this every day."

"You really do cook every day?"

"How else would I eat?"

"Most men I know who are single eat out."

"And just how many single men do you know?" I shrugged my shoulders, something that always aggravated the heck out of my mother. "Since my moms was never big on cookin', junk food and cold cereal was all I knew for a long time. So once I got my own crib, I taught myself how to cook."

"You taught yourself very well, Mr. Knight. The only time I get to eat anything this healthy and good . . . " —I started to say, *Is when I'm with you.* But finished—"is when I pay for it. It really was good."

"I'm glad you liked it. But I guess I'll have to make tilapia more often since you didn't compliment me on the veggie lasagna I made last week or the homemade fettuccini or—"

"Yes, I did. You know I'm always tellin' you how everything you've made for me has been delicious." So delicious I could easily see myself indulging in it every day.

With the kitchen back to its showroom self, Alex and I went into the room across from his master suite and next door to his guest bath. He had left the stereo on WNUA. Celine Dion and R Kelly were singing "I Am Your Angel." He sang along with them while sorting through his collection of movies and calling out his latest purchases.

I sat on his futon and took off my sandals. "Let's watch *The Five Heartbeats.*"

"Didn't we see that last week on cable?"

"And?"

He popped the movie in and rolled the ottoman over to where I sat. Alex placed my feet in his lap. I laid my head back and closed my eyes while he massaged my anxious toes. He worked his magic on them as I listened to my favorite movie, visualizing each scene in my mind. When I woke up, the credits were rolling. Alex was sitting next to me.

"You wanna get comfortable?"

I stretched out on the futon, laying my head in his lap. He took the twist off my ponytail and ran his fingers through my hair, paying careful attention to my temples. I drifted back to sleep. When I woke up the second time, a rerun of the *Cosby Show* was on the television. And "I Get So Lonely" by Janet Jackson was playing on the radio.

I sat up. "Why did you let me sleep so long?"

"Because you needed to."

I looked at the time on the cable box. "It's ten o'clock. I better get outta here."

"You're more than welcome to stretch out in my guest room. I got clean sheets. And they match." I knew he was referring to the conversation we had, and me insisting I couldn't sleep if all of the linen on my bed didn't match. A mental thing I developed after only being allowed to use the oldest and most worn bed coverings and towels when I lived with Mother.

"Thanks, but I've been here too long."

"Says who?"

"Where did I put my purse?"

"You left it in the kitchen."

Man, I wanted to stay—not just for the moment, but forever. Alex wouldn't stop staring at me. And thinking about going home, and having Jeff meet me at the door, probably greasing on some restaurant food he would leave wherever he finished it, I almost wanted to cry. I rubbed my eyes. They were a little crusty.

I jumped up. "Can I use the bathroom?"

"Like you have to ask. The washcloths are in the closet behind the door."

He followed me into the bathroom, decorated with hunter and white accessories. He took a washcloth out of the closet and turned on the hot water. Alex lifted my face toward his and cleaned it with the softness of the cloth, smelling Snuggle fresh.

"You know you don't have to leave."

My heart was beating so fast I felt it thumping against his chest. I swallowed hard, hoping my breath didn't smell like sleep. "I gotta . . . uh . . . you know . . . um . . . go . . . back to my office. To—"

He came closer. "To do what?"

"Because I might—"
"Nikki, spend the night with me."
I mumbled, "I can't."
"Why not?"

I thought about Jeff, although he really didn't have anything to do with it. I knew if I stayed I would never want to leave. I was going to say, "Because I can't," but he pulled me into his arms. And his kiss prevented me from saying another word.

Him unzipping my dress as he led me to his bedroom was another reason I was speechless. Even though I kept thinking, *Nicole, you know better than this*. Yet, I wanted his tongue in my mouth, on my breasts, his hands rubbing my hips, touching my thighs, taking off my clothes. Laying me down.

Still, I tried to say, "We shouldn't be doin' this." But he was kissing me with so much passion—he set fire to my soul. Then he touched me in places I had never been intimately touched. And I helped him take off his pants. I throbbed for him and welcomed him in sheer delight as he entered me so gently, but with so much rhythm that I held him close, kissing him feverishly. His face. His eyes. His mouth.

And he said, "I love you, Nikki. I've always loved you," as he stimulated my desires to the point of *please don't stop* and like a volcano—we erupted together. And I cried, holding him even tighter, caressing his head against my heart until he started to love me all over again and like two dominate forces of nature—we exploded into each other. Again.

15

Lying on Alex's feather bed, I wondered if the clouds were as soft. For a quick second, I thought I heard something vibrating on the hardwood floor. But again he had relaxed me so much it seemed as if I was hallucinating about being in his arms. I closed my eyes. I heard the *hm-m-m* again. I turned on the lamp next to his king-size bed.

He woke up, snuggling closer to me. "What's the matter?" He heard the *hm-m-m-m*. "What's that?"

I felt around until I found my pager under my dress. I glimpsed at the time. It was one forty-five a.m. Jeff had paged me fifty-eight times with 9-1-1. My heart stopped for a millisecond, then started pounding. Alex kissed my neck and down my shoulder as if it was something we did every day. I tried to ease away from him. He pulled me into his arms. "Just ignore it."

I threw my hand over my mouth. *Nicole, what did you just do? You just had sex with Alex. You're twelve years older than him. You knew him when he was in high school.* Then I remembered, *He said he loved me.* Then I wondered, *Did he say it because I'm in his bed or does he really? It can't be. It ain't no way.*

He said, "You gonna call him?"

Suppose he's tryin' to get rid of me now since I just gave myself to him so easily. Oh God, I just committed adultery. I can't believe I did that. With Alex of all people. What am I supposed to do now? I turned away from him. Tears dripped from the corner of my eyes onto the pillow. He turned my face back to his. "It's okay, Nikki. Nothin' has happened or is gonna happen that I can't see you through."

DAYLIGHT COMING

I thought about Limmell—then LJ. "Suppose something terrible has happened?"

"Suppose it ain't."

He smacked a kiss on my lips, then got up to get my cell phone. I stared at him as he walked away. What a temple to behold. I had never wanted a man as badly as I wanted him, and by the way he was putting it on me, he wanted me just as badly. He was moaning my name and kissing me everywhere as if the pleasure was all his to have me in his bed.

He handed me my phone. I dialed my message center, hands shaking so bad it fell on the floor. He picked it up. I threw my free hand over my face as he watched me listening to Jeff.

"Nicole, where the hell you at? I know you with whoever that son-of-a . . . " He hung up and called again. "Nicole, I don't know where you at but there was a damn fire on Lake Street. The damn garage burned down and you somewhere f—" I clicked the telephone off.

"What happened?"

"There was a fire at one of my houses. The garage burned down."

It was just like Jeff to panic and page me a hundred times. I started laughing, but my laughter turned into more tears, then downright bawling.

"Nikki, it ain't that bad."

I believe in the power of insurance, so the garage catching on fire was the furthest thing from my mind. I was more concerned with what he thought about me. He sat next to me and ran his fingers through my tangled hair.

"Nikki, why are you cryin'? And don't tell me it's over your garage." He kissed my lips. *Because I was moaning and oow-ing and ah-h-ing like a dog in heat. I'm married, so how can I ever look in your face again.*

"Nikki, look at me." *I'll never be able to look at you again. I was working my body so tough, you probably think I do this for a living.* "Look at me."

I turned over on my side, not making eye contact, waiting for him to laugh. For him to say he knew I was a whore. Because that's what Jeff had been calling me and told me I would be if I ever let another man touch me as long as I was married to him.

He had said, "In the eyes of God, you'll be considered a whore."

Alex lay beside me and wrapped his arms around me. He kissed me like he did when we were in his bathroom. Then he loved me even harder than the first time and I enjoyed every inch of him so much that I could have died right there in our ecstasy, a very, very happy woman.

It was close to six in the morning before I was ready to face Jeff. Being with Alex—no matter how I chose to view it, what excuses I made—in the eyes of God, sex with anybody other than my spouse is adultery. I knew it. But I never had anyone who wanted me like him or taught me what it meant when R Kelly sang about giving his woman some of his "12 Play."

I left Alex's house knowing—not just because I had slept with him—that all of the love he confessed for me, he had it, and so much more. It made me not want to leave him, but he encouraged, "Handle your business, baby, and call me if you need me." He pulled me to him and rubbed the small of my back while kissing down the front of my dress. "You know I'll go with you." I had already refused him six times.

"That's okay."

"And I ain't forgot. We are gonna talk and you are gonna tell me what's been gettin' you so down, because I can't have your back if you won't let me."

I snapped out of the trance our final kiss left me in, and got into my Volvo. I knew I would eventually have to tell him, if we were going to be together. Because as we showered, even though I was embarrassed as hell, he said, "You know I want you here with me now more than ever, right?"

I didn't respond to his comment. "Just so you know, I have never touched another man's wife before. And even though I know your husband is a ass, I don't take pride in it. And I know you with me is causin' you a lot of static, but I've loved you ever since the first time I saw you. When Jeff opened the door and you were sittin' on the couch, wearin' your pink baggy pajamas and bunny house shoes, I fell in love. And the whole time I was gone, you never left my mind."

We'd had plenty of conversations about the years he was away while having breakfast, lunch, or dinner. We talked about his dead-end relationships and the feelings he had about not knowing where he belonged. Coming back to Illinois for his grandfather's funeral reminded him where home was so he decided to apply for the job in Lake Forest. Although he didn't want to deal with his mother's drama—walking around in a drunken stupor and cursing everybody out—he still wanted to be nearby just in case she decided to change the way she lived.

After running away, five years passed before any of his family knew where he was. He never knew his father, and his mother had never been anything more to him than someone who birthed him when she was thirteen. Ever since he could walk and talk, he had to fend for himself the best way possible. He felt no connection to her or anyone else in their family other than his deceased grandfather. Now that he was back, he just wanted to be somewhere he could make himself a home and be comfortable doing it. He loved his job and his house, the first one he ever owned, and by us making love, he assumed I would someday be his.

He said, "When you know in your heart who you want, can't nobody, I don't care how good they are to you or for you, they can't fill the void. That's why I've been goin' from place to place, not wantin' to commit to anybody. Yeah, I've broken a few hearts. Not because I'm a vicious animal or anything like that. It's just some women who chose me, I didn't choose them. They wanted more than I had to give. And when I couldn't give it, I would book. I know better now. And I promise you, Nikki, I'll never leave you alone. Not unless you want me to."

We talked on the phone as I drove to Evanston. All the while we chatted, those same tingles I got every time he touched me kept creeping up and down my spine. When I got lost in thinking about what he had done to my body, I trembled.

He said, "I enjoyed it, too."

I smiled to myself, happy for a change not to be feeling so lowly and thinking it might be the one time something in my life was really meant to be. But I had still committed adultery. Yet, my heart said, *So what? Jeff's done it! As a matter of fact, he's been doin' it ever since Pastor said, 'Dearly beloved, we are gathered here.'*

16

"I love you", Alex said, just before I called Isaac to meet me on Lake Street. Jeff was the last person I wanted to talk to, so I avoided calling him. I knew he was highly pissed and by now everyone in Evanston knew I was MIA. We parked in the alley at the same time. Isaac was already there, standing next to the garage's charred remains, smoking a cigarette, and looking crisp and clean in his starched blue jeans, white pocket T, and leather work boots.

Jeff barreled over to my car. "Nicole, where the hell you been?"

I got out and walked past him as if he wasn't there. Since he had supposedly hired this young girl, who couldn't have been any more than nineteen, as his secretary, he had started to wear a lot of the clothes the younger guys wore, especially the brand-name stuff. He was sporting a gray Adidas sweatsuit and a pair of Adidas jogging shoes. He had also started to grow his hair longer and comb it back to hide the thinning spot on the top of his head.

"Good mornin', Isaac," I said, continuing to ignore Jeff.

"Mornin'."

"Don't be actin' like I ain't ask you a damn question, Nicole! This fire started at five o'clock. I been pagin' you ever since. Why the hell you just gettin' here and where the hell you comin' from lookin' like that?"

"Isaac, you workin' on anything big or do I need to take a number?"

"I'm booked for the next six weeks. And right now I'm working on two decks, a family room, a unfinished basement, and *your pastor* has been buggin' the hell outta me to build her a green house."

"You sure that's all she wants."

He smiled. "You okay?"

"I would do a helluva lot better if this idiot would disappear."

"Well, it ain't that easy." Jeff continued to rant about me not coming home and doing him wrong while I ignored him to the best of my ability. I could feel Isaac didn't like being caught in the middle of our drama, but was very gracious about it. "Jeff, just calm down. We can't solve nothin' by yellin'."

I nodded. *But we would be a helluva lot better if you would drop dead. Damn, I wish somebody would kill him!*

Isaac said, "You wanna go get something to eat and talk about what you gonna do? Unless you ate already."

I pretended to check the time on my pager. "Might as well." I was already embarrassed he knew where I was coming from. It felt like being caught with your pants down. "Were you here with the fire department?"

"Yeah."

"What did they say?"

"Oily rags and little Victor out here tryin' to smoke cigarettes. Him and some of his friends. It was a accident. But . . . "

Jeff walked between us. "You better start explainin' where the hell you comin' from."

Isaac motioned for me to go to my car. He walked behind me. I asked, opening my door, "Where's Pablo?" Because it was unusual for me to come on the block and not be greeted by him. And his wife always gave me a plate of something, because she knew I loved her cooking.

Isaac said in a lowered voice, "Your husband kicked them out."

"Please tell me you're jokin'?"

"Told him to get his shit and his banana boat-ridin' children and get the hell off his property. But don't say—"

"Jeff, what the hell did you do?"

"What the hell you mean? Where the hell you been?"

"You kicked Pablo and his family out?"

"That bastard's—"

"Let's get this straight. You don't own nothin' here nor did you have a right to say shit to my tenant. You should've learned that from goin' on Lake Shore Drive!"

"Well, you should never rented to his—"

I threw my hand up. "Do not call Pablo, his wife, or his kids another name or you'll have to kick my ass, because I'm sure as hell gonna try to kick yours."

He rushed over to where Isaac and I were standing. "Damn them. You never shoulda rented to them . . ."

I kicked him. He grabbed his shin, then reached for me. Isaac stepped between us. Jeff threw his arms up.

"You see how she is, man? Stay out all night long, dressed like she been out partyin'. Then won't give me a word of explanation. I'm her husband, man. I got a right to know." Isaac peered over his shoulder at me. Jeff yelled around him. "You gonna tell me where you been or I'm gonna beat it outta you."

I took out the pipe wrench I kept under the front seat of my car. "Just try it."

Isaac said, "Jeff, why don't you go somewhere and cool off." But he went on a rampage calling me a slew of whores and bitches. I stared at him all through his tirade with my defense weapon in my hand, glad somebody else got a chance to see how ignorant his saved and sanctified behind could get. When Isaac couldn't take any more of his disrespecting me, he grabbed him by the back of his jacket and threw him into his car.

"What you takin' her side now?" Jeff said. "You screwin' her, too?"

I think Isaac turned a new shade of black and probably did all the praying he knew how to do to keep from giving Jeff an old-fashioned ass kicking. I sped away, tires spinning in the gravel. I'm not sure when they left or what else was said, but Isaac found me sitting some blocks down the street so humiliated I couldn't look at him. He knocked on my window.

"You all right?"

I let it down. "Isaac, I am so sorry."

"Can we talk?"

I opened my door and got out. The last thing I wanted was for Jeff to drive by, see us in my car and add more fuel to the fire he had already started.

"You know I don't normally pry into your personal affairs, but since your husband seems to think . . . uh . . . " Isaac shook his head. "Nikki, whoever this guy is, I hope he's worth it."

"How do you know it's a he?"

"Are you gay?" We both laughed. "Because my sister bought me the same bath stuff for my birthday." My chin fell into my chest. And a tear sneaked from my eye. "Don't cry, because I'm not tryin' to put you down. Who the hell am I to judge anybody? All I'm tryin' to say is, as one friend to another, just be careful. Because you're playin' a dangerous game. And make this dude respect you, whoever he is, and you keep on respectin' you. You love him?" I wanted to say, *More than anybody could ever know.* But nodded instead.

We parted with me feeling somewhat better that my secret was finally out and determined not to let the morning pass without finding Pablo and his family. I drove over to his brother's house in the Rogers Park community, which was a dash across Howard Street into the city. I figured he would be there, because they owned a lawn and garden business together and were very close. He was still upset when he came to the door with his wife on his heels. I felt even worse seeing their five children, huddled in the corner saying, "No, Papi," when he said, "Okay, we go back, but I no want to deal with your husband. He a hateful man." Hateful wasn't even close to describing Jeff. He was evil! Even more evil than I perceived him to be!

After Alex made me a scrumptious Jambalaya omelet, then treated me to some of him, he left me in such a state of euphoria I almost forgot I was supposed to meet Isaac at the Evanston Civic Center. If he hadn't paged me three times, I would have spent the rest of the morning in Alex's bed comfortably wrapped in his jersey-knit sheets.

DAYLIGHT COMING

Although the brief conversation we had following the scene at my garage was Isaac's way of letting me know my indiscretions had no bearing on our relationship, the air around us seemed different. I couldn't think of any more to say to him than he could think of to say to me. In the past there was always something for us to discuss or debate. Alex blowing up my cell didn't make things any more relaxed. I excused myself to the bathroom to call him.

"Hey, beautiful, where you at?"
"With Isaac pickin' up a buildin' permit."
"You okay?"
"Yeah."
"You sound kind of down."
"He knows about us."
"So."
"Alex."
"I love you and you love me, right?"
"Yeah."
"So what could be so bad about that?"
"I'm still married, remember."
"That's only temporary, right?"
"Yeah."
"So cheer up. Can I buy you lunch?"
"I would love it, but I gotta get started tearin' down the rest of the garage."
"You, by yourself?"
"I told you I'm good at manual labor."
"Are you as good at it as you are at makin' me say, *umph-umph-umph*?"
"You tell me."
"Only if you promise that I'll be seein' you this evenin'?"

Common sense said *don't do it*, but I couldn't help myself. Besides, I couldn't see myself going home to Jeff. He was sitting in his car when I pulled up to the garage, after having paid for my permit. I walked past him and straight to Pablo and his brother, who had already started to tear down the charred mess. Jeff sped off, but rode through the alley three times. Each time he said, "Nicole, let me talk to you," as if what he had to say was more important than what I was doing.

Finally I snapped, "If I wanted to talk to you, don't you think I woulda done it the first time you rode through?" He didn't return. He just called my cell phone from Mother's.

"You better watch how you be talkin' to me in front of them people. And you better tell that Mexican to keep his damn nose outta our business, because next time I see him near you, I might have to hurt him." Then he started with the same old, "Where you been stayin'? You plannin' on leavin' me?" while smacking in my ear.

I asked myself the same thing on my way to Alex's house. He welcomed me into his home with a tantalizing kiss and a tasty dinner of baked chicken-breasts, steamed carrots, and penne-pasta followed by a bath in his garden tub and a massage. I woke up in the middle of the night, sore all over and asking myself once again, *Nicole, what are you doin' here?* But Alex was so addictive that getting up to leave him was like a crackhead leaving the crackhouse when the crack is free.

I was hooked on him so tough I made up my mind Jeff and I were through. But there was the issue of getting Jeff out of my house.

17

At least once a week Alex and I had lunch at Ming's, a tiny Chinese restaurant, we just happened to stumble upon, not far from his job. I couldn't get enough of their shrimp with lobster sauce, and he always had their General Tso's chicken with vegetable fried rice. We always ate in the same corner, farthest from the door, smiling at each other and sampling from each other's plates. The mother of Jeff's firstborn son walked in with four other women while he was paying our check and helping himself to the complimentary chocolate mints on the counter.

She rushed over to him. "Alex Knight? Is that you? I ain't seen you in years. Where in the world have you been?"

Stunned that he was recognized, he held a brief conversation with her while I slipped out the door. I had already been dreading what would happen once Jeff found out who I was seeing, but not as much as Mother's birthday celebration, which—as some would say—was just around the corner.

Mother was already laying into me as hard and as often as she could and I had been avoiding her as much as possible. If her party hadn't been planned six months in advance, with me responsible for all of the cooking, I wouldn't have gone. Not one to often break my promises, I had to make myself get up on her special day since I never wanted to leave Alex. And he always made sure I had a reason to come back.

He rolled out of bed behind me and followed me into the shower. Streams of water ran down his back, flowed over his abs, biceps, and triceps, forcing me into pulling him into my arms and kissing him as if it would be our last. Aching for me just as bad as I was dying to have him, he picked me up. And I wrapped my legs around his waist. With my back against the shower wall, he left me barely able to catch my breath after our love came down. I pushed him out of the bathroom, knowing if I was one second later than Mother thought I was supposed to be, I would be accused of ruining her birthday.

I threw on the black A-line skirt and leotard and a white crochet-knit sweater he had picked out for me. Then I ran to the Factory Card Outlet and purchased everything in gold: the balloons, cups, napkins, plates and banner, she told me I needed to bring and drove to Evanston. Jeff was already there, but in a mood so lively, it was shocking. Still, I watched him with a suspicious eye as I placed everything for the cornbread stuffing I was going to make on the kitchen table. I was close to having all of the onions, bell peppers, and celery diced and sliced when the doorbell rang. Mother went to answer it with him directly behind her.

She said, "Thank you," to whomever had come in a cheerful voice. I kept chopping away, hoping we could get through the day without somebody jumping on my case and me having to snap. I was already somewhat pissed that RudyAnn was once again nowhere to be seen when work needed to be done. And Mother was acting as if I had as many hands and feet as an octopus. She and Jeff charged back into the kitchen. Her complexion was bright red and he was huffing and puffing like he was going to blow the house down.

"How dare you!" she snapped, slamming a vase full of red roses on the table. "If I haven't taught you anything, I have taught you to respect yourself, your marriage, and your family. And I don't appreciate whoever he is sendin' these things—" she slapped across the top of the flowers— "to my house." Four petals flew off and fell on the table.

"What are you talkin' about?"

She threw the gift card at me. I picked it out of the bowl. I knew Jeff was the sender before I even read, *"Happy Birthday, from your future son-in-law, Alex"* scribbled on it.

DAYLIGHT COMING

Jeff fell in the chair closest to him. "Oh why, Nicole, why-y-y?" He dropped his head on his arm. "How could you do me like this?"

Mother stood over him. She patted his back while he howled. "Now what do you have to say for yourself?"

Jeff looked up at her. "Mother Borge, he used to wash our cars." He dabbed his crocodile tears with a paper towel she handed him. "He spent nights in our house. You remember him, don't you? That skinny little kid with the big Afro. He used to be with Nicole all the time. I pray to God . . . " He wailed. "That she wasn't sleepin' with him way back then."

Mother's mouth dropped into a perfect "O" and her eyes got extremely big. I grabbed my purse and ran out the door, desperate to be anywhere other than near Jeff because I almost went Freddie Krueger on his ass!

By me having a full-blown affair, I refused to step a foot inside Holy Hill. I had seen too many hypocrites to set myself out like them. Alex had taken an interest in Islam just before moving back to Evanston, so we studied and meditated together. My motto was regardless of how bleak your life may seem, there is still something to thank God for. Mother didn't want me to even have that satisfaction. She was constantly calling me, threatening me with the fires of hell, as if she would be the first one to enter *The Pearly Gates*, the way she judged and belittled people.

After having labeled me a Jezebel and an adulteress, she left a message stating, "It's very important, Nicole." Unaccustomed to anything distressing coming from her, I anxiously dialed her office number. "This is Nicole. What's wrong?"

"How you doin'?"

"O-o-kay. I guess. What's the matter?"

"What are your plans for lunch today?"

"Meanin'?"

"Do you have any plans for lunch?"

"Not at the moment. Why?"

"I wanna go to Dixie Kitchen."
"O-o-kay. And?"
"I want you to join me?"
"What's goin' on, Mother?"
"I just wanna talk to you."
"Why? You ain't damned my soul enough?"
"No, I just wanna talk."

Over jerk chicken, hot cakes, red beans and rice, we discussed the weather, and her up-and-coming retirement. She made most of the conversation, because I was waiting for her to slap me upside my head with an insult. Anything. She just chitchatted about nothing until she found a way to orchestrate what she really wanted into our conversation. By the time our plates were collected and she had a final cup of black coffee and paid the check, I had promised I would chair, Dreams and Wishes, an annual Christmas charity event I had founded and coordinated for Holy Hill for the past ten years.

We always had three nights of families signing up for toys, food baskets, and whatever else our many supporters donated. Jeff, knowing most of my days were being spent at the church, would stop by, trying to talk to me. I was standing in the recreation room showing several volunteers how I wanted gloves and the matching skull caps sorted. He approached me with the same ole, "Nicole, when are you gonna stop all this foolishness and come home?"

Mother was passing by. She stuck her head in the door. "Jeff, come here." A smile slithered across his face. He hurried over to her.

"Yes, ma'am."

"I'm sure things are gonna get better for you two, but right now let Nicole do what she has to do. I'm sure all of the work she's been doin' in the name of the Lord is makin' her tired enough."

Shocked and embarrassed, he sat a few chairs away from me, helping the volunteers while gawking at me. I rolled my eyes and left the room. He followed me out the door to Pastor Dorthea's office.

DAYLIGHT COMING

"Nicole, the lease is gonna be up soon over on Benson. What am I supposed to do about relocatin', since you controllin' all the money?"

Knowing his landlord would probably try to commit us to another year, I mailed him a notarized and certified letter the same day he dropped the keys off. It stated any lease signed by Jeffrey Kingston for NCS Management Company, would be Jeff's sole responsibility and that I refused to be held financially or any way responsible for any deals made without my knowledge or consent.

Mother said, coming from who knows where, "Jeff, can't you see Nicole is handlin' church business and don't have time to discuss where you're gonna move your office? I asked you to let her be."

"Yes ma'am," he said, but sat in the parking lot waiting for me to leave. Alex had warned me many times, "Nikki, you need to stay away from him, because you don't know what this dude might try to do to you. I wish you would quit bein' so stubborn and let me take you wherever you need to go because you never know when this dude may snap. At least if I'm with you, I can defend you. But half the time, I don't know where you at."

"Alex, the last thing on my mind is what Jeff is gonna do."

I pulled onto the street from the church parking lot. He zoomed behind me, flashing his lights from low to high beam, then sped up next to me, shouting, "YOU BRINGIN' YO ASS HOME TONIGHT!"

I gave him the finger and hit the gas. He rode my bumper until I threw on brakes. He swerved around me and almost collided with another car. I took advantage of his near miss and made a quick right up a one-way street. He managed to catch up with me. He honked his horn and shook his fist at me. I drove to our house on Sheridan Road.

He pulled in behind me and barreled out of his car. "I'M TIRED OF YOU . . . " I gave him the finger again, made a U-turn across the lawn, and sped away.

Since things seemed to be working out just fine between Mother and me, I contemplated asking her to speak to him about his steady streams of telephone calls and always trying to follow me. But I figured, why ruin what was turning out to be a very pleasant experience?

Two days before Christmas, the families on our wish list came to pick up their gifts and food baskets. We also put together toy bags for the children who had missed our deadline, using what we had left over. By Christmas Eve, all we had to do was pass out the turkeys and hams and keep smiling for the many reporters who dropped by to interview and get pictures of the two hundred families. I always laid low and let Mother and Pastor Dorthea have their minutes of fame.

By eight forty-four in the evening, except for the garbage that had to be taken out, the gym was clean. We passed out every donation, down to the last package of dinner rolls. A homeless man, who volunteered to help with cleaning up, asked if he could have it.

I said, "Sure," giving him thirty dollars and wishing him, "Merry Christmas and a blessed New Year."

"Thank you kindly sister, but can I bother you for a ride to Chicago?"

"You surely can. Where you goin'?" I had seen him around the neighborhood so I knew he was harmless.

"Over on Paulina and Howard by the El station."

"Let me get my coat."

Mother said, "Let Jeff do it."

The expression on his face clearly showed he was against it, but he said, "Okay," just to appease her. I was anxious to be spending my first Christmas with Alex, although he didn't celebrate it, because of his Muslim beliefs. I was glad she made the suggestion, until she said, "Nicole, I need to see you before you leave."

"I'm tryin' to get home, Mother. I'm tired."

"I know. But this'll only take a minute."

I walked slowly behind Mother to Pastor Dorthea's office. The moment she opened the door, my heart sank because I knew she had played me. Still I silently prayed, *God, bless me not to say or do anything I may regret. Please, Lord. Hold my tongue and protect my heart. Please, God!*

Pastor walked over to me. She wrapped her arm around mine, pulling me to the center of the room. I tried to resist her, but she wouldn't let me go.

She said, trying to force me to sit down, "You know, Nicole, you're such a beautiful woman and God has blessed you with so many talents. Not too many people can coordinate such an awesome event for the needy. You have truly been a blessin' to this church.

"Not just tonight, though. Because your help with the Teen Ministry and the Youth Choir has been tremendous as well. And God is lookin' down on you. He's got so many plans for you. And I hate to bring this up, but you can't keep livin' like you livin' and expect Him not to bring damnation upon you and that boy you layin' up with."

I turned to the picture of *The Baptism*, painted by some unknown artist that hung on the wall to the right of her desk.

"Now don't get upset with me because I know the devil comes to us in all kinds of ways, disguisin' himself in the form of a man you may think you love. But if a man truly loves you, he ain't gonna make you leave your home, honey. Or steal from your husband."

My blood pressure shot up a couple of notches, but I kept my eyes on the young girl being emerged in the blue waters even after Mother hummed, "A-a-men."

Pastor continued, still holding on to my arm, although I was trying to ease away from her as gently as possible. "Nicole, I know you and Jeff have had your share of ups and downs and a lot of them weren't your fault. But you know as well as I do that he's overall a good man and a great provider."

Mother added, "Jeff has taken excellent care of you over the years. You've got a beautiful house with beautiful things. And look how he helped me get my car last year." It was my first time hearing it. "But that boy, who you think you're in love with, is he worth you walkin' out on a man of God? Will he ever be worth your salvation and your soul? Because look at where he came from. Look at his mother and her brothers. They're disgustin'! All they've ever been are alcoholics, drug addicts, and trouble and that's exactly what that boy is. Trouble. He's no good and just after whatever change you got."

"How is Alex trouble, Mother? And what makes him no good? Because you say so?" I stared at her, waiting for her to answer. She just kept her nose in the air.

"You know, Mother, you and Pastor…" I snatched my arm away from her. She jumped back like I had pulled a gun on her. "Stand here praisin' Jeff like he's God. Well, what about all of those children he has? All born while we were married. Ain't that adultery, too? Or are y'all readin' from a different Bible than me? And you're talkin' about me stealin' from him. I don't have to steal from Jeff or anybody else.

"Because I. Yes, I, Mother, own…" I didn't want to go into details for fear of her repeating every word I said to him. "A buildin' or two. He doesn't have a job, so what money does he have to steal? He's got you all fooled, but you know what, that's your problem. Because I don't have to explain myself or the decisions I make to you or anybody else. I've been out of your house for twenty years so I think you tellin' me what to do is long over."

Pastor shook her head. "Leola, you just can't talk to them when they're like this. They start lustin' after these young devils and lose their minds."

"You don't know what a devil is until you've lived with a man like Jeff. You know as well as I do that he's slept with just about every woman in this church. But I'm wrong to have left him. I can't say movin' in with another man was the right choice, but my life with Jeff was hell! And Mother, you've seen me beat up too many times to even pretend he's the kind of husband God wants him to be."

"I also see that you're a slut!"

It had always been in the back of my mind, but I wouldn't dare allow it to move any further. To say it and even think it is a sin. A humongous one against God. Because you can go to the Bible, the Qu'ran, or the Torah and it all means the same thing. We are to obey our parents. We are not to curse or disrespect them, regardless. But, "you bitch", was pressing against my teeth, trying to force itself off my tongue, and escape from my lips. But I held on to those words, squinting, trembling, and glaring at this woman who had just said what she said to me in the house of the Lord. It was by His grace and His mercy that I didn't drop her where she stood.

Pastor said, "But God has a way of changin' everybody, Leola. Nicole knows that thang she's livin' with ain't worth the time she spends with him. And from what I hear, he's one of them Muslims. So it won't be long before he'll be beatin' on her and married to other women."

"At least he'll be screwin' them legally," I added.

Mother gasped and Pastor said, "Jesus! What has gotten into you, child? When you were livin' with Jeff, you were never this disrespectful. That's because in spite of what he's done in the past, he loves you, Nicole."

"Yeah, he loved me so good that he got your niece pregnant in my house."

She damn near swallowed her tongue when I threw that bone at her. Mother had to help her sit down.

"Jeff is lucky I didn't leave him way before now the way he's been sleepin' with everything that comes his way. But y'all don't see it. Because y'all too busy lookin' at the dollar signs he's been flashin' before your eyes and those fancy gifts. Ain't that right, Mother? You're always throwin' 'money is the root of all evil' in my face. If it is, how come you saints never turn down any?"

Old gripes were about to surface and things no daughter should say to her mother came to mind. I got the heck out of there before I took it any further. But they had pushed me in a corner and all I knew how to do was to come out fighting.

Pastor's niece had worked as my assistant on one of our spring candy sales. She had stopped by the house to drop off the last of the monies she had collected. Jeff talked her out of the cash *and* her panties probably no sooner than she walked in the door. I could tell when I got home something had gone down even though I wanted to believe she was my friend.

Afterwards, she would barely speak to me, but would always be in his face. She wasn't pretty like his other full-figured women, so he ignored her most of the time. I guess until he wanted some. When Pastor, whom she was living with at the time, found out the girl was pregnant and she was insisting Jeff was the father, I'm sure she asked him for money for an abortion. Of course, he didn't have it, so she had Mother ask me if she could borrow eight hundred dollars to have something fixed on her car. The day after I gave her the money, which she never paid back, one of Isaac's employees saw Jeff picking her niece up from an abortion clinic in Chicago.

18

With so much rage storming inside me, I couldn't be anywhere near Alex. I drove to my office. The lights were on upstairs. I watched my tenants on the second floor decorating their Christmas tree. I wondered why I couldn't have their kind of happiness and why every time I tried to do something right, it turned out all wrong. Which really wasn't true. I was just throwing myself a pity bash and crying uncontrollably. I sat in my car for at least an hour before Isaac rode past. He saw me and backed his new Tahoe up. I dried my eyes and tried to smile.

"Evenin', Nicole. What are you doin' sittin' out here all by yourself?"

"I'm gettin' ready to go inside. I thought I would spend the night here."

"And why's that?"

I sighed. "Same old drama."

He parked behind me, then got into my car, smelling like fresh-baked sweet potato pie. "You always welcome at my sister's. All of her kids are over there and her grandkids."

"That's okay. This is your night and I would probably—"

"You know you're special to us. Besides, what's one more mouth to feed?"

"So what are you doin' out here ridin' around if all of your family is at your sister's?"

"I had to take our cousin home. He came from the Westside on the train, drunk, to fight one of her sons."

"I guess I better turn in for the night and let you go join your family."

Isaac followed me to the door. He let us in and flipped on the switch controlling the track lights he had installed over my workspace. He sat in the leather chair across from my desk. I went into the kitchen to get him a ginger ale.

"You wanna talk about it?" he said, as I flopped in my chair.

"No." I logged on to AOL to see what properties were listed for sale.

"Nikki, why are you alone on Christmas Eve? Is everything all right between you and your . . . friend, I presume?"

"Everything is always right with him. It's me who has all the damn issues!"

Isaac listened attentively as I rehashed the last eight hours of my life. I had to excuse myself to the bathroom to hide how heartbroken I was when I got to the part about what happened between Mother, Pastor, and me.

"Nikki, what do you want?" he asked, when I came out, holding a box of Puffs tissues in my hand.

"Alex always asks me the same thing."

"We're not talkin' about him. Let's focus on *you* for a change. What do you want outta life?"

"Just to be happy and to be with Alex."

"Well, do you think you and Alex can ever be happy as long as you still lettin' Jeff control your life?"

"He doesn't—"

"He steals from you and you allow it. He's had I don't know how many other children by other women and you still payin' for his mistakes." He knew I had paid for Pastor's niece's abortion. And a couple of times when his children were in need, I sent checks. "Nikki, you can't live this way forever. Tryin' to keep what you have by caterin' to him and livin' with Alex. You'll never be really happy unless you let something go."

"You know I don't wanna be with Jeff. I don't love him and never will, but if I divorce him, he's gonna try and take everything I own. And I . . . You just don't know."

"And all of it can be replaced. But it still leads me back to the same question: Do you ever plan on being happy in this lifetime? When are you gonna learn how to walk away from the bullshit and live your life?"

"Well, how am I supposed to know how to do that when all I've ever known is what it feels like to be kicked in my ass? I can't do shit right. Every time I think I've found happiness—what happens—it gets snatched away."

"You just feelin' sorry for yourself because of what Leola and Dorthea said."

"And they're right. I am an adulteress. Which isn't any better than a harlot. Or better yet a whore in the eyes of God."

He frowned as if he couldn't believe I was saying those things about myself.

"I can't condone what you doin', because we've all made mistakes. And I ain't saying lovin' Alex is a mistake. But when we do wrong in the end, we always pay. Still we all do some messed-up things in our lives, but that's how we learn. From our mistakes. I lost twenty years of my life and my children were grown by the time I was released from prison. And I don't have a clue where any of them are. You know that.

"But you keep on keepin' on and you focus on the good things and if things around you become too messed up, you gotta learn how to walk away from it. I can't stand Jeff. I wished you would've left him the moment you told me who you were married to, because I know his whole family. And yes, I was shocked Leola let you marry him of all people. But how many more years of your life are you gonna spend takin' his bullshit? So what if you lose a house or two. Which would you rather have, a piece of property or peace of mind?"

"What about Alex?"

"I can't advise you. But you still have to ask yourself, what is Alex givin' up for you? You're the one bein' followed and chastised, criticized."

"Almost circumcised."

He laughed. "Yeah, you're right."

The doorbell buzzed. Isaac got up and opened the door. Alex rushed inside with so much worry on his face I felt horrible for not calling him. "Nikki, didn't you get any of my messages? You got me worried like crazy."

"I'm okay."

"Nikki, I was scared as hell. You know how stuff is always happenin'. Are you alright?" I nodded. "I been out lookin' for you for I don't know how long. I rode over on Sheridan Road, over by the church, and by your mom's. Then I figured you had to be here since I didn't see your car anywhere else. Nikki, what is goin' on? You were so happy this mornin' when I last saw you."

I threw the mound of tissue on my desk in the garbage. "I'm okay. Really I am." I looked at Isaac. "Thank you."

Alex was as confused as he appeared to be. Isaac said, "I rescued her from sittin' outside in her car all night."

"But man, what is a brother supposed to do when he loves a woman, knows she's goin' through drama and married to a ass, and she won't open up and tell him what the hell is goin' on?"

"I would just keep on lovin' her, bein' there for her until she decides to talk about it. Sometimes the things our loved ones go through is downright humiliatin'. But if you love them, *really* *love* them, you have to be patient until the time comes for them to open up. Because if they love you, *really* love you, one day they will. Because they'll know they can trust you. And on that note, I think I'll say goodnight." Isaac looked at both of us. "Merry Christmas, you two. And Nikki, give the brother a chance. Talk to him. He might just understand and be able to help you sort out some things."

Before daybreak, Alex and I drove home after spending the rest of the night talking until we went to sleep on the daybed in the back of my office. He had made most of our dinner, so all I had to do was soak in the tub filled with the essence of cucumbers and melon and get some more rest. I slept until he woke me up to get dressed for our company. LJ and Bethany with their two little ones, Limmell and Tyson, were the first to arrive, both boys dressed in identical light-blue sweats. They were so cute and adorable that I couldn't resist sitting them on my lap and kissing one cheek after the other.

Prior to their arrival, I had been nervous LJ wouldn't like Alex since both of them associated with very few people. But they hit it off immediately talking about everything from fatherhood to sports cars to the latest in electronics. Still, I sensed LJ was thinking about Limmell just as I had been—how nothing would ever be the same and how great it would have been to share these moments with him, especially the birth of his first son. Regardless of how much he smiled, there was still an air of sadness about him. I almost had to excuse myself from the room as I stared at him—handsome as they come and looking like Limmell's twin.

Bethany must have sensed the sadness that came over me. She laid her hand on mine. "Thanks for invitin' us over. LJ needed to get out of the house." For such a young woman, she was a lot more mature and compassionate than I had given her credit for being.

I thanked her for coming, then decided I was going to enjoy my day with my most favorite people and see to it that LJ enjoyed it as well. In spite of my intentions, I was still somewhat worried about how Alex's mother, Roxanne, would react once she figured out who I was. The first time Alex and I visited her together, although intoxicated, she kept staring at me, insisting, "I know this girl from somewhere."

She pulled into our driveway at noon in her loud black Corolla, along with her brother, Gene, and his wife. We weren't aware they were coming. Very little had changed about Roxanne over the years. Still a small woman, maybe ninety pounds wet, but looking far older than her early forties. I took their coats, then offered them a little something before we put dinner on the table. His uncle said, "I don't want no carrots and dip. I want some real food." He stuffed a piece of celery into his mouth and chopped down on it with his gums.

"She's just tryin' to be sociable, honey. Besides, some vegetables won't hurt you, not at all," his wife advised.

He glanced down at the bulge hanging over his green polyester slacks and sat on the couch, grabbing some carrot sticks. First to the table, he was impressed with how good of a cook Alex was, since Roxanne was never skilled in the art of preparing a meal. After a scrumptious dinner of lamb paprikash, homemade pan-seared noodles, sautéed yellow and green squash, shrimp scampi, and peach tea, we sat around, at first awkwardly. But Gene relaxed us with his sense of humor and stories about them growing up on the Westside of Chicago.

He said, "We was so po' even the rats turned their noses up at us. Remember that one Christmas when Daddy came home drunk with eight brown paper bags and gave all of us one with our names wrote on it in crayon."

Roxanne hummed, "Uh-huh," picking something out of her brown teeth.

"And we all looked inside and won't nothin' in them bags but a plastic candy cane."

They laughed heartily. "Them sho was some rough times. But now . . . " He nodded. "Look how far we come. And I think we oughta toast to it."

"I think you right, " his wife replied, pulling a brown paper bag out of her oversized purse. She waved her hand at me. "Honey, get us some glasses."

Alex said, "We don't drink and I would prefer if you didn't either, especially with children being here. "

Gene said, "Man, get us some glasses. I think it's time we toast to the Knight family and us being reunited for the first time in months. Look like you doin' mighty good for yo' self. And we just wanna celebrate with you and yo beautiful wife."

"Right on," Roxanne said as she hurried into the kitchen, holding up her oversized blue jeans. She returned with an eight-ounce tumbler she had grabbed out of the cabinet. She shoved it at him, then snatched her hand back.

"Gene, what the hell did you buy brown liquor for?" Alex and I reached for the napkins on the coffee table at the same time. "Can't nobody drink that shit, but you."

"Roxanne, watch your mouth!" Alex snapped.

"You need to quit drinkin' anyway," Gene said. "Cause you look like shit. And smell like it, too. Most of the damn time."

His wife fell back in the loveseat, rolling with laughter.

DAYLIGHT COMING

"Bitch, what you laughin' at?" Roxanne asked.

The woman leaped from the couch, snatching her wig off. "Who you callin' a bitch?"

"Who you thank?"

It got uglier than the tiny plaits on the woman's flat head. So bad that LJ rushed Bethany and their frightened kids down the hall to our room. Gene and Alex tried to intervene, but couldn't calm the squabbling women. Alex stormed over to the closet and seized their coats off the hangers. He threw them at his aunt and mother.

"Get out!" Both women stopped arguing and stood with their mouths tore open. "Get the hell outta my house!"

"Pardon," Roxanne said.

"I didn't stutter."

"I guess I better go before I have to hurt somebody feelings up in here," she replied.

"Well, it won't be mine," Alex emphasized.

Roxanne rolled her eyes, picked up her worn coat and walked over to the door. "Well, where my gifts at?" she asked. "Don't make no sense to come this far and leave with nothin'."

Alex glared at her with a chill I only saw whenever Jeff's name was mentioned.

Gene said, "Might as well get ours, too."

Alex grabbed the four presents I had bought for Roxanne out of the closet and threw them out the door. Roxanne and her sister-in-law raced behind them, grabbing them up like they didn't care as long as they got something.

"Ain't you got some nerve actin' like we beneath you?" Gene said, as he marched out the door.

"It ain't about you bein' beneath me. I know where the hell I came from. Y'all just ought to know how to act in somebody's damn house."

"Well, you ain't got to worry about me ever steppin' a foot in yo castle again." He sneered. "King!"

Alex slammed the door in his face. "Now you see why I can't be around them. I don't have patience for bullshit. I don't care who it is. Anybody want me to stay out of their life, all they gotta do is bring too much drama my way. I don't know why I thought for just once we could get together and nobody show their ass. But that's how my people are. Ignorant as hell!"

I felt awful because I was the one who insisted he invite his mother to dinner. I also knew he was humiliated, considering he was meeting LJ and Bethany for the first time. Yet, behind his anger, I saw how pained he was. He apologized to them and me several times for what had happened. Each time we accepted it with understanding. Still, it didn't take a genius to see that if I didn't hurry up and get rid of my excess baggage, as easy as it had been to kick his mother out of his house, I was living and loving on borrowed time.

19

With my mind made up to start the New Year off with more control over my life, I decided Jeff and I could come to a neutral agreement on how to end our marriage without a lot of drama. I went to his office on the third day of the year.

"Jeff, can we talk?"

I tried to negotiate a way he could earn a salary by helping me manage an apartment building. He loved the idea of me giving him some responsibilities, even though to him, allowing him to be the landlord meant I had to let him collect the rent.

"Why are you all of a sudden bein' so nice to me, Nicole?"

"Because I'm tired of fightin' with you."

"Does that mean you comin' back home or are you gonna keep livin' with that grease monkey?"

It always stung when he called Alex names, yet once again, I dismissed his ignorance. "No, I'm not comin' back. I'm just gonna keep livin' in the back of my office."

"If you livin' there . . . " He reached in his middle drawer and dangled some keys on a State Farm chain in front of my eyes. "Then you must be invisible, so quit lyin'. You know you livin' with that young-ass boy you used to baby-sit for. And you know you was screwin' him way back then."

I closed my briefcase and stood up.

"You also know you headed straight to hell. God don't like ugly and leavin' your husband for another man is ugly. Do you ever think about that when that grease monkey is tryin' to knock your backsides out? While he's got you on your knees whimperin' like a sick dog? Have you? While's he's rammin' his self all up in your ass? Have you ever thought about what if you should die while he's screwin' your brains out? Little Nicole with her perfect little ass would go to hell just like the rest of us heathens."

God, I wish somebody would kill this bastard. "Thank you for the advice, Jeff."

He followed me out the door. "Nicole, remember this. Stop, Jeff, stop. O-o-h it hurt." I stopped as if a boulder had just dropped in my path. "It hurts, Jeff. Stop. Please, stop." I turned around and stared at him, wondering how he could even bring that up. "All the while lovin' every minute of it. You stankin'-ass slut!"

Later in the day when I met Alex for lunch, I was barely able to consume the broasted chicken and Greek salad he treated me to. Because every filthy thing Jeff had done to me that I had worked so hard to put out of my mind seemed to have come back to haunt me, all at once. Concerned with my picking over my food, he said, "Nicole, please! Talk to me."

To tell him the truth would have made me look like the sick freak Jeff had called me, but not telling him anything only made Alex angrier. He would get this eerie look in his eyes whenever he suspected I was stressed by something Jeff-related. The same look he got the first time we discussed the night he ran away.

For months after he left, with only thirty dollars to his name, he was homeless until this girl, who he met in a shelter, took him in. Sasha, also a runaway, was trying to escape an unplanned pregnancy and a domineering married boyfriend. She and Alex had formed a friendship and he had become her protection on the streets of Atlanta. He convinced her to call her parents three weeks before her daughter arrived still-born. They came and took the two of them back to Miami.

They parted because of her addiction to heroin. From there Alex was in and out of relationships, earning money by being a street mechanic and boarding mostly with older women who kept a roof over his head and his belly full. This was his life until a jealous lover named Christine taught him a big lesson.

"After Chris tried to stab me, I decided no more tryin' to get what I wanted if I had to get it from anybody else. So I took a room at a boardin' house, found a job in a factory that made videotapes, then put myself through college.

"It was the wisest choice I ever made, because that's how I got my first job at one of Miami's largest foreign repair shops. And I worked as many hours as I could get, because I got tired of bein' alone and havin' no one to love. Or no connection to anybody. I guess it's because most of the time when I thought about you, that was when I would really feel lonely. Like I keep tryin' to tell you, something in my heart kept tellin' me you and I were meant to be."

"But I never thought about you beyond bein' like my little brother."

"I know and would get pissed at you for always treatin' me like a kid. You would take me by my hand and say, 'Alex, one day everything you desire is gonna be yours. Because you're special.' Man, when you used to hug me..."

"So while I was tryin' to play the big-sister role, you were thinkin' about gettin' your groove on."

"You have always been beautiful to me and I have always envied and hated Jeff, because he never knew how to treat you. Or appreciate you."

I found it hard to believe Alex had been in love with me all that time. It seemed too much like something you read about in a novel. I loved him, too, but in a different way. Even then he still accepted what I was willing to give. As we became closer, he continued to show me just how much he loved me, even when some of the decisions I made tested his patience to the core.

It took three weeks before I was able to face Jeff again after his malicious taunting. The things he reminded me of seemed to all come barreling at me at once. Not just a thought here and there, but every gory detail. Every time I closed my eyes, I could hear, see, and feel him. I lost my desire to eat anything, was constantly nauseous, and wasn't able to sleep more than two hours a night.

Seeing my demeanor change before his eyes, Alex said, "I know he's done something to you. And I'm tired of him sweatin' you and you not trustin' me to tell me what it is. See, this really makes me wanna—"

"Please, Alex, just let me handle this. I'm workin' on some things I need to do. But please, just give me time to sort it all out."

I decided to meet Jeff at Buffalo Joe's for their infamous chicken wings, celery strips and Ranch dressing, my treat. I gave him the keys to one of my buildings, the one I was making the least profit off.

"The tenants pay nine-fifty each. All you have to do is pay the water, gas, and light bills. Monthly of course. And the rest of the money is yours. But as the manager, you gotta keep the property up." I handed him a list of everything that had to be done in and around the building periodically. "Because if you don't, the tenants will stop payin' and the property value will go down."

A week later, the grass still wasn't cut and it hadn't been cleaned up around the place. Passing by daily, I finally couldn't take it anymore. I mowed the lawn, weeded out the flower garden, then vacuumed the halls and cleaned the doors as I had instructed Jeff to do.

I called him, asking, "Why?"

"I forgot."

But he didn't forget to give the tenants a friendly call to remind them where their checks or money orders were to be mailed. A month later, things weren't any better. I decided to call him once again, rather than to be in his presence. I got straight to the point reminding him about the importance of paying the bills on time and keeping his tenants happy.

"If it concerns you so damn much, then you keep doin' it," Jeff replied.

"That's not the agreement we made. I turned the property over to you, because you—"

"Damn them people, when are you comin' home?" He belched in my ear.

DAYLIGHT COMING

I shook my head, disgusted by how gross it sounded. "Why would I?"

"Because you know you miss this good lovin'. Stop, Jeff, stop. O-o-oh it hurt." I slammed the telephone down.

After two months of going back and forth with him about his responsibilities—me picking up his slack, him collecting the profit—I sent his tenants a certified letter, apologizing for the entire mess. I gave them a month's rent free and asked them to forward their payments back to me. When he found his mailbox empty, he came to my office so furious his eyes were bulging out of their sockets. He walked in the door, slapping my matching accessories off my desk and kicking over my garbage can.

I tried to remain calm, but our disagreement became so heated, I threatened, "If you ever come near me again, I'm gonna have you arrested."

"You better call the police," he shouted in my face. "Because you gonna need 'em."

"Jeff, you ain't gonna do a damn thing to me."

"You just better watch your back. Because I got something for you!" It was more taunting—only with more horrid details and destroying my house.

Even though Alex was forever pleading with me to stay away from him, to not put myself in any awkward positions, I couldn't resist my urge to go there. Or my desire to try to clean it up even though just about everything I'd left behind was either gone or had become junk. Every time it would be even more heartbreaking, but I would still clean and attempt to piece together as much as I could.

Trying to pry off a plastic bowl Jeff left melted on the stove, I got the bright idea to hire weekly cleaning people, thinking it would force him to take better care of the place. Or maybe embarrass him into it. The owner called me two weeks after they started.

"I'm sorry, Miss Kingston, but I can't send my girls back over there. They're scared to death of your brother."

There was no way after hiring Mighty Maids I was going to tell them I was married to such a filthy creature, who answered the door in his boxers every day they were scheduled to come, demanding they cook him something to eat. When I heard about it, I thought, *Jeff must be losin' his damn mind.*

"So you're quittin' on me."

"I'm sorry, Miss Kingston, but I can't jeopardize my employees' safety or sanity for you or anybody else!"

Alex figured out once again something was horribly wrong. He tried to be patient about me keeping whatever it was from him, but finally confronted me one evening when his kisses weren't doing anything but making me cringe.

"Nikki, don't you think I get tired of tryin' to guess what the hell is goin' on with you? If we're gonna be together, you gonna have to tell me what's troublin' you. If you trust me and love me the way you say you do, then you gotta tell me. Even if it's painful as hell. There's nothin' he could've done to you to make me ever stop lovin' you. You gotta believe me, baby."

"I can't."

"Yes, you can, because it's *our* problem now."

He turned the television down and sat watching me with begging eyes. I don't know if it was the desperation in them or the fear I would lose him that made me say, "Jeff raped me." Or if it was because those words had been screaming inside of me, needing to be released.

"That son-of-a-bitch. That's what I thought." He raced to the closet for his jacket, where the keys to his truck were.

I ran behind him. "Alex, please."

"What the hell do you expect me to do? You keep all of these secrets from me. Why I don't know?"

"Because I don't want you actin' like you're actin' now!"

"Well, have you ever thought that you got me feelin' *and lookin'* like a damn punk?"

"How?"

"Because he's messin' with you every day. I see it on your face. Hear it in your voice. And all I can do is sit back and watch you bein' miserable. I don't know when I last saw you smile. I try to pamper the hell outta you, do everything for you I know he didn't do, and you walkin' around lookin' like you on the verge of suicide. And now you say, he raped you."

"It's old."

"How do I know?"

"Because I said so."

"You keep so much from me, how do I know it wasn't yesterday."

I rubbed my forehead with my fingers. "You would've known."

"Nikki, when?"

I sat on the couch. I grabbed a pillow and wrapped my arms around it. "Every time he touched me."

He sat next to me. "What is that supposed to mean?"

I sighed. "My mother made me marry him."

"Why?"

"She didn't want me there with her and RudyAnn anymore."

"Let me get this straight. Your mother made you marry Jeff. And he used to rape you. I'm missin' something."

"I never wanted sex with him. So he used to just take it, sayin' he was exercisin' his marital rights. And he used to hurt me. Real bad."

"Nikki, I'm sorry I snapped on you the way I did. I just get so frustrated when I think about the hell he put you through and I wanna help you, baby. Honest, I do. And I'm not tryin' to judge you. But you take so much off him that I don't understand."

"Most of this stuff is old."

"It can't be so old if it's stressin' you like it is. You don't see how sad you look. And it hurts like hell. I understand a little, knowin' that sick bastard used to rape you. But, why didn't you have him arrested?"

"Alex, I really don't want to talk about this."

"See, this is what you do every time I try to get to the bottom of what's goin' on. But tonight you're gonna talk to me. Because I need some answers. When was the last time he did that to you?"

I closed my eyes and sighed. "The night you ran away."

His hand froze on the small of my back. And I covered my face with my hands to tell him what I had revealed to no other.

"After I convinced you to go home and let me handle Jeff, which meant fightin' him with everything I had until I couldn't fight him any longer. I let go of the door and he snatched me inside. And . . . I tried to stab him, but as he always did, he overpowered me. It had been years since he'd come near me like that, so it was like he was tryin' to kill me.

"After he was through, I was in so much pain. Oh God, I hurt like you wouldn't believe. So bad I couldn't get up. So I just laid there, starin' at the knife he had kicked under the kitchen table. I wanted to cut his throat so bad that I had to pinch myself over and over again to snap out of it. Then I thought about you. The look on your face when I chased you away.

"That's when I started to cry. Not for me. But for you, because I was worried about what was gonna happen to you. To our friendship since we were all each other had. I don't know how long I laid there because I couldn't stand up. I had to crawl to the bathroom. By then, Jeff had taken a shower, gotten dressed and was gone for the night."

"Damn, baby. I didn't know it was that bad. And like I said, I'm sorry for the hell he put you through, but that was over ten years ago. So why are you all of a sudden turnin' cold whenever I touch you?" I started chewing on my thumbnail. He pulled my hand down. "Why, Nikki?"

"Because . . . " I whispered.

"Why?"

"Because he won't leave me alone about it. He used to hurt me every time when we first got married. Because I wasn't used to sex. And he was so rough and wanted to do things. That were so . . . I just wasn't familiar with. Now every time I turn around, he's callin' me makin' crying noises in the phone, laughin' about how I used to beg him not to touch me and braggin' about the things he did to me."

"Nikki, you could've told me and I would've put a end to it no sooner than it started."

"But I thought . . . "

"I don't think you're nasty or anything like that. I just think he's a sick son-of-a-bitch and if he ever touches you again, I'll kill him!"

"He ain't worth you goin' to jail."

"It ain't like I ain't been there before."

While out on the street, Alex was often so broke he did what he felt it took to eat. One night there was a raid at one of his buddy's house. He told the police about Alex's hustle to get off. He served ninety days for possession.

"Man, that was the worst time of my life. And I swore I would never go to jail again. But Jeff would be more than worth it," Alex added.

20

After promising Alex I would be extra careful, I started keeping my office door locked whenever I was on the premises. I even called Isaac about helping me choose an alarm system.

"Nicole, is there something I need to know?" he asked.

"I just think it would be a good idea."

"And I told you this when?"

"When I first opened my office. So are you gonna be able to help me?"

The doorbell buzzed. I didn't have to look at the face to know it was Anna. I could tell by the three-inch heels and the way she was standing.

Isaac said, "I'll get back with you in a day or so. I'm swamped right now."

"Okay. I'll talk to you later."

"Okay. And call me again sometimes. When you don't want something."

"Yes, sir."

I clicked him off and let Anna in. She gave me a big hug. "What's up with the door being locked?"

"I've been feuding with Jeff. He wants me to come home. I won't, so he's been having tantrums."

"You better watch your back, Nicole. Because there's no telling what he could do to you."

I nodded, then asked, "So what's up? I ain't seen or heard from you in a long time."

"And I ain't seen or heard from you in a while, either. Don't know a sista no more."

"You know how it goes."

DAYLIGHT COMING

"Yeah, I do. But, Nicole, we need to talk."

"About?"

"I've been hearing some things."

"Such as."

"You and Alex."

"And..."

"Did you?"

"Did I what?" I thought about it. "Anna, you know me better than that. Have you ever heard . . . "

"It doesn't matter what I heard back then. It's what I'm hearing now, that my best friend is sleeping with this young guy she used to baby-sit for. Were you—"

"No! And first of all, I didn't baby-sit Alex. He was in the eighth grade when we met, so I think he was a bit too old for a childcare provider. And another thing, we've been together for a year. So why are you all of a sudden comin' to me about this?"

"Because I just am."

"I know everybody in Evanston is talkin' about me. I can just imagine how many whores and sluts I been called. And cradle robbers."

"You know that doesn't faze me with my track record."

"Then why would you ask me something so ridiculous?"

"I don't know. I guess the way your . . . "

"I know damn well you ain't comparin' me to RudyAnn."

"It's just that everywhere I go, I'm hearing something about you and Alex and how y'all used to be together all the time . . . "

"Anna, you know for a fact that I was a virgin until my senior year. And you know I was never with anybody else after Styles dumped me until I married Jeff. So you should also know I ain't one to sleep around, let alone with a kid in junior high. My life may have been jacked up, but I would never stoop that low."

"Nicole, you're right. And I'm sorry, but—"

"You should be. You out of all people should know I would have never seduced Alex as a child." I smiled. "I don't have a problem doin' it now."

She laughed. "I don't blame you because the brotha is fine as hell. But your ex is dragging your name through the mud like you won't believe. Telling people you stole all of his money. I hear he's stressing the hell outta your mama."

"That's because she's lettin' him. Girl, I can't believe you would even try to compare me to RudyAnn. Now that's a low blow."

Anna laughed. "I know I've done some thangs, but she *was* nasty."

"And Lennox got the nerve to act like her crap don't stink. He knew when he married her LJ wasn't his. Then gonna treat him and Limmell—" I hadn't mentioned Limmell's name since his funeral. I shook my head. "Man, I miss him."

"Me too. He was a great kid."

"But LJ's doin' great at Northeastern."

She frowned. "I thought he was goin' to Northwestern."

"He transferred."

"Why?"

"He had some lame excuse. But he's hangin' in there."

"What's he majoring in now?"

"He still wants to be a teacher, but it ought to be Planned Parenthood, because Bethany is pregnant. Again! She's six weeks so you know I had to tell him about himself. I ain't gonna keep helpin' them with Pampers and milk if they can't start usin' protection."

"You know all LJ has to do is make a phone call and you're breaking out your checkbook, so you should've kept those words to yourself."

"I know I got it bad, but I'm learnin' to say no."

"Was it before or after you bought him a new Altima?"

"He wanted a Escalade."

"You're a wonderful auntie, Nicole."

"Sometimes. But gettin' back to the subject." I threw a paperclip at her. "You actually thought . . . "

She ducked. "I didn't know what to think."

"Why didn't you just ask?"

"Because, how often do we hear from you now? You hardly ever answer your phone or return any of my calls. I had Isaac over the other day, because he's remodeling my downstairs kitchen, and, girl, he looks so lost without you. You just kicked all of us to the curb."

"Y'all ain't the ones I wanna kick to the curb. It's that bastard I'm married to I can't seem to get rid of."

"With the reputation he's got, just plead temporary insanity. Trust me . . . the judge will understand, especially now since he's moved that girl in your house."

"What girl?'

"The one who he claims was his secretary. I'm telling you, if she ain't living with him, she's there an awful lot. You know I'm always over in the area. Three times in a row, I've seen her coming out of your house."

"That black—"

"Nicole, look. One friend to another. If it's over between you and Jeff, go ahead and decide what is what and get your divorce. What are you still holding on to him for?"

"I ain't holdin' on to him. It's just that . . . I can't explain it right now."

"Well, whatever the case may be, how much longer are you going to be living with Alex and married to him? And considering Jeff doesn't have a job or any income. Taking care of him? And now his hoochie!"

I don't know, but one thing's for sure, that bitch is gettin' the hell outta my house!

21

Although I had promised Alex I was going to stay away from Jeff, I woke up with my house on Sheridan Road on my mind. I had an impending need to see if he really did have his girlfriend living there. I dialed his cell number. It was disconnected. I checked the time. I thought, *He's probably somewhere having breakfast.*

I grabbed the bottle of pepper spray Alex had given me and his Louisville Slugger. I hurried to my house and walked inside, startling his guest and some young guy hugged up on my once-was-white leather couch in the living room. He was a cutie, but I saw wannabe-thug with his pants-down-to-his-knees, silver-chain-swinging, tattoo-covered self. Not that I'm trying to say everybody who dresses like that is a thug, but he tried to get hostile with me after I politely told them, "This is my house. And you gotta go."

"We ain't goin' no damn where," he said.

"Y'all gettin' the hell outta here."

I ran up on them, swinging the Louisville like I was deranged. Both of them raced out the front door. He threatened to burn the house down as he stood in the yard calling me every kind of bitch he could think of.

"It's insured. So go ahead, burn it up. I'm still gonna get paid and your ass is goin' to jail!"

I was alone for maybe five minutes before Jeff slipped in through the patio door. Dishes were all over the kitchen. The soles of my gym shoes kept sticking to the floor and unidentifiable foods had turned into mush inside the refrigerator.

Seeing me standing next to the stove, he asked. "What are you doing here? And where's . . . "

"I kicked her and her boyfriend out."

"What the hell you mean her boyfriend? He was her kid brother."

"They were hugged up on the couch with his hands in her crotch. Unless they were committin' incest, they ain't hardly brother and sister."

"You're just jealous."

"Of what?"

He jacked on his slacks. "'Cause she's gettin' all of this man and you layin' up with a boy." He looked like he was extremely tired, had huge bags under his eyes, and had lost a noticeable amount of weight. It was the worse I had ever seen him.

"Yeah, Jeff, whatever. Carrie called my office yesterday sayin' she needs some money to buy your son some new sneakers, so go shake your thang at her. Man!"

Their affair had lasted for about three years. He had given her a bad case of gonorrhea so she quit him. She had given birth to his last born, Lamar, in 1983. Jeff never gave her a dime for him just like he did the rest of his kids.

"Fuck you, Nicole."

"You wish."

"So you'll be screamin', 'Stop, Jeff, stop.'"

"Since I'm with a real man now, I'll probably laugh at your ass." He didn't appreciate what I said. I apologized to clear the air.

"So you back to stay."

"Jeff, don't start."

"Well, get out then."

"Okay." I started out of the kitchen. He dashed in front of me with an evil smirk on his face. I backed up, looking around for my purse and the pepper spray I had tossed in it after getting rid of his guest and her friend. Jeff swooped me into his arms. "I know what you want." His breath was hot and strong like pork sausages.

I tried to wrestle away from him. He pinned my arms behind my back with one hand, then jammed the other between my legs. "Beg me, Nicole." He dug his nails into my thigh. "Beg me to turn you loose. Beg me like you used to. 'Stop, Jeff, stop.' Beg me or I'll bust your insides." I stomped his foot. He scratched harder. The pain was excruciating, but I was determined not to break in front of him.

"Turn me loose, Jeff."

"You know you want Big Poppa."

He pressed his erection against me in a hard grind. Keeping his body close to mine and his nails in my skin, he bumped me toward the living room. I knew once he got me near the couch, it would only be a matter of seconds before he would have my shorts down to my knees. He did it once before with a pair of jogging pants. I was refusing him one day after work. He snatched them down quicker than I could get them back up, then leaned me over the sofa, knocked my legs apart, and jammed his erection in as far as it would go.

Petrified it would happen again, I dropped down, then threw myself back with so much intensity that I thought I had cracked my skull when the back of my head slammed into his face. He threw his hand over his injury.

"Got-dammit, Nicole. You broke my fuckin' nose!"

Blood gushed from it as he paced, trying to shake off the pain. I snatched my purse off the table, determined to get out the door before he came back to his senses. He grabbed my arm, digging his nails into my skin and ripping away some of my flesh. I clawed at his face. He backhanded me. I slammed into the wall. Instant pain shot up my spine as I landed on the floor.

I grabbed the pepper spray out of my purse, spraying wildly. He screamed, then slapped himself in the face and rubbed his eyes violently. I jumped to my feet and barreled out of the front door, unlocking my car door with the remote as I raced to safety.

Jeff charged out of the house with the bat in his hands, wheezing and ranting, "I'm gonna kill you." I snatched the door open and dived inside my car. My hands were shaking so bad I don't know how I started it. But I put my Volvo in reverse and raced out of the driveway.

DAYLIGHT COMING

I parked in the alley behind Isaac's garage and dashed to his back door. I banged on it, like my life depended on it. He opened up in a hurry. "Damn, Nikki, you . . . " Horror covered his face. "What the hell . . . "

"I was at my . . . " I stopped to catch my breath. "I was at my house on Sheridan Road . . . "

"Is that damn house worth all this? That sick bastard could be buryin' you in the backyard right now. And how in the hell would we know? Get in here!"

He pulled me into the kitchen and took a first-aid kit from off top of the refrigerator. Isaac poured Peroxide on a cotton ball and dabbed at my wounds. It stung, but I tried to be a woman about it by not screaming like I wanted to. Next he applied globs of Neosporine to my injuries, while staring at me like he wanted to knock some sense into my head.

He pulled a chair away from the table. "Sit down." I eased into the seat, because my inner thighs burned worse than the Peroxide and wouldn't stop throbbing. He stood over me, glaring at my legs. I tried to pull my shorts over my wounds so he wouldn't see the blood oozing from them.

"Nikki, did Jeff rape you?"

"No."

"Do you expect me to believe that? Look at your damn self."

"He didn't, honest," I mumbled, "but he tried."

Isaac marched over to the telephone. I ran and snatched it up. I held it behind my back. "I can't go to the police, Isaac."

"Why the hell not?"

"Because there are so many things that you don't understand."

"Make me understand, because normal people don't claw between somebody's legs like that. I ain't never seen nothin' like that before in my life."

"I can't, Isaac."

"Nikki, do you not understand what just happened to you?"

"I do, but . . ."

"Then what the hell are you waitin' for? For Jeff to kill you?"

Whenever hours went by and he didn't hear from me, Alex automatically panicked. He had gone to my office and checked out all of my buildings and houses to no avail. Unable to find me, he decided to swing by Isaac's to see if he had heard from me. Even though I begged him not to, Isaac said, "Yeah, she's in here."

Although he really didn't like me hanging around Isaac, he was relieved to see that I was okay until he saw the bandages on my arm. "What the f . . ." And on my thighs. "Nikki, tell me that son-of-a-bitch didn't do this to you?"

Alex charged out the front door. Isaac rushed behind him. He had to stand behind his Land Cruiser to keep him from going to find Jeff. Alex jumped out of his truck.

"What in the hell am I supposed to do? He used to rape her. And now since she ain't with him no more . . . Man, what the hell was she doin' alone with him in the first place?"

Alex rushed toward the house. Isaac followed him inside. I ran into the bathroom. Alex shook the doorknob. "Nikki, let me in. Nikki, let me in this bathroom, because you got some explainin' to do!" I was crying so hard, I couldn't utter anything, but sobs.

"Let me talk to her," Isaac said.

Alex punched the bathroom door. I heard the front door slam again. Isaac said, "Damn," and left out behind him. Hearing the sound of squalling tires, I ran out of the bathroom. Isaac rushed back inside, grabbed his keys, and pulled me to his truck. We got to my house just as Alex was ringing the bell and bamming on the door. Jeff barely opened it an inch. Alex kicked it open the rest of the way and dived inside.

By the time Isaac and I reached them, Alex's hands were wrapped around Jeff's neck. One of Jeff's eyes was swollen shut. And he was on his knees with his tongue hanging out of his mouth. I raced over to them.

"Alex, please, let him go. Please, baby. Let him go. I don't want you goin' to jail. Please. Let's go home. I'll press charges. I'll do anything if we can just go home." Isaac tried desperately to pry his hands from around Jeff's neck. There was so much rage in Alex's eyes I didn't think he would but he let Jeff go.

Jeff fell over gasping. "Man, I don't know what Nicole told you. But I ain't touched her!"

Alex looked down at him like he was ready to pounce on him again, but I grabbed his arm. "Baby, please. He ain't worth you goin' to jail."

He stared at me—eyes still so furious I backed away from him. Isaac patted him on the shoulder. "Thank you, man. Now let's just get outta here."

"Man, she ain't worth all this," Jeff said, getting off the floor.

Alex lunged at him. Jeff screamed like a frightened child, then hightailed it to the bathroom. Isaac grabbed Alex's arm. He snatched away from him and dashed over to Jeff's place of safety. He kicked the door and slammed into it with his shoulder.

"Man, I ain't done nothin'. I swear," Jeff shouted.

"Alex, please, don't do this," I begged.

He kicked the door even harder. His foot went through the wood. Jeff yelled, "I ain't done nothin' to Nicole. She lyin' on me, man. She lyin'."

Alex punched the door with his fist. "Open the damn door, you punk-ass bitch!"

It took Isaac and me, I don't know how long to talk some sense into his head. It gave Jeff leeway to escape out the bathroom window. I don't know how he squeezed out of it, but by the time Alex finished tearing the door down, he was long gone, his car still parked out front.

I tried to apologize to Alex for the mess I caused, but he brushed past me like I was a stranger. Isaac and I followed him home. He parked in the driveway, got out of his truck, and went straight to the backyard. I opened my door to go behind him.

Isaac said, "Stay here."

He walked around to the back of the house. There was a brief moment of discussion, then Alex snapped, ranting about how bad he wanted to kill Jeff's pathetic ass. Once his rage was somewhat out of his system, we finally said goodnight to Isaac with Alex promising, "I'll take care of her. Thank you, man." Isaac had insisted he would feel better if we spent the night with him. I wanted to since Alex wouldn't talk to me. But being the compassionate man he was, he ran me a tub of hot water adding two cups of Epsom salt and several capfuls of Aloe Vera oil. I soaked for a half-hour waiting for him to come and say what he had to say, but he stayed in the bedroom.

I dried myself off, doctored my wounds, threw on a mega-sized T-shirt, and went outside. I sat on the deck. Alex came to the doorway, then went into the back of the house. He turned on the sounds of Walter Beasley. I listened to the smooth jazz until the CD played out. Thinking he was in bed, I crept inside. He was gone. I called Isaac. He wasn't at home. I paged him and rang both his and Alex's cell phones repeatedly while pacing and praying until Alex came home. I met him at the door.

"Alex, where've you been?"

He went into the bedroom, slamming the door. I sat on the couch too bummed to cry anymore, wondering, *where do I go now*? I pulled the Yellow Pages from the closet near the front door.

Alex came into the living room. "Where do you plan to go?"

"I don't know," I whispered, pained by the thought of him wanting me to leave. He took the telephone book out of my hand and tossed it on the coffee table. Alex sat next to me. He took me into his arms. As if he knew I was uncertain if I should touch him back, he wrapped mine around him.

"I know I've said this a thousand times. Nikki, would you talk to me, please. What is goin' on? And why do you keep . . . I don't know how else to say it. Why do you keep puttin' yourself in danger—goin' around Jeff? And why do you keep lettin' him do these things to you and not have him arrested?"

"Suppose . . . " I sighed. "Suppose I do have him arrested and have to tell all of the things he's done to me. And they'll ask, if he did all of that to you, why would you go back there alone?"

"And what would you say? Why did you go there?"

"Because he's destroyin' it."

"Let me get this straight. You went back there, jeopardizin' your life. Not knowin' if he's capable of killin' you or not over a damn house?" Alex stared at me like my mind was stapled to the wall. "Answer me, Nikki. You went back there because you were concerned about your house."

"Jeff has sold my big-screen TV, stereo set, bedroom set, den set, all of my jewelry, and poured bleach all over my shoes, leather coats, and silk blouses. And the place is filthy."

"And that's more important to you than your life?"

"No."

"Then what the hell were you doin' there?" I never lied to Alex. Not opening my mouth was my way of not incriminating myself with any more irrational explanations. "Are you still in love with him?"

"You know I've never been in love with Jeff."

"Then why should you give a damn if somebody else *was* livin' with him?" I froze. "Isaac told me."

"He told you what."

"I know he had another woman . . . "

"I could care less who Jeff is with, but I ain't gonna keep a roof over his head and hers, too."

"What the hell is that supposed to mean?" I sighed again. "Do you mind if I get into your business enough to ask, why are you still payin' the mortgage and the bills, I presume, over there, and you ain't lived on Sheridan Road in over a year?"

"Because Jeff won't pay nothin'."

"Why the hell don't you put him out then? That muthafu… Nikki, that bastard has raped you, stole from you, got I don't know how many credit cards in your name, and had five or six damn kids by other women, while you were married to him! And you're still takin' care of him!"

I resented him bringing up what I had shared with him and ignored him waiting for a reasonable explanation, which I couldn't give.

"Well tell me this, what is he doin' to you, Nikki? Blackmailin' you because I know it's gotta be more to it than you just takin' care of him for the sake of takin' care of him."

22

For the brief amount of time Jeff left Alex and me alone because Isaac had a heart-to-heart talk with him, we lived out our fantasy of being together in peace. Alex had gone back to the house to have another man-to-man discussion as well, but Isaac was already there when he drove up, assuring him, "You don't have to worry about him ever botherin' you two again."

Of course it took more than that to convince Alex to turn around and go back home. But whatever Isaac said or did, it worked for a while. I was elated to finally breathe without having to worry about Jeff's stream of phone calls. I also didn't have to worry about when and if he would pop up, since his threats had become more frightening. I even felt more at ease being out in public with Alex.

We began having strolls along Lake Michigan like old times, went to a couple of Steppers' sets—even though neither one of us could step a lick—and outdoor concerts. We even started frequenting our old favorite hangout, Navy Pier.

We had been discussing him going into business for months. Having taken up accounting classes and business management along the way, he knew what he had to do. He just hadn't saved enough money to get started. I offered to give it to him several times. But each time, he said, "Nikki, this is something I have to do on my own. I love you for wantin' to look out for me. But I wouldn't feel right takin' from you. I got a plan, baby. It'll just take me a minute before I can execute it."

After being in the industry for years, he could spot a master mechanic in a heartbeat. He was always getting addresses and phone numbers for potential employees. If we were somewhere and there was a car tech on the premises, he or she and Alex would connect instantly. As little as I knew about cars, other than how to drive them, I loved hearing him talk shop, watching him check my oil and other fluids, and making sure my Volvo was in top running condition.

We walked a great length of the pier before we found a place to sit. He said, "You know, Nikki, even though our first year together has been crazy as hell, I'm glad we're still together."

"Me, too."

"Lately, I've been doin' a lot of thinkin' about us." I got an instant pain in my stomach. "And like I said, we've been through some things. But we overcame them. Because we're a team. Right?"

"Yeah."

"And since we're a team and since I know I love you more than life, baby, will you marry me?"

"You want me to marry you?"

"Yeah. Why not?"

I could not believe after all the drama I had brought into our relationship he still wanted me to be his wife. Sure enough I wanted to spend the rest of my life with him. But what we shared was good enough for me just as long as every morning when I woke up, his face was the first one I saw.

He took my left hand into his. He slipped a rock on my finger. I really started bawling. People passing by looked at me like, *What's your problem?*

Alex said, "I just asked her to marry me." The word spread and some twenty or more people congratulated us. I called Anna on our way home.

Alex asked, "You sure she's up?"

"She'll wanna get up for this."

Anna said, "Nicole, this better be good for you to be calling me at two o'clock in the damn morning."

"Guess what?"

"What?"

"Alex asked . . ."

She screamed. "I knew it! I knew it! Roger, wake up."

"How did you know?"

"I told you every time we're together and I'm watching him looking at you. I could see how much he loves you."

"Yeah, you did."

Alex held my hand as we cruised down Lake Shore Drive, the lake on one side and streams of high rises and other elaborate places to live on the other. "What's she sayin'?"

"Tell him I said congratulations," Anna replied.

"She sends her congrats."

She and Roger met us at the neighborhood IHOP to celebrate. She hopped out of her 4Runner no sooner than he pulled into the parking lot. For me to have woke her up, she looked mighty jazzy in her designer jeans, cashmere sweater, and spiked-heel sandals.

"Let me see," she said, smiling as if she was the one proposed to.

I held my hand out. I waved my diamond before her eyes. "O-o-w, Nicole, it's so beautiful! I know who's gonna be standing right next to you." I got a little misty-eyed, because after I moved in with Alex, we hadn't spent as much time together. "Did you think I was gonna say no?"

"Who said I was gonna ask you to be my matron of honor?"

"Because you know I would've turned that mutha out." We laughed and the guys shook their heads. "Nikki, the only thing I would've said no to would've been you getting married and not asking me to be in the damn wedding. You know you're my girl. Just like my little sister."

"Excuse you, but I *am* the oldest."

"By two months. But I still feel like I'm the big sister." In many ways she was. Still there are certain things big sisters and best friends just can't help you with.

Lying on my back on the couch, I tapped my forehead repeatedly, trying to figure out what I was going to do about Jeff. I wanted him out of my life so bad, hiring somebody to kill him was something I was taking into consideration, to avoid a messy divorce and to keep his hands off anything I had worked hard to pay for. Living in my house without upping a dime was bad enough. And constantly interfering in my life. Whether it was by his degrading phone calls that kept me awake at night or his threat, "You'll never be happy with *that boy* as long as *I'm* alive."

As if he knew he was on my mind, he rang my cell phone. The minute I said, "Hello," wondering who was calling me so early in the morning from a pay phone, he said, "I need to see you."

"Jeff, I don't have time for—"

"Oh, I think you wanna make time. If not, I hate to think what would happen if what I found out just happened to leak out."

I was on Sheridan Road in less than twenty minutes, red bandana still on my head, wearing one of Alex's hooded FUBU sweatshirts and a pair of his sweat pants, both sagging off me.

"What's this all about, Jeff?"

He winced and rubbed his left arm. "Have a seat."

"I'd rather stand."

"Suit yourself."

"Can we get to the purpose of you callin' me? I have things to do."

He walked over to the mess of papers on the acrylic coffee table in the living room. With my hand in my pocket, I followed him, keeping my fingers wrapped around the new can of pepper spray I had bought, just in case his mind was in his zipper again. He sat on the couch. He picked up a fat white folder, stuffed with more papers.

"I want my half."

"Half of what."

"They say forgery is a federal crime, Nicole."

"What are you talkin' about?"

"Cut the bull. You forged my signature on every piece of property you ever bought. Signed my name as if I was so fuckin' stupid I would never find out that the law says you can't buy property without my consent."

"I don't need your consent."

He slammed his fist on the table, then grabbed his chest. I jumped back. "All this damn time, I been doin' whatever I can to survive, beggin' folks for money to eat. Livin' in squalor."

"How do you call livin' in a ten-room house rent free, livin' in squalor?"

"And you makin' thousands of dollars without givin' me a damn dime."

"I been keepin' a roof over your head. And you been takin' whatever you want."

"Oh, I see, so you just been pacifyin' me so you could keep all the money for yourself. Like I was so… " I looked down at the new gym shoes Alex had bought me so I could start jogging with him. "Look at me."

My heart seemed to be beating in slow motion and the apple-cinnamon pancakes Alex made me for breakfast rose up in my throat.

"What do you want, Jeff?"

"Half."

"What do you mean?"

"You know damn well what I mean. Every piece of property you own, I want half of everything you got. All eight of your buildings. Your three houses. No, better yet, I want them all sold and I want sixty percent profit."

"But you never invested—"

"I never had to because the minute you forged my name made me entitled to everything. The three graystones on King Drive. Your house on Gray. The one on Mulford. Need I go on, because you knew I would never agree to that bullshit. So I want eighty percent or I will go to the police, then the newspapers. I will ruin you, just like you been tryin' to ruin me!"

"How? When I worked—made all of the business deals, rehab— "

"I don't give a damn if you sold ass for it! Startin' tomorrow mornin', I want my name on every credit card, every checkin' account. I even want my name on the title to your car. And also startin' tomorrow—no, you got until six o'clock this evenin'—I want everything you own, down to your funkiest pair of drawers back here . . . " He pointed at the floor. "In this house."

"But— "

"But my ass! Now get on your knees." I couldn't move. I couldn't breathe. "Drop to your damn knees because you owe me. And I plan to collect." He unzipped his pants as he rushed towards me. "I said, drop..." His face twisted. He grabbed his chest. He balled his fingers up in his shirt. "My heart," he gasped. "I been havin' . . . Call a ambulance."

Part Three:
It's A Mighty Thin Line

23

Mother was the first person to call me to say, "Nicole, you need to get over to Evanston General."

While I listened to her message, it seemed as if my entire body was screaming, *Now what are you gonna do?* Going to see Jeff wasn't one of my options.

Alex knew something was wrong, even though I kept Jeff's illness from him for three days. He said to me, after he came home from playing basketball at the Y with LJ, "When I asked you a couple of days ago, what was goin' on, what was wrong with you, why didn't you tell me Jeff had a heart attack?"

"Because it ain't that important."

"So what's troubling you, then?"

"Nothing."

"Then what's with the change in your demeanor? Like I always say, talk to me."

He sat next to me on the steps of the deck where I did most of my thinking. He ran his fingers through my new hair-do. "Didn't we agree we were gonna talk about everything? And not keep any more secrets?"

I nodded. Still I couldn't bring myself to tell him my whereabouts when Jeff had his heart attack no more than I could reveal the many other secrets I had. I just put them in the back of my mind, hoping to forget about them and that maybe my nightmare was finally over.

Uncertain if it was the flu-like symptoms I was experiencing, chills, runny nose, body aches, or guilt, but I had to make myself eat the garden salad and black bean soup the waitress at Bennigan's placed before me. By the time she brought my chicken quesadillas, I lacked the energy to open my mouth.

"Could you package this to go? My fiancée is sick," Alex said to the waitress.

"Sure." She was back in less than five minutes. She wished me a speedy recovery and told Alex, "Drive careful. I hear it's snowing pretty bad out there."

He put me to bed after we got home, then took my temperature. I had a fever of 103.5. Considering I'm not one to get sick often, he had to hide my car keys to keep me home. He also called in for three days so he could take care of whatever needed to be done around my buildings and to nurse me back to health. Isaac insisted, after calling to see how we were, that he could get someone to handle things. He knew my routine and was accustomed to looking out for me anyway.

"Can you ask him if he can go and check on my house?" I asked Alex. My throat hurt so bad, it brought tears to my eyes to speak.

The night Isaac had paid Jeff a visit, I'm assuming he was too furious to notice how filthy it was. After he dropped in this time to make sure all the doors were locked and no one had broken in, he said, "I ain't never known nobody to be that damn nasty." He paid a friend and her daughter-in-law to clean it up.

It took them almost two weeks to make the house livable again. Isaac and Alex promised they would paint it, considering how frantic I was that it would lose its value because I was thinking about selling. Alex and I had discussed buying a house together, one big enough for me to put in an office, and for him to have a mega-sized entertainment room and weight room space. As much as I loved planning our future together, I knew our dreams would never come true unless Jeff died, because I couldn't foresee him letting me go any other way. But how often do we find what we want and what we get are two entirely different things?

My cell phone rang three different times before Alex answered it. My illness had me confined to bed with him playing my nurse much longer than either one of us anticipated. My chest and throat throbbed. My lips were chapped. I kept running a fever and had a severe case of diarrhea. I also couldn't hold anything down.

After listening to the person on the other line, he said, "I'm sorry, but right now Nikki is too sick to come to the phone." He took a pen and paper out of the nightstand on my side of the bed.

"Who is it?" I groaned.

He covered the mouthpiece. "Jeff's mother."

I held my hand out. He frowned, but still put the phone to my ear.

"Please, Nicole, Jeffy's about to leave here and all he keeps askin' for is to ask you to come see him. He says he needs to talk to you and don't wanna die unless he makes his peace with you," his mother, Vanessa, pleaded. "I don't know what happened between you two that you won't come, but don't these years you were married to my boy mean nothing at all? He's dyin' and wants to see you? Can't you come, please?"

His sister, Doreen, took the phone away from her. "Listen, heifer." I clicked her off. The last time we heard from her, Jeff and I were still living together. She asked to borrow five hundred dollars to get her transmission rebuilt. Jeff had said, "You screwed to get the car. So screw to get it fixed," and slammed the telephone down in her ear. She called back cursing him out on the answering machine. As far as I knew it was their last contact.

When Jeff and I married, although he had me fill out invitations for his family members, none of them showed up. The Kingstons were a mystery to me until his father, Earl, had a stroke. I took the message and only drove Jeff to the hospital because he called Mother for prayer after I told him the news. And she insisted it was the Godly thing for me to do, considering he had just finished working a fourteen-hour shift. Or so he claimed. I never saw his paycheck or stub so when and if he did overtime was also a mystery yet to be solved.

I was even more reluctant to go inside, but he begged, "Please, Nicole. It just don't seem right for me to come and my wife not show up with me. Besides, you know you told Mother Borge you were gonna see me through this."

I hadn't told her. She had told me. Knowing he was going to tell her word-for-word my each and every action, I let him hold my hand the entire seven blocks we walked, because parking was ridiculous. After getting directions, we found his family on the third floor. Dressed in a red housecoat with white and blue flowers, run-over black moccasins, and white sweat-socks with a big burgundy band around the top, Jeff's mother rushed over to us after spotting us getting off the elevator. Her hair was all over her head like she had been riding in the wind, and she was grinning her raggedy smile as if she was glad to see us.

Jeff said, as she hugged me, "This is my wife, Nicole." She turned to him when she was done squeezing me as if she was expecting a bigger hug. "How's *he* doin'?" he asked, shrugging out of her reach.

Obviously disappointed by his lack of compassion, she said, "Better," and nodded. She was as dark as he was—as tall as he was—but on the fragile side and smelled like she had just finished frying chicken.

"This is my mama, Nicole," he said. He then walked over to a window far away from his family. His mother grabbed my hand. She pulled me over to her only daughter, Doreen, who was just as homely as she was. She muttered, "Hey." And went back to conversing with the other two women sitting across from her.

Vanessa rushed me over to Jeff's brothers, huddled in a corner of the waiting room. From the moment we met, I noticed that dog ran deep in them, too. His brother Bobbie's wife was standing next to him and he was eyeballing every behind walking past. The other brothers, June and TommyLee, both had white wives. They seemed to be the closest. They had roaming eyes, too, and only grunted when she introduced us.

Jeff's mother anxiously led me over to meet her husband, Earl, as soon as he woke up. He barely spoke when Vanessa introduced us and acted as if he didn't hear her when she said, "Jeffy's here."

On our way home, Jeff asked, "What did my old man say to you?"

"Hello."

"That's it."

"What else was he supposed to say?"

"What did he say when mama said I was there?"

"Nothin'."

Vanessa called to thank me for coming the following morning and to give me an update on Earl's condition. We also had a very informative conversation.

While Jeff and I were at the hospital his brother, TommyLee, implied several times how surprised he was *the king* would bring his royal ass into the county. He was talking about the city-owned hospital. Jeff eventually asked, "Man, you got something you wanna say to me?"

TommyLee rushed at him. Vanessa dashed between them, one just as big as the other. She had to beg them to calm down. TommyLee told Jeff, "I'll see you somewhere and we *will* finish this."

"We can finish this now," Jeff replied. But we left immediately following their confrontation.

According to Vanessa, they had an ongoing feud over some girl who had been living with TommyLee when he caught her and Jeff in his apartment in their waterbed.

Another major disagreement included the rest of his siblings. "You know, Jeffy's our youngest boy," Vanessa said. "I don't know how he did it, but he talked Earl into gettin' a loan for him and usin' our buildin' as collateral. Jeffy didn't pay a solitary dime of that thirty thousand dollars back. Forty-five years Earl was a janitor at that oil refinery in Indiana. And had to use some of his pension to pay off that loan or we would have surely lost our home."

"Wow," I said, unable to think of anything else and really not caring.

"Jeffy ought to be ashamed of his self for trickin' his daddy. I didn't want Earl to do it no way, because Jeffy has always been selfish and will do just about anythang to get his way. I still ain't never think he'd do Earl like that since he was closer to him than any of the other boys."

What she said about Jeff was true. He would do just about anything to get his way. And money. So I knew once again I was backed in a corner. But I didn't have a clue how I was going to come out fighting.

24

Alex tried to keep me as comfortable as possible, but the actions I had taken and had been taking wouldn't allow me to sleep. The cold I had was kicking my butt even worse. Still I said to him, "You can go to work, I'll be fine."

"I'm not leavin' you here like this. Beside, my guys can handle the shop. And they know where to reach me."

He made me a piping hot cup of Theraflu and attempted to feed me a bowl of homemade chicken noodle soup. My cell phone hummed in my nightstand drawer.

"Didn't I tell you to cut that thing off?"

"Somebody might need to reach me."

"Somebody like who?" He opened the drawer. "It's a cellular call. 847-555-1203."

"It's Mother." I answered.

RudyAnn said, "Your wish is finally comin' true," before I even finished saying, "Hello."

"Meanin'?"

"Your husband is finally dyin'. We're at the hospital now. Mother wants to know how soon can you get here because the doctors don't think Jeff is gonna make it through the night."

I pulled the covers up to my chin and told Alex. The thermostat was set on eighty, but I was sweating like crazy and was covered with every comforter we had. I was still freezing.

"Nikki, I hate for you to go out of the house like this, but it's your call. But I can't let you drive. And you know between your mother and his people, they're gonna give you hell." Hell was too kind of a word.

I was groggy as heck, but the frigid air quickly reminded me of what time it was even though it was short walk from the house to the Land Cruiser. I shivered as the wind blew through my scalp. Prior to getting sick, I had treated myself to a layered cut after seeing a model sporting it in *Essence* magazine. I thought, *Wow, that might look good on me.*

Alex had said, "Long or short, you're still beautiful to me. But you really look like a kid now."

I was in and out of consciousness as he cruised to the hospital. It was colder than the Arctic out and he had to be extra careful not to slide on the streets. It still seemed like we got there too fast. We hurried inside to get out of the cold and stepped off the elevator into a waiting room full of looks that were even icier.

Jeff's brother, Bobby, who was a year older than him, jumped up, almost hitting their mother in the face. Vanessa grabbed the back of his jacket as he stood huffing like a miniature Jeff. Mother swelled instantly, her eyes mainly on my new cut. The rest of Jeff's family just stood gaping at us. RudyAnn, who was sitting next to Pastor, grinned as if she couldn't wait for something to go down.

Alex sensed my reluctance to go any further. "Don't worry. Ain't nothin' gonna happen as long they don't put their hands on you. You want me to go in with you?"

"That's okay. But thanks for comin'. I know this is awkward for you."

"They're the ones with the problem."

I let go of his hand. He took a seat in the waiting room just like everyone else. Jeff's brother, TommyLee, the one who acted like he hated Jeff the most, rushed inside the bathroom followed by his two sons. He said, "That bitch got a lot of nerve," before the door closed behind him. I was almost inside Jeff's room by the time Mother reached me.

"Nicole Kingston!"

"It's over between me and Jeff, Mother, and I'm only comin' now because he's sick. Alex and I are engaged . . . " I held up my ring finger. "So you might as well get used to it." She turned bright red and I left her standing in the ambience of it.

I eased inside Jeff's room, letting the door close behind me. I stood there, struggling to breathe through my congestion. He sucked on the oxygen as if it was his last breath. I held onto the door handle anxious for him to exhale. As he did so, his eyes opened on me. He waved for me to come closer with his finger, weighted down by a mechanism monitoring his blood pressure. I was hesitant at first, but feared his steady waving might be too much of a strain on his heart.

He pointed to a pad of paper next to his bed that had, *"please call my wife"*, sloppily written on it.

He wrote, *"I'm glad you came."* I couldn't think of anything to say to him and was relieved when one of the nurses pushed the door open.

She said, "You can go closer. He can't bite you," smiling at her own sense of humor. "So who are you? I seemed to have met everyone else, except for that hunk of a man sitting in the waiting room wearing that white Phat Farm sweater."

I said, "I'm Jeff's ex." And considered letting her know, *"the hunk you checkin' out is my fiancé."*

"So you're the missin' wife. Nicole, huh. Well, Nicole, it's nice to finally meet you. That's a cute haircut you got."

"Thank you."

"He's been beggin' us to call you ever since he regained consciousness."

"I heard. But I've been sick."

"I was wonderin' why you ain't been around. What's wrong?"

"I got the flu."

"You should've told somebody at the nurse's station. As sick as Jeff is, he can't afford to catch anything."

I lied. "That's why I'm standin' so far from him."

Jeff took the mask off and wheezed. "Don't make her leave. I need to talk to her." He put it back on, inhaling deeply.

She opened the cabinet over the sink. She handed me a comfort mask. "Now come over here and wash your hands. How long you been sick?"

"A week goin' on two."

"You been to the doctor?"

"No."

"Well, if whatever your symptoms are don't clear up soon, you need to go so you won't catch pneumonia. How you gonna take care of your husband if you sick yourself?"

Jeff tried to raise his head to see what I was going to say. The nurse took a seat in a chair at the far end of the room. She picked up a sales paper somebody left there.

"You can go on and talk to him if you like. I'm doin' a double today and my dogs are killin' me." She kicked her shoes off and slipped down in the chair, stretching her legs.

Jeff wrote, *"How are you?"* while I was avoiding looking at him.

"I'm fine."

He wrote. *"I'm dying."*

"Don't think that Jeff. I'm sure your doctors are doin' the best they can for you."

A tear rolled down the side of his face. He wiped it away to the best of his ability, then scribbled, *"I'm tired & ready."*

A cough lodged in my throat. I tried to suppress it, but more followed until I was gasping to catch my breath. His nurse poured me a cup of water out of the pitcher on the table next to his bed. Jeff took his time scribbling the next message as I tried to regain my composure. As he was doing so, I remembered the time Alex and I went to Great America Theme Park. We got lost because the directions he wrote for me were almost illegible.

I also remembered returning home late in the afternoon and the smell of Opium perfume smacking me in the nose. We had a big argument about it. He said, "If you're so insecure, then why don't you stay home sometimes."

He wrote, *"I don't have much time left."*

I said, "You believe in God don't you? You know all things are possible through Him. So why are you thinkin' your time is up?"

He took off his oxygen mask. "Because I gotta pay for what I done."

I sympathized with him for giving up on his life so quickly, but also wondered what was he up to? Because Jeff could milk the hell out of a situation. And I wasn't about to be taken by another one of his con jobs.

He put his mask back on, took in a breath of air, removed it, then said with his eyes closed, "Nicole, I know . . . " He paused. "I know I have done some bad stuff. But . . . " He put it back on and slowly wrote, "*I don't want to die in here.*" He started to cry and cough.

His nurse said, "He really needs to get some rest, sugah. His family has tried to be in and out of here all day. But the doctor put a stop to it." She mumbled, "They more interested in where he's bankin' as opposed to if he's gonna survive anyway."

The wonder on my face made her clarify her statement. She walked over to me. She spoke with her back to Jeff. "His one brother. I think his name is Tommy. He was drillin' Jeff about how much he was worth and where was the deeds to the property he owned. One of the day nurses heard him and told Doctor Marshburn. That's why we've been keeping an extra eye on him. Because those people are ruthless."

"So how is he really?"

She continued to speak low. "Although we got him hooked up to all of this stuff, it's by the grace of the Lord he's still hangin' in there. On the day they brought him in, they had to do a quadruple bypass. He was blessed to make it through that."

"How much time are they givin' him?"

"Not much. But he keeps on tellin' us he . . . " Jeff waved his finger for me to come closer. He had wrote, "*Nicole, I'm sorry for how I treated you. Please forgive me and let me die at home.*"

She patted his hand. "Jeff you ain't goin' no where until the good Lord calls you. What I tell you about feelin' sorry for yourself?" More tears streamed down the side of his face. She grabbed a tissue out of the box next to his bed. She dabbed his eyes. "You ain't gonna ever get well if you layin' here drownin' in your sorrow." She smiled at me. "Ain't that right, sugah?"

She let Jeff's hand go and grabbed mine. "It's time for you to say goodnight, Misses Kingston. Visitin' hours will be over in ten minutes and I promised his mother and mother-in-law they can come and say goodnight. Just them two though."

I said, "Bye, Jeff." He reached for me, his hand trembling and his eyes full of sadness, something I had never seen. I knew it was going to keep me awake.

The second I opened Jeff's door, Mother, RudyAnn, and Pastor Dorthea zoomed in my face. Alex rushed to my side. "Mrs. Borge, can't you see that Nicole is sick? Can't you discuss this later?"

Mother rolled her eyes at him, then asked the girl at the desk, "Is there someplace where we can go and talk in private?"

"Visitin' hours are over. Y'all can talk wherever you want. Just not up in here."

Mother cleared her throat at her like, *do you know who you're talking to?* She stared back like *I could care less.* She grabbed my arm and pulled me so close her lips were on my cheek.

"What in the world have you done to your hair? And you should be ashamed of yourself for bringin' that boy here."

"Mother, must we discuss this now? Because the last thing I wanna do is to put on a show for Jeff's family."

She snatched me even harder, shoving me around like I was still two years old. "Don't talk to me in that tone, because I am still your Mother and you will respect me whether you respect yourself or not."

DAYLIGHT COMING

I stared at her hand as she held on to my arm. Her nails embedded in the fabric of my sweater.

"You wanna hit me, Nicole?" She stepped back, then threw her arms down. "Well, just go ahead. You've already shown what kind of woman you are by bringin' this boy here. You should be ashamed of yourself."

"I really don't feel like listenin' to this, Mother, because I've said all I'm gonna say. It's over between me and Jeff. So you can just deal with it. Or stay the—"

She slapped a drop of blood from my nose. And I swung at her with all of my might. Alex caught my fist, then grabbed me and locked me in his arms, while I tried to get my hands on her. Because I never wanted to beat anybody down so bad in my life. Other than Jeff.

I can only blame it on the Theraflu because there is no way I would have cursed my mother to her face or had to be carried out of the hospital to keep from killing her. Not me. She had scolded me numerous times before, but was known to be capable of keeping her cool under the tensest circumstances. But she showed her ignorance in public just as tough as I did by taking her coat off and insisting Alex let me go. Jeff's family cheered in the background.

The following morning she called my cell phone and said to my voice mail, "I have never been so humiliated before in my life. I won't ever be able to show my face in that hospital again. The nerve of you talkin' to me like that. But this is the final straw. You wanna be by yourself. You want me to stay out of your life. Well you got it, Missy."

25

I hit Alex with a couple of snowballs and he threw a few at me, missing me on purpose. He didn't want me outside, but I loved watching him shoveling snow, because he always fascinated me with his sexy way of doing the simplest tasks. Mother cruised her Cadillac around our cul-de-sac, then backed up and drove into our driveway. We both looked at each other with *what-the-hell* on our faces.

"Nikki, go in the house. You're just gettin' over being sick for almost three weeks and I ain't havin' her upsettin' you again. Not like she did at the hospital. I know she's your mother, but this is *our* house, and she will show you some respect or she can keep goin'."

"She won't leave even if you say so. So we might as well get this over with."

Mother opened her door and got out. RudyAnn rolled her window down. Mother came around the car. "Nicole, I need to talk to you." She cut Alex an icy glance. "Alone."

"As I told you at the hospital, Alex and I are engaged. So whatever you have to say to me, you can say it in front of him."

"Even if it is about your husband. You are still married, you know."

"Yes I do and so does Alex," I replied, looking from her to RudyAnn. RudyAnn was damn near foaming at the mouth checking him out. I went and stood in front of him. She smiled. "Would you like to come in?"

Mother cleared her throat. "Only because this is important."

DAYLIGHT COMING

Alex grabbed the shovel he had left leaning against his truck. He walked around to the back of the house. RudyAnn threw her door open. She almost knocked Mother down trying to get inside. I smelled their jealousy coming in the door just like I had when I purchased my house on Sheridan Road. Alex came in through the patio and took his boots off on the rug. RudyAnn brushed past me, headed for the kitchen.

"Let me get some water?" she said, standing over him with her coat open and her hands on her hips.

"Okay, but can you back up?"

She didn't budge. I went to the refrigerator and got her a bottle of Dasani. She twisted over to the couch and dropped next to Mother, who was sitting on the edge like it was a dirty toilet. Alex shook his head and walked down the hall.

I sat in the loveseat after removing off my boots. "So Mother, how did you find me?"

"What difference does it make?"

"Just curious."

RudyAnn said, "His Uncle Gene told us." She stared in the direction Alex had gone.

"And you saw him..."

"He works at the convenience store by the house."

"Okay, now what can I do for you?"

"I . . . we've come here to talk to you about Jeff," Mother said.

"What about him?"

"His people."

"Meanin'?"

"They've been callin' us repeatedly askin' questions like where are his insurance papers, the deeds to the property he owns; who's his attorney? Since you haven't been to your office, that brother of his, TommyLee, has been callin' me every day wantin' me to talk to you about turnin' Jeff's stuff over to him.

"So I need for you to tell me where his information is so I can get him off my back. I don't know what he might be plannin' to do to me since he can't locate you. Besides, I really don't know what that man is talkin' about because Jeff told me a while back if anything happens to him that I could have the house on Sheridan Road. And he has two policies with me as his beneficiary."

"If he does, then I don't have a clue where they are, because when he quit his job, he stopped makin' payments on his insurance so they cancelled it. So as far as I know, the only policies he has are the two I took out on him."

"Don't you still have the keys to the house? One time he showed me a safe built in the wall of your bedroom. They could be in there. Don't you have the code?"

The safe Jeff had shown Mother was in my bedroom. I had never kept anything in there other than my jewelry. He got the combination some kind of way and hocked all of it. Or gave it to some of his girlfriends.

"If you don't wanna go there, you can give us the keys," RudyAnn said. "He promised the house to her anyway and you already got this one."

"In a court of law, maybe Jeff can fight me over it and they may award it to him, but unless I die, he can't will it or give it to anyone."

Mother stood up, then straightened her coat. "That's just like you, Nicole, to suck up all you can get without considerin' those who put you where you are today."

"Mother, you know I worked hard to pay for that house and paid for it without help from you, Jeff, or anybody else. Y'all were the ones who was callin' me foolish and insisted I was wastin' money on it."

She sniffed. "Well, I can only say I didn't raise you to be this selfish."

"How am I being selfish?"

"Because that's what livin' in sin and crawlin' in the gutter does to your soul."

RudyAnn added, "And you ought to be ashamed of yourself. You old enough to be that boy's mother."

"No, you two ought to be ashamed of yourselves. Jeff ain't even dead yet and y'all ready to cash in on whatever you can get. Y'all ain't no better than his family. The least you could do is to let him die. It does seem more human than kickin' him out of his house."

DAYLIGHT COMING

Mother said, "I thought you said it was *your* house."

"It is. I just let him live there. You want proof?"

She rolled her eyes and marched out the door with RudyAnn on her heels. I slammed it behind them, then sulked about us never being able to be cordial to one another unless it was for one of her selfish reasons. Anna and her mother ate lunch together at least twice a week, shopped together all of the time, and talked on the telephone so much her husband insisted she should just move her in with them.

Their relationship had gone through its share of turmoil also, because Anna's mother had been a prostitute and an alcoholic, in and out of one abusive relationship after another. After Anna went away to college, one of her mother's tricks put her in the hospital for a month after she took five dollars from him for a quart of beer and a pack of cigarettes. So she quit both habits and has been straight ever since.

Although they had become inseparable, Anna still often stated, "I love Mama dearly, but there ain't no way we could live under the same roof ever again." I couldn't see anything more than hate for me from my mother and it hurt, even at 39.

Jeff spent Christmas, his favorite holiday, and New Year's Eve in the hospital going from good to better, then back to worse. I thought about him as Alex, LJ, Bethany, their three boys, and I watched Dick Clark and a host of others bring 1999 in with Prince's former hit blasting in the background. Still working at Dominick's grocery store and going to school, LJ had found his family a cute two-bedroom apartment just inside Chicago. Several times I had offered to set them up in one of my three-bedrooms, but LJ insisted, "Nikki, could you let me do something for my wife and kids for a change?"

Still, I was forever popping in on them with diapers, groceries, toys, and designer clothes. As I watched him — both of his sons piled on his lap—I couldn't help but feel proud of him. How he had grown into such an exceptional father in spite of his childhood. Glad to see him so happy, I wiped away a tear that escaped and silently thanked God for making him into the man he was.

Yet, my happiness only lasted a little while because Jeff would not leave my mind. His condition was also putting a serious strain on my relationship with Alex. His physician, Dr. Marshburn, called me every time something went wrong with him. And every time he could take a breath he would cry, "Nicole, please don't let me die alone."

Even though I was trying to be a Good Samaritan, I was still more worried he would tell what he had found out regarding my business transactions, so I made sure I visited him regularly. Still, I wasn't prepared to make any kind of decision about what I was going to do about him, when his doctor said, "We've done all we can for him. And it makes no sense to keep spending money to keep him here. So you're either going to have to take him home with you or find a nursing facility for him. Or turn him over to his family."

The latter Alex would have certainly agreed to. Every day he stressed his displeasure at me being so attentive toward Jeff. He argued, "Spendin' so much time with him is only givin' him high hopes, Nikki."

"I made it very clear that it's over between us."

"Then why are you lettin' him control you from his hospital bed?"

"He really is dyin', Alex."

"They said that weeks ago and he's still here."

We never disagreed so much and there were nights we slept in separate rooms and mornings he left without saying good-bye. That was minor compared to what I felt was yet to happen.

26

Alex and I had called a truce and were finalizing our wedding plans, although Jeff was in no condition to sign the divorce papers and I wasn't so cold to ask him to. We had made juicy love, prior to him leaving for work and I was lying in the ecstasy of what he could always do to my body and how much I enjoyed doing the same to his. The telephone rang. Not checking the Caller ID, I grabbed it, thinking he was calling me to say, "I love you, Nikki."

It was Jeff's physician. "Nicole."

I rolled my eyes to the ceiling. "Yes." *What the heck does he want now?*

"I'm calling to see if you've made arrangements for your husband yet." I had told him a thousand times Jeff and I were history of the worst kind.

"No."

"Well, his brothers came in here about an hour ago and they're trying to move him to their parents' house."

"That's between them." I hung up on him.

But my conscience wouldn't let me go back to sleep. It wouldn't allow me to reminisce over the way Alex was calling my name and holding me so tight as he loved me that my passion overwhelmed me three times compared to his two. It was too busy putting pictures in my head—how I could go to prison if Jeff breathed a word of how I obtained all my property without his name on anything. It taunted me so much I took a quick shower and rushed to the hospital.

As if he knew I was coming, Dr. Marshburn had made all of the arrangements for Jeff's release. After I signed the paperwork the nurse shoved in front of me, I thought, *Nicole, what in the hell are you doin'? Didn't you just promise Alex you were gonna focus more on your relationship and let Jeff's family deal with him? Didn't you, Nicole? Where are you gonna take him? And what are you gonna tell Alex?"*

Jeff's social worker had given me a list of private care nurses and I happened to luck up on one who was willing to start the same day. She showed up at the house at 3 p.m. as promised along with some medical equipment I didn't care about learning how to operate. Before her arrival, I had paced the floors trying to figure out what to do. With each step, I felt more and more like I was backed into a corner with water gushing at me. I knew to hold my breath because it was going to hit me hard and heavy.

Alex had already called me ten times on my cell. Each time, I let the calls go to my voice mail. I didn't know what I was going to say to him when he came home, but I didn't expect him to become so irate. Telling him I was moving back on Sheridan Road to take care of Jeff was the most difficult thing I had ever done. There was so much pain and disbelief in his eyes I thought he was going to cry.

"Nikki, are you outta your mind? Say you didn't do that. What about us?" I had no answer for him. "Please tell me you're lyin'. That you're jokin'. But please don't tell me you're walkin' out of my life like I don't exist. Like our love never existed." My chin slumped on my chest, confirmed what he was afraid was true.

He threw his hands up, then dropped them down. "So let me ask you this? All of those times we were together, that I made love to you and you made love to me, what was that all about? What am I, your boy-toy? You lay up in my bed. I cook for you. Massage your back. I do everything for you. Wash your hair. Everything most men would never do.

"And you just gonna walk out on me? Answer me. You're leavin' me. For a man who treated you like shit! Oh, so now you don't have an answer. Well, I tell you what. You don't have to say a damn word. But you do have to get your shit and get the hell outta my house."

I wanted to say, *Alex, I know you don't mean it. Just give me some time to get Jeff situated. To get myself together because I have done some things I don't know how to fix, and I could go to jail.* But Alex went into the bedroom and slammed the door. I raced down the hall with those words still on the tip of my tongue.

I opened the door. "Why are you still here? Don't you have a husband to take care of?" Then he lay down on the bed looking up at the stars. I had talked him into getting a skylight, so every time we made love we could look up at the heavens and thank God for each other. I touched his leg. He jumped up. He pulled me into the living room, snatched my purse from off the couch, and pushed me out the front door.

I wanted to tell him, "Alex, I'm sorry." Yet I knew our engagement was over and I would never be Mrs. Alexander Julian Knight.

When Jeff's family found out he was out of the hospital, they came to the house riding six cars deep. They cursed me outside my door, threw clods of dirt and grass they pulled out of the front lawn at the house, and spit all over my car. And somebody even peed on my steps. I sat on the stairs listening to them calling me "greedy bitches", "sluts" and "whores" and daring me to bring my bony ass outside, until they were satisfied we weren't there.

I was on Sheridan Road for a week before anybody called me or stopped by. Isaac knocked on my door around 2:45 in the afternoon to drop off the junk mail that had been piling up at my office. I was reluctant to let him in, because I couldn't recall the last time I had combed my hair or brushed my teeth. And I knew I looked anorexic.

He stared at me, when he finally convinced me to open the door even though he had a key. "Damn, Nikki, you look terrible." Tears I had been trying to suppress broke from the dam that held them. "You know I was pissed when I heard what you did. But I ain't so messed up I don't understand. But you look bad. And if this is what it's doin' to you, then you need to put him in a home with people who are better equipped to take care of him."

I hung my head. He started giving me the 4-1-1 on what was going on in the business world. I wanted to ask about Alex so bad he felt my vibes.

"He looks just as bad as you do. You broke his heart, you know. And the last time I saw him, he didn't wanna speak to me. But I talked to him anyway."

I wanted to ask, "Did he say anything about me?" But I felt it would have been selfish since I had kicked him to the curb trying to hold on to my so-called empire. I took my mail out of Isaac's hand and laid it on the table in the foyer. He glanced at the time on his cell phone.

"Well, I gotta go. I got two appointments I can't miss, but I'll be back later this evenin', because we need to talk."

I didn't want to talk. I just wanted him to leave so I could resume my position in the corner of my bedroom. Jeff had gotten rid of all of the furniture upstairs, except his. But I refused to go near anything he called *his* even though I had set him up in the family room in a hospital bed I had rented. Except for some clothes in the basement I was going to give to the Salvation Army, I had nothing to wear, so I walked around mostly in sweats with no underwear. I was too out of it to go shopping and dreaded doing anything for myself.

Because not only did I feel like I was underwater, suffocating—unable to breathe—but bath time made me think of Alex. He loved to give me sponge baths, wash my hair, and rub me down with scented oils while candles burned. Trying to fix myself a meal was even worse. I could barely stand to go into the kitchen, because we did a lot of kissing over the stove. Up against the refrigerator. And sitting at the island.

Everything around me reminded me of him even though he had only been in my house once. Even sitting on the deck brought back memories like the one time we got courageous or crazy enough to make love outside. He was reading poetry by Nikki Giovanni to me and looked so enticing under the patio light I got those tingly feelings I always got when I was near him. Or thought about him. I turned it out just as he closed the book.

He said, "What are you doin'?" Wearing a lime sheath and lime sandals, I slid one leg across his lap, kissing him. He had on a pair of Nike shorts without a shirt. I reached inside them. "I thought you were shy."

I smiled and his eyes smiled back as I guided him to where I wanted him and he took me where I wanted to go. As soon as I stood up, lightheaded and feeling oh-so-good, our neighbor turned his porch light on. We looked at one another and laughed. That was something I missed more than anything—his laughter and the way he could make me feel better even when things were at their worst.

Anna rushed over no sooner than Isaac left. I knew he must have called her and told her how terrible I looked. She let herself in. She found me in my room, sitting in the corner. I was wrapping what hair I had left around my finger.

She marched over to me. "Nicole, get up from there." I looked up at her with tears in my eyes. "I ain't going through this with you again."

I put my hands over my face. She stooped next to me. "I know I sound harsh, but you have too much to live for to be letting yourself go like this."

"Like what?"

"Don't start that mess with me. Now get up. You're gonna take a shower and comb your hair and we're gonna have some lunch and a long talk."

"I can't take this, Anna. I just can't."

She pulled me into her arms and immediately started to pray while crying just as hard as me. I wanted to tell her it was a waste on me, because just as Pastor Dorthea and Mother had told me earlier in the day, I was hopeless.

Pastor had called me at seven in the morning for three days in a row, each time starting the conversation with, "How are you, Nicole?" Then she'd ask about Jeff.

I always said, "He's about the same."

And she would cheerfully remind me, "Don't forget the five hundred dollars he owes me once everything is taken care of."

Her five hundred dollars was the last thing I wanted to discuss that early in the morning. I wanted the call to be from Alex. Finally, I asked, "Did you ever pay him back the two thousand you borrowed for the piano you just had to have?" She got silent. "Then you owe him."

"It was a gift and you know it."

"I don't know anything except you borrowed from him."

"That's just like you, Nicole, always draggin' up the past."

"That's just like you, Dorthea! Always thinkin' about yourself. I didn't borrow from you. So if you want your five hundred dollars so bad, get it from Jeff yourself, because I'm sure you'll see each other in hell!"

I know she was dialing Mother's number before she got another dial tone. After her call, I refused to answer the phone again. One of our deacons had called me three times about his seven hundred dollars, and a host of other Holy Hill parishioners had called as well. At least she did ask about Jeff.

27

I knew Mother was pissed by the way she walked into the house with her nose up in the air even though Jeff had just lost his biles and his nurse was cleaning him up.

"I need to see you on the porch." I closed the door behind us. "So how's he holdin' up?"

I looked away from her and spoke with my heart in my hand. "I can't take too much more of this."

"Take too much more of what?"

"Of being cooped up in this house every day and waitin'."

She waved her hand across my face. "It's just the will of the Lord, Nicole. Besides, you dug this grave for yourself. So quit whinin'. Because if you had been here takin' care of Jeff like a good wife should, and not runnin' after that young boy, he might not be goin' through this."

I shook my head and went back inside. I sat down at the kitchen island. I opened a bottle of Dasani water, Alex's favorite brand and mine. The thought made me tear up.

"There's no need to cry now, because like I told you time and time again, you have to pay for what you do whenever you do wrong. So it's not goin' to help you sittin' up here actin' like you're two years old."

I went into the living room, taking a seat on the couch. I spun the bottle of water on the glass table, pleading silently with God to please send her home before I said something I would later regret. But she wanted to nag me like she had every day of my life. I decided not to acknowledge her by going into the basement. She claimed she was claustrophobic, but was right behind me.

"See, there you go, tryin' to run away from the truth. I told you that boy was trouble. But no, you don't listen. Never have. Always want things your way. You should've never left Jeff for him. Now he's dyin', so where is your young lover? The man you claim to be engaged to. He's probably found him somebody else and forgot all about you."

Talk about beating a woman when she's already down. I rubbed my finger across the diamonds in my engagement ring. A tear fell on my hand. I quickly wiped it away, since seeing I was in agony didn't do a thing to make her want to remove her foot from out of my behind.

I sighed. "Are you through, Mother? Anything else you gotta say to remind me of how much you hate me? How you have always hated me from the moment I was conceived?"

"What on earth are you rantin' about now?"

"Admit it. You hate me so much that I can't remember you ever payin' me a compliment. Givin' me a hug or a kiss. I can't even remember you ever smilin' at me."

"You're just makin' up stuff to justify your wrongdoings."

"I'm makin' stuff up. Well, tell me this—did I imagine you beatin' me with extension cords? Me havin' to clean RudyAnn's room, cook and wash all of our clothes? You makin' me marry Jeff when I begged you not to. And I guess I dreamed up you scrubbin' my skin until I bled while callin' me dark and ugly and sayin' I looked like a mangy mud puppy?"

"I never said such a thing."

"You know you did. So admit it." I threw my hands on my cheeks. "Oh, that's right. That would make the saved and sanctified Mother Borge look like she's lyin'. And she doesn't lie because she's so damn perfect that she walked across the water with Jesus. Well, Miss Saved-And-Sanctified, do you know what Jeff did to me on our wedding night? No, you don't because you don't care, but I'm gonna tell you.

"Jeff hurt me! He made me bleed and he made me cry. I begged him to stop and he hurt me even more. And did you care? No, because you were so busy trying to get rid of me. Jeff was a year older than RudyAnn and you made me marry him when she was the oldest. That's because he wasn't good enough for her, was he?"

She looked away from me at the old computer he had bought at a yard sale that never worked.

"You have always treated me worse than her and you know as well as I do that Lennox wasn't LJ's or Limmell's father and that she had six abortions after Limmell was born. Yet, you love her, but not me. And even as a little girl, even after you used to beat me, I would wish you'd come and hold me and tell me you loved me. But you never came. Because you were too busy tryin' to find another chore for me to do as more punishment. Or another reason to beat the hell outta me."

"Nicole, I never . . . "

"Well, who left these . . . " I turned my back to her and lifted my T-shirt. "On my back? Maybe they're almost gone now . . . " Thanks to Alex rubbing cocoa butter on them. "But did I do this myself? You can remember everything I ever did wrong, but you can't remember RudyAnn lyin' sayin' I stole five dollars out of your purse. And you beat me with a extension cord until I was bleedin'. You can remember how much of a rotten daughter I was, but you can't remember how I was on the floor tryin' to crawl away from you, and you were tryin' to block me from gettin' out the door, and my tears fell on your new patent leather shoes. And you snatched some napkins off the shelf, threw them in my face, then beat me harder until they were dry. You dislocated your shoulder.

"And you know it's all because my father ran out on you when you were three months' pregnant. He left you for another woman. And she stabbed him to death on the same day he came to you and borrowed five hundred dollars to get his car out of the shop and swore to you he was comin' back home. The woman caught him in her bed with her sister and stabbed him to death."

"You don't have a clue what you're talkin' about."

"How come I don't, when I've heard you and Pastor talk about it so many times that it's etched in my brain? Just like you tellin' her how you wished you had got a abortion when you found out you were pregnant with me. You were hailed in the church as a saint and got gypped by a womanizin' bum who wouldn't work and screwed anything that moved.

"And Jeff was just like him. You know you saw it, but you still made me marry him. You were so damn eager to get me out of your house that you didn't bother to tell me anything about sex. But you made damn sure I knew that I was supposed to cook his meals, wash his clothes, his back, his feet. And anything else he didn't wanna scrub. And wouldn't let me come home even after he almost beat me to death."

"You must be losin' your mind."

"Am I? Well, let's see, now am I right or am I wrong that I caught Jeff and Sallie Parker in our bed in our house? And yes, I did attack Jeff with a fryin' pan. But he beat me like I was a man. I called you screamin', beggin' you to come help me and you rushed over and gasped, "Jeff what in the world?"

And he said, "I didn't know it was her, Mother Borge. I swear I didn't. I was here alone, takin' a bath and she came home and jumped on me. I didn't know it was her so I thought I was defendin' myself against a burglar."

"I barely weighed one hundred pounds, so how could he have not known it was me? And how many burglars my size would attack a man his size? But you, my mother said to me, "Nicole, quit cryin'. You're not hurt that bad. Besides, you should learn how to keep your hands to yourself and your mouth shut!"

"I was black and blue all over. Barely able to see or move and you stood over me, callin' me evil, manipulative, and a compulsive liar just like my father. Everything you wanted to say and see happen to him, you rejoiced in watchin' it happen to me. So Jeff knew from that moment on that he could get away with murder as far as you were concerned. So guess what he did after you left? He raped me to teach me a lesson about tellin' our business."

She shook her head. "You are too much, Nicole. You'll say just about anything to have your way."

"You know you condoned all of those things he did to me. And no matter how much I begged him. I even wore extra clothes. He would still just walk up to me and force me on the floor or drag me to the bedroom. I couldn't even take a bath when he was home because he broke the lock off the bathroom door.

"That was what I was subjected to as a new bride. Jeff's sexual abuse. Until I started sleepin' with knives, hammers, and screwdrivers and hidin' all kinds of stuff all over the house to protect myself. And you know for a fact you saw most of my scars, but all you could think of to say to me was, "Jeff is a good man, Nicole. A man who lives for God." But please tell me, Mother, what damn God?"

"How dare you use the name of the Lord in vain?"

"Please! You don't think what you have done in the name of the Lord ain't evil? You forcin' your daughter to marry a hypocrite and badgerin' her every day so that she would stay with him, knowin' he'll screw anything with a hole. He's has had five children, if not more, while he was married, and is also a deacon of the church you attend. You were the main one pushin' for him to be a damn deacon, knowin' what kind of man he was. And not to even mention the anger that you been holdin' on to for years that you been takin' out on me.

"And all of the other things that went on under your roof that you turned your back on. Like RudyAnn bringin' all of those men and boys into the house and havin' sex with them. Even after she got married. But that's right, her father was the love of your life and those are her sins, right, because you're incapable of committin' any? You're just holy-holy! Holier than Christ!"

"Are you through now?

"I guess so, because dynamite couldn't dent your heart when it comes to me. But that's okay. Because I'm through with you, Leola! So could you leave now?"

She looked at me as if to say, *What?*

"You heard me. You need to leave. Because I'm tired of you and tired of tryin' to make you love me. And I'm tired of my life bein' centered around Jeff."

"It wasn't that centered."

"How come it wasn't? I wanted you to be proud of me. I wanted to be a good wife. Better than RudyAnn. I wanted to take care of him better than any woman you ever seen. That's why I stayed with him and was faithful until I met Alex, even though I never loved him. I hated Jeff. But you loved him so much so I stayed. And the more I stayed, the less I gave a damn about myself until Anna came along and helped me to start my business, and Isaac, and then Alex came along sayin' he—"

She grunted. "Humph!"

"Until them, I didn't care whether I lived or died. I just lacked the courage to kill myself. I guess that's why I was so mad at Limmell for havin' the courage to do what I was too weak to do."

"You have just lost all of your God-given mind."

"No, I've found it. And I've realized you don't and never have given a damn about me, and you never will. And I'm sure if you could switch places, it would be me lyin' in that bed right now instead of Jeff. You told Pastor you should've aborted me. Well consider me aborted. Consider me dead to you. Consider me out of your life. Forever. From this moment on—I ain't your daughter and the only family I have is LJ, Anna, and Isaac."

"You're ridiculous."

"No, I'm just being truthful for a change. I've done some things I ain't proud of and come tomorrow all that I own could be taken away from me. But it doesn't matter anymore because what's having everything you want if nobody gives a damn about you? Can I show you out?"

I walked up the steps. She followed me. When she got near the front door she said, "I guess you had your say, Nicole. And I forgive you for talkin' to me like I'm somebody off the streets. I tried to teach you better, but you were rotten from the beginnin'. So like I said, you made this bed. You lie in it and don't bother to ever call me for anything."

"What could you possibly give me when you have kicked me in the behind so many times that it don't even hurt no more. It just makes me mad."

"And that's exactly what you are. Mad! And hopeless. And headed straight to hell."

"I'll see you when I get there!"

After Anna left, I felt so much better I gave Jeff's nurse the night off. Her granddaughter had been operated on that morning, so she was more than glad to leave. And even happier when I said, "My treat."

I finished eating the sweet and sour chicken Anna ordered for us and ate a bowl of orange sherbet Jeff's nurse had left in the refrigerator. He noticed the good mood I was in when I entered his room to check on him. "What's goin' on? Why are you so happy?"

"I had a long talk with Anna. She pointed out some things to me and I got some things off my chest."

Anna said, after I confessed what I had done, "I always wondered how, as greedy as Jeff was, how you got him to sign off on all of your purchases. And I wanted to ask, but I didn't want to believe you would do such a thing."

"I never thought I would either because other than speedin', I've never broken the law—that I'm aware of. But after I wrote the letter sayin' we were legally separated, signed his name and had it notarized, anything else I filled out, I just didn't bother to indicate we were together. So are you gonna report me?"

"You know better. But you could've got me caught up in some serious stuff. But let's just say we'll let it be buried with Jeff when the time comes."

"And I have one more confession to make."

"Do I wanna hear this?"

"I was with Jeff when he had his heart attack."

"No shit?"

"He fell on his knees and I grabbed the papers he was threatenin' me with and ran. But I couldn't just leave him so I drove to the payphone down the street, disguised my voice, and called 9-1-1."

"You were desperate and scared."

"It's no excuse."

"No, it's not. But it ain't like you left him for dead. Because you know I would have in a heartbeat."

28

I made Jeff homemade chicken and rice soup while snacking on orange sherbet. I took him his dinner. He hesitated before receiving it, then stared at me as he slowly chewed his food.

"Why are you starin' at me? You don't think—"

"No-o-o. It's just that you're so beautiful." He had never told me that before. "I have always thought you were the most beautiful woman in the world." He looked away. "Regardless of how much I've done and how bad I treated you." A tear rolled down his cheek.

I wiped it away. "It's old now. And in a lot of ways, I was selfish myself. And could've been more understandin'."

"How could you've been understandin' when I've always been such a jerk to you? No, I was an ass. And I'm sorry. Not because I don't know how much time I got left, but because I should've treated you better than I did. And respected you."

"It's okay. Because like I said, it's over now."

"Nicole, I have a confession to make."

"Jeff, it really ain't necessary."

"For me it is. Not because I'm trying to hurt you anymore, but because it's the right thing to do. And I suspect you already know."

"What?"

"I paid this girl I know to trace your Social Security number. That's how I got the information on the property you bought. And I was lying when I said I had copies."

"I know."

"Nicole, I owe so many people."

"I know. They've been callin' me like crazy and I've been hangin' up on them like crazy."

"You will hang up on somebody in a heartbeat."

"Jeff, I hate to say it at a time like this but—"

"I know, Nicole. I got a lot to answer to."

"Yeah, you do. But what's most important is that you get well and do right by those you took advantage of."

"It's too late now, but I been praying real hard that not only God, but you'll forgive me. Please, Nicole. I know He's forgiving, but what about you? I know I put you through hell throughout our entire marriage and I did some…"

I handed him the box of Puffs next to his bed. With trembling hands he wiped his eyes and nose. "Will you forgive me, Nicole? Please? I don't wanna die carryin' this burden."

A few hours prior, I would have spit in his face. Not to mention I had stood over him several times while he lay sound asleep with a knife in my hand willing myself not to slit his throat. "I forgive you, Jeff." He smiled and lay back on the bed. "But do you forgive me, too?"

"For what?" he asked.

"Any and everything, I may have done to you."

He cried harder. "We could've had a beautiful marriage if I hadn't—"

"Like I said, it's old." And I didn't want to lie to him.

"But you never would've had an affair or lied about… you know."

"But I did and you know as well as I do two wrongs don't make a right."

He wiped his nose again and blew it. "You're right."

"You want some more soup?"

"I'm too tired to eat."

"You sleepy?" I fluffed his pillows.

"No, I'm just tired and I'm ready to go home."

"You are home."

"No, home to God. I made my peace with Him and I prayed that all of the people I hurt, used, and abused will forgive me."

"I'm sure they will."

"Even my children."

"I'm hopin' they will."

"Even though I'm leavin' them with nothin'."

I really didn't want to discuss his death with him, but felt he'd be relieved to know, "Whatever money I receive after . . . you know . . . from the insurance, I'm splittin' it among them. And I'm thinkin' about sellin' this house. "

"But I promised—"

"I know you did and you had no right. But you do have five children, so it's the least we can do for them."

"You remember how many?"

"You have your oldest son by Sharon Stovall. Sophia has the twins. The other girl—what's her name, the one who married the man who used to be our church janitor."

"Jeanette."

"She had your fourth son. Then there's Lamar by Carrie. He's your youngest."

"Nicole, I am so sorry."

"It's okay now. It was embarrassing. But what can we do?"

"I wonder why we never had any—"

"Because our marriage was never the right type of atmosphere for us to even think about having children." He put his head down. "But I'm gonna make sure, as I said, that your children get something."

"You would do that, wouldn't you?"

"I don't mind."

"That's why I've always loved you. You have a big heart and you're so forgivin'. Even to me. Not many women would've tolerated the stuff I did."

He had lost more weight and his skin was sagging off his bones. I felt sorry for him and cuddled next to him, knowing in my last days, I would want somebody, anybody, to hold and comfort me. Jeff tried to move over to make room for me, but lacked the energy. I fitted myself in what space was left on his bed. I flipped the TV on. He was always a movie man and it just so happened his favorite one and mine, *The Five Heartbeats*, was on HBO. We watched it together, him enjoying every bit of me being next to him. And me enjoying not being weighted down by hate. He went to sleep before the ending. I eased off the bed to get another bottle of water.

When I returned, he said, "Can you do something for me?"

"What?"

"Can you read to me from the Book of Isaiah?"

I took his Bible out of the nightstand. "Where do you want me to start?"

I snuggled next to him, turning on my side so he could put his arm around my waist. "The fifty-third chapter," he said, his voice even weaker. I stroked his temple as I read and he lay listening, holding my free hand. His grip tightened. He smiled and took his last breath.

I sat by his side uncertain what I should do next. Then relief overwhelmed me like none I ever felt before. I cried from deep within. Not because Jeff was dead, but because those last moments with him not only saved his soul, but mine as well.

Jeff's family complained about everything from having the service at Holy Hill to his white Armani suit with the matching tie to me putting three of his gold rings on his fingers. TommyLee said, just before the funeral, "She could'a gave them to me. It ain't like they gonna serve a purpose on him now." He and Bobby got into a fierce argument about it, because Bobby insisted, "Me and him was the closest."

Their sister, Doreen, assisted in separating her brothers, then marched up to Jeff's white casket, trimmed in gold. She screamed a piercing cry that made everybody stop whatever they were doing. Her boyfriend wrapped his arms around her and led her away from the coffin. She stopped when she got near me, rolled her eyes and started back sobbing loudly.

As if on cue, one of the nieces, whom I had never met, yelled, "Uncle Jeffy, Uncle Jeffy. I'm gonna miss my uncle."

I turned around, surprised by the outburst, because I never recalled any of them ever spending any time with Jeff, let alone calling him. TommyLee stuck up his middle finger.

DAYLIGHT COMING

RudyAnn came from the far side of the sanctuary and sat next to me.

"Just ignore them. How you doin' today?"

Momentarily shocked by her saying something to me that wasn't negative, I said, "I'm okay."

Lennox took a seat next to her. She sighed, shaking her head. He said, "Good, mornin', Nicole. How you doin'?"

I mumbled, "I'm all right," looking over my shoulder for Anna, who had called and said, "Nicole, I'm running late. But I'm on my way."

I spotted Isaac a few seats over and felt relieved he was nearby. Seldom wearing anything other than blue jeans, he looked extremely handsome in his chocolate pin-striped suit, white shirt and brown tie. I smiled at him and turned back around just as the senior choir began "Speak to My Heart" by Donnie McClurklin. It was one of Jeff's favorite songs.

They all looked exceptionally regal in their purple robes, even though I had to give two of them the money Jeff owed them before they agreed to sing. Lennox hurried to the podium to read the cards and the obituary as soon as they were done.

Although I asked him not to, because I wanted to keep the services very short, he said, "Deacon Kingston was so well loved and I know so many of you would like to pay your respects with comments about him. Since he was such a family man and a blessin' to this church and community. So come on up and please try to limit yourself to three minutes."

TommyLee was the first one to fly up to the front of the church. He started his speech, lying about how close he and Jeff were and how Jeff was such a good baby brother. He ended it with how much he was going to miss him. Next was Doreen who moaned about how much she loved her brother and how good of a man he was. After her was a cousin I had never seen and a nephew who looked just like Jeff and lied just as hard as Jeff, talking about all of the advice his uncle had given him. Jeff used to call all of his siblings' children, raggedy little bastards with no home training.

I wondered if Mother was going to say anything, but she just sat there staring at his coffin with a blank look on her face. I also wondered if it had been me lying there if she would have shed a tear, since I never saw her cry. As I watched her, the need for her to love me overwhelmed me once again. I wanted to touch her. To tell her I loved her and ask if we could start all over. At least be friends like she was with Jeff. Since he was gone, could she give me just a little bit of what she felt for him? Even if they did have a connection from the first time they met. They would talk and giggle and he would follow her around the house going on and on about nothing, and she would listen as if it was something of great importance.

But if it had been me, she would have said, "Nicole, don't you have something to do other than be on my heels?"

Jeff really did love her and I resented it for a long time. He bought me gifts while we dated and during the first two months of our marriage, but she always got the biggest box of chocolates, the better-looking roses, and the very best of him. He charmed her and other women, whereas from day one he felt a strong need to control me with whatever methods he deemed necessary.

Both of them had their share in making me feel like I was nothing, but Isaac and Anna saw me differently. So did Alex, the man whom I wanted to be with so much that I wondered if it would have been selfish to call him after the funeral, considering we had been more than lovers. We had this fire, this connection that whenever he was around, I could feel him out and my mind wouldn't stay on anything or anyone else. I thought about the reaction Mother would have when and if we did get back together.

She had said, "That boy never cared about you, Nicole. He was just seein' dollar signs. You know he was raised with nothin'."

Alex never asked me for anything. Whenever we went anywhere, I didn't have to fork over anything, even after he found out I was still paying all of the bills for Jeff, while living with him. As much as it hurt him, he still stuck to, "The mortgage, gas, oil, etcetera is my responsibility. I wanna take care of you, Nikki. That's what a real man does. He takes care of the woman he loves."

I don't know if RudyAnn sensed how lowly I was beginning to feel, but she grabbed my hand. I looked up at her, even more stunned. She said, "Don't worry. Everything is gonna be all right." I wondered, *Where the heck is Anna? Because this chick is trippin' me out!*

Pastor Dorthea's eyes moved from my face to Mother's and throughout the congregation as she said the closing remarks of her eulogy. I missed most of it, because my thoughts were wandering all over the place. I wanted to see Alex, say hello to him, and thank him for the happiest time of my life, breathe in his cologne.

By the time RudyAnn nudged me back into the here-and-now, a choir member was singing, "His Eye Is On The Sparrow," the all-time get-the-congregation-crying-at-a-funeral-song. Jeff's mother was surrounded by some of his family members. They were trying to fan her back to consciousness. Others were just screaming all over the place.

It was four-thirty before we were on our way to the mausoleum, Anna walking in the door while we were on our way out. Jeff's siblings tried to fight me on him being cremated, but he had told his mother that was what he wanted. His father was dead-set against it also, but she was determined to follow Jeff's last requests.

Inside the icy gray walls, I could barely sit still as Pastor Dorthea said a final prayer before Jeff was to be incinerated. His family didn't cut-up as bad, but made plenty sarcastic remarks about me finally getting what I wanted. With Pastor's final, "Amen," I bid a few people, "Thank you for coming." And hurried outside to my car. I sensed they couldn't wait to get me alone and spit their nasty threats into my face about what they were going to do to me if I didn't turn all of Jeff's things over to them. Still I kept my composure, ignoring their angry glares and hoping my supplications for peace would be answered. But some folks just don't believe in peace.

I hurried inside Dominick's grocery store for some last-minute items before heading home and getting everything ready for my guests: Isaac, Anna, her mother and husband, and a few more. I even invited LJ and his family to come dine with us. He said, "You know if I go anywhere near Lennox and he look at me wrong, I'm gonna want to kill him. So I ain't comin' over to your house and you know I ain't goin' to Jeff's funeral. I didn't like his black ass no way."

"If Lennox comes, it'll be because he's following RudyAnn. Because you know he didn't get a personal invitation from me. Still, when are you gonna forgive him?" He didn't answer. "Well, you gotta let it go at some point. Because how can you teach your boys to forgive if you won't?"

"Okay. And how can you preach to me about forgivin' and you won't?"

"I forgave Jeff."

"But what about your mama and your sister?"

"I'm workin' on it."

"Nikki, I don't hate Lennox as much as I used to. I just don't have nothing to say to him. I also can't see him bein' around my kids. I'm no son of his. So how can he be around my boys and fake the funk like he gives a damn about them. RudyAnn comes over and she's even babysat while me and Bethany went out. But as far as Lennox is concerned, if he died tomorrow, I wouldn't give a damn."

"I'm glad you're now spendin' time with your mother."

"Yeah, but she's still hot in the ass."

"LJ."

"I'm just callin' it like I see it. I don't care where we're at, she's flirtin' with somebody. That's because she's miserable. She don't love Lennox. Never have if you ask me. Not with some of the stuff she used to do."

"Then why is she still with him?"

"Why were you still with the bear?"

"We need to talk about that."

"I know it has a lot to do with your mama."

"Amongst other things." I sighed. "There's so much I gotta tell you."

"Whatever it is, I don't wanna know and I forgive you."

"But you need to know . . ."

"All I need to know is that you're gonna be all right. Whatever happened in the past is the past. And if it has no effect on me, Bethany and our kids, or me and your relationship, I could care less."

"You sure."

"Word is bond. And just so you know, changin' the subject—Bethany and I are thinkin' about lettin' RudyAnn move in with us."

"I know you ain't . . ."

"Nikki, like I said, she's miserable and . . ."

"LJ, you only got two bedrooms."

"You get in wherever you can fit in around here anyway."

"Well, I offered to give you a house."

"And I appreciate it. But like I keep tellin' you, I'm a man now and real men take care of their family."

"Mother included."

"If I have to. You've been payin' my way through college and footin' my bills—"

"I don't mind."

"But I do, so can we get back to the subject at hand?"

"Yes, sir."

"Regardless of what went down in the past, RudyAnn is still my mother and we've been talkin' and I know she wants something more than what she has now. And if she's here, Bethany can finish school after she has the baby. It'll work. And if it don't, you know me."

Yeah, I did. LJ could be as sweet as they come. But he would check a soul in a heartbeat. Even me.

29

I felt like cooking and Anna and I had been up most of the night putting a spread together that would put Emeril Lagasse to shame. After leaving Dominick's I zoomed up Sheridan Road to pull the aluminum pans out of the refrigerator and light the Brunson burners so everything would be piping hot for my guests. I pulled into my driveway. Who else, other than TommyLee, was standing in front of a moving truck with three other men and his oldest son. His white Lincoln Town Car was parked next to it.

I jumped out of my car and went straight to him, talking smack right in his face. His son and the other men, who looked like the neighborhood crackheads, circled me.

Still, I insisted, "You ain't put shit in my house and you ain't takin' shit out. You didn't even like Jeff and he damn sure couldn't stand your ass. So you need to get off my damn property."

"And if I don't?"

"Then you're gonna have to answer to me," Isaac said, coming from the side of the house.

"This ain't got nothin' to do with you, Mackey."

"This has everything to do with me, if you messin' with her."

"Why? Is she one of your whores from back in the day?"

Isaac's face hardened. "Nikki, get in the house."

"I ain't leavin' you." I was more afraid they would hurt him than me.

Isaac glared at me. I started moving, but not far. He said to TommyLee, "I believe she asked you to get off her property."

DAYLIGHT COMING

"I ain't goin' nowhere without gettin' my brother's stuff. Kingston money bought it and a Kingston is takin' it." TommyLee insisted.

"Well, that's gonna be a problem," Isaac said.

He spun TommyLee around, then bent his arm behind his back. TommyLee dropped to his knees, moaning and wrenching in pain. With his forearm pressed into TommyLee's neck, Isaac continued applying so much pressure TommyLee started to pale.

His son said, "Please, mister. Please. We'll leave. Won't we, daddy? We'll leave and never come back."

TommyLee nodded to the best of his ability. Isaac let him go, then snatched him to his feet by the collar of his jacket. "Man, look at her." TommyLee turned his head away from me. He was panting, trying to catch his breath. Isaac slapped his face back around. "Look at her, man." TommyLee cut his eyes at me. "Look at her real good. Because if she ever tells me you called her or come near her or was seen in Evanston, I'll hunt you down. And trust me, you don't want me to do that. Now get the hell outta here."

He shoved TommyLee into his car. His head slammed into the doorframe. He grabbed it and fell inside, rocking back and forth in agony. Isaac stopped his son as he tried to run over to the driver's side. He was so petrified, he was crying and trembling worse than his father.

"Grow up, boy, and be your own man."

He said, "Yes, yes, sir," and jumped into the car. He backed up so fast he almost sideswiped my Volvo.

One of TommyLee's henchmen walked up to Isaac. He held out his hand. "Man, I knew I knowed you from somewhere. You remember me, man, Pete Black from over on Congress and Central. We grew up together. You was on Central and Jackson. Man, you sho was the shit back in the day."

Isaac's cold stare made the snaggle-toothed man drop his head. He shoved his hands into his pockets and went got into the truck.

"Dag, Isaac, I didn't know you cared so much about me," I said.

"I don't see why not. I taught you everything I know and I'm always savin' your behind."

"That's true."

"But what in the hell made you get out of your car like that? I suspected he was up to something. That's why I came straight over here from the services and parked in the back of the house."

"Thanks."

"But do you know what could've happened to you? A woman and all those men."

"I was just mad."

He shook his head. "I ain't always gonna be around to save you, Nicole. So you gotta start . . . how can I say this?"

"Usin' my brain?"

"You use that but, bein' more conscientious of what you're doin'. You don't see danger in a lot of situations. I guess you act on impulse. But you leave yourself open to get seriously hurt."

"Isaac, so much has happened to me in my life that I can't foresee anything worse than what my mother and Jeff did to me."

"That's another thing. You gotta quit feelin' sorry for yourself. All of that stuff is behind you. Many died goin' through the same stuff you went through and you're still here. You could've easily become a drug addict. A alcoholic. Been in and out of jail."

"But there's a possibility I can still go."

"Are you gonna tell?"

"No."

"Then neither am I. So that's another thing you need to put behind you. You dwell on the past too much, Nikki. Let's talk about *now*. What are you gonna do?"

30

Mother, Pastor Dorthea, RudyAnn, and Lennox rang my bell two minutes after Anna, her mother and I had everything set up and ready for my hungry guests. Mother walked in with her nose so far up in the air, I'm surprised she didn't bump it on the ceiling.

RudyAnn said, "Ignore her," as she walked to the kitchen, followed by Lennox who was holding on to the fingers she had accidentally slammed in the car door. "Go find a seat, Lenny, and I'll get you some ice. Nicole, where do you keep your dish towels?"

"They're in the drawer next to the dishwasher."

"Thank you."

I looked at Anna. "What's up with her?"

"I don't know." She pushed me into the kitchen. "But appreciate it."

RudyAnn said with her back to me. "I know I never said this before, but I'm proud of you." I was stunned, once again. "And you were wrong. Anna—meanin' no harm—and Isaac ain't the only family you got." She pressed the button on the icemaker. The cubes dropped into the towel. "And another thing. Thanks for what you did for Limmell. Because I didn't . . . " Her voice broke. "You were right. I didn't do right by him. And if it wasn't for you, LJ wouldn't be the man he is now."

She wrapped the towel around the ice and walked out of the kitchen. I asked Anna, "What the hell just happened here?"

"Sounds like she's apologizing to me."

"Or is she tryin' to get this house? Did I tell you that LJ said she may be movin' in with them?"

"Nikki, she was sincere, because you know I can spot a fake in a heartbeat."

"Mother must've told her what I said. Because I did say you and Isaac were my only family. And LJ, of course."

"Whatever the case, enjoy your big sister wanting to make peace with you."

"Maybe, but I still wonder what she's up to, because this is a overnight thing. I can't even say when I last saw her or even talked to her. She didn't even come over here while I was here with Jeff or call to check on me."

"But she's here now. That's what matters."

We joined my guests in the dining room. Everyone was lined up with their plates. Anna's mother was instructing them on what was what, while smiling sweetly at Isaac. And he was smiling right back. Lots of talking was going on about how beautiful the service was amongst other things. Everybody seemed to be enjoying being together, except Mother and Pastor Dorthea.

"Would you like for me to make your plates?" I asked them.

"I'll get one when I'm ready to eat, thank you," Mother said.

"I ain't hungry," Pastor said, staring at the food like it was the Last Supper.

"Okay, just let me know." Mother grunted.

I smiled at her and went to assist Anna with the drinks. "Did Isaac tell you his good news?" she asked.

"Oh yeah, I forgot." I picked up a glass. I tapped the side with a spoon. "Before y'all start eatin', first of all, I'd like to thank you for comin'. And second, I have some great news."

I looked at Isaac. I knew he was going to kill me later. "Isaac bid on a contract to remodel a apartment complex that will house abused women and their children—the largest and first of its kind in the area. And he got it. He got the contract. And I'm so proud of him." Everyone clapped. He smiled, shaking his head.

"Nicole, you have something to celebrate as well," Anna added.

"I do. What?"

"I wouldn't have gotten it if it wasn't for you," Isaac said.

"Okay and you wanna explain that to me."

Anna said, "Nicole, look at how many people ostracized him when he got out of prison. Remember some of the stuff they were saying to you for associating with him."

"Yeah and . . . "

"You gave me a chance when nobody else would. You had no idea what kind of man I had become bein' locked up for all of those years, but you still reached out to me. You trusted me." I was still confused. "Before you asked me to come work for you, nobody wanted to be bothered with me."

Anna replied, "But look at him now. Look at where he is now, because of you. You looked past him being a once convicted man and saw a person who needed to breathe again."

"And as long as I live, I will always be grateful. Daughter." Isaac grabbed me in a big hug, something very unusual for him.

We laughed and he, Anna and I shared our first group hug. Mother and Pastor cut their eyes at each other. I had never thought about accepting credit for his thriving business or the new house he was planning to build from the ground up or any of his accomplishments. I viewed them as gifts from God like I had been taught since I was a child. All good things are gifts from God. But he and Anna insisted I had laid the foundation. It gave me leeway to tell myself once again, *I'm not so bad.*

RudyAnn walked over to us. "Nicole is an awesome woman. And she has done so much for me, too. And although we've had some rough times, Nicole, I want you to know that as I said in the kitchen, I'm proud of you, too. And if I ever had to pick anybody as my hero . . . " She looked at Mother, then back at me. "It would be you."

Mother rolled her eyes and went into the kitchen.

"Your mother does love you, Nicole, even if she does have a odd way of showing it," Anna said.

"If I could only feel it. Just once in my life."

"Regardless of how she may act, don't let it stop you from being the best daughter you can be. I know how hard you try when it comes to her and I've seen your tears many times when you didn't know I was looking. But you've got to be bigger than her. Just like you were bigger than Jeff. Because Roger's ass would've been burned up long before now."

Anna had Roger locked on so tough he didn't question a thing she said. I laughed. "Girl, you are so crazy."

RudyAnn cleared her throat.

"Are you okay?" I asked her.

"Well, I need to get this off my chest. You know, I've been doin' some thinkin'. A lot of thinkin'. And . . . well . . . I'm miserable."

I asked, "What's wrong?" as if LJ hadn't told me the exact same thing.

"First of all, I'm not saying this because I want anything from you. I just want a life. Here I am almost fifty and I'm still livin' with my mother. And still married to a man I never loved." Surprised by her openness, I let her continue to vent. "I'm just tired, Nicole. Tired of beggin'. Tired of everything I have comin' from you or Mother. I want my own place. I want Lenny to go away. I want to be able to buy things for myself and to be able to buy gifts on birthdays and holidays for my grandchildren. But I don't have a clue where I'm supposed to start."

"The place to start is with a job."

"But what can I do?"

"I can teach you how to use a computer. Word processin', spreadsheets, and I can train you on usin' the telephone. The right way. Because I know how smart you were in school."

Anna said, "I have a friend who owns a temp agency in downtown Evanston, but you have to get some training before she will even consider hiring you. But if you learn fast, I know she'll hook you up."

"It sounds good, but—"

"Why don't we talk about it later?" I said. "Anna and I are goin' away for the weekend to Wisconsin to the Interlaken Spa and Resort and you can come—"

"Nicole, you know I can't afford—"

"Can I finish? Anna is treatin' me, so I'll treat you."

"I'll pass, because if I go I'll still be in the same boat—there lookin' for a handout."

Anna said, "A treat isn't a hand-out, RudyAnn. Just consider it as a career move. You'll come and we'll map out your future while we're getting our nails and toes done. So what do you say?"

"Well . . . "

"Come on, RudyAnn, it'll be our first vacation together and it'll be so much fun."

"You would do that for me after all . . . "

"No doubt."

Anna said, "Y'all about to make me cry. Now go on and hug."

We laughed and reached for each other. Mother walked between us. "Rudalia, I'm ready to go." She carried a plate of food wrapped in aluminum foil.

"Well, I wanna hang out with Nicole and Anna."

"*Well*, I'm ready to go. Now!"

"Lenny!" He stopped talking to Isaac and hurried over to RudyAnn. "Mother is ready to go. Take her home because I'm gonna be over here for a while with my sister."

Mother stared at her, her eyes angry and cold. "Suit yourself. Nicole, get my coat."

"I'll get it," Anna said.

"I asked Nicole."

Anna followed me to the coat closet. "I just can't win, can I?" I said.

"She'll come around. Start spending more time with your sister and see don't she start feeling left out and wanna be with you."

"I don't know."

"You guys have been through a lot, Nicole."

"I was the one goin' through a lot. She used to beat the shit outta me."

"Used to. But as they say, 'Time heals all wounds.'"

I wondered when it would begin to heal Mother's, because after I passed her her coat, she dropped her food in the small garbage can in the foyer and walked out the front door.

Isaac came and stood next to me. "You just keep on respectin' her and bein' as kind as you can."

"I'm gonna try."
"Either way, you still got me!"
"Yeah, but how long? I see you checkin' out Anna's mother."
"When you're hot in demand, you're just hot in demand."
"Well, do your thang, Mr. Hot Stuff."

31

As soon as RudyAnn and Anna were out the door, I rushed upstairs and jumped into the shower. I slipped into the red silk pajamas I treated myself to from Victoria's Secret and went into the kitchen. I took a Pepsi out of the refrigerator, then walked around admiring my spacious cove while taking sips from the bottle. RudyAnn and I had cleaned it, and the marble floors and ceramic tile walls sparkled by the moonlight. So did the stainless steel refrigerator, stove, and dishwasher. Everything else was white just like Alex's.

I thought about him for a few minutes. "Well, if we don't get back together, I'll be alright. Because I'm through waddlin' in my misery," I said to myself.

I took another sip of my pop as I headed into the study. I grabbed the *Evanston Review* from off my desk and sat on the floor in front of the chair closest to the fireplace to read. Jeff's picture was in it along with his obituary. "Local resident succumbs at the age of 48." It didn't hurt knowing he was out of my life, but it did seem strange I would never see him again.

I glanced through the rest of the paper, then got up to turn the radio on to WGCI. Whitney Houston's latest hit, "My Love Is Your Love," was going off. Lauren Hill's "Ex-Factor" came on. I sat at my desk and sang along with her as I wrote out my agenda for the next couple of days. Once done with my *to-do* list, I walked over to the window facing the backyard. I dug my toes into the carpet that kept me awake for three nights while I pondered over which color would work best with the white marble fireplace. It took me even longer to choose the eggshell color for the wall. I had selected everything in my house down to the crown moulding. I got on Isaac's nerves with my indecisiveness. A couple of times he left me standing in the aisle at Home Depot to go get something to eat.

Together we painted my bedroom china-white, then dipped tips of feathers into gold paint to give the walls a marble look. Jeff ruined it after I left him by throwing paint thinner at the oil painting I had paid a Northwestern student to do for me of the house. The thinner splattered the wall, leaving it a dirty-looking beige. The oil painting was thrown in the garbage.

When I saw what he did, I took the picture down, held it to my breasts and cried like it was a child. But it wasn't. None of the things I was so foolish over were as valuable as having someone to love me, call me family, or be my friend. Besides, everything I called mine-all-mine was replaceable.

I went back to my desk and turned on my PC, one of the few things Jeff hadn't destroyed or sold. I guess because he enjoyed the explicit websites too much to get rid of it. I typed up a standard letter to all of his children who were all still living in either Evanston or Chicago and printed checks for each one of them. In each letter I explained more money would be coming at a later date in the form of a trust fund my lawyer would be drawing up. I knew it wasn't my obligation, but I wanted them to have at least one good memory of their father, even if it was only monetary.

The next letter I wrote was to my tenants living in my buildings on King Drive. I informed them I was converting their apartments into condominiums and was granting them the first option to buy. I figured the profit from one of the graystones would be a substantial amount of money for paying off all of Jeff's debt and giving to his children. I also considered maybe getting to know them, provided they wanted to get to know me.

With a plan in mind, I looked forward to making a difference in their lives and using the skills I acquired, thanks to Isaac, to patch up my house. I thought about the six copies of *Custom Home Magazine* in the backseat of my car. Anna had given them to me, insisting, "Nicole, it's your dream house. So enjoy it."

Yet, I couldn't help but think, *what's the use of havin' all of this house and livin' by myself?* Still, I thanked God for her as I walked upstairs to Jeff's room. I pulled one of his cashmere coats out of his closet and slid my feet into a pair of his leather slippers. I hadn't thought about what I was going to do with his clothes since he owned so many. He had even more shoes. I would have liked to have given them to his father and brothers since they were all the same size, but really didn't want any more contact with them, considering them having labeled me as a gold-digging bitch.

They didn't even try to hear my side of the story. Or wait to see if I was going to offer them anything. The minute they heard he was sick, they thought they were going to take whatever they wanted and I was going to sit back and say, "Okay."

I shrugged my shoulders. "Oh well." I went back downstairs, grabbed the keys to my car off the hall table, and opened the door. Alex was getting ready to ring the bell. We looked into each other's eyes. He glanced over my head.

"How you doin'?"

"I'm fine." And I meant it until he looked into my eyes again.

"I was just in the neighborhood."

"Visitin' who?"

He smiled. "Can we talk?"

"Yeah. You wanna come in?"

"Is it okay?"

"I don't see why not. But first, I gotta get somethin' outta my car."

He stood in the doorway watching me as I grabbed the magazines off the back seat. "Nikki, I'm sorry."

"For?" I closed the door.

"Being so selfish I couldn't see you were doin' the right thing."

"But there's a lot more to it than me doin' the right thing. I did some terrible things—some illegal things." I told him about my indiscretions and the attempted blackmail on Jeff's part. He stood staring at me as if he really couldn't believe I would do such a thing.

"And I ran out on Jeff when he was havin' his heart attack. So my intention wasn't to take care of him. But to make sure he didn't tell his family I lied on all of my applications for loans so they wouldn't try to take away my property."

"Wow. You did all of that?"

"Yeah."

"And I understand."

"How could you when I walked out on you tryin' to hold on to— "

"Don't get me wrong, I'm not condonin' what you did, but understand that your life dictated the decisions you made. You were scared and made some bad choices."

"Really bad. "

"We all do. But you learned your lesson, right?"

"Yes."

"And I should've been here for you instead of sulkin' like a kid."

"I needed to sort out my mess on my own."

"So is forgivin' me a possibility?"

"I was never mad at you, Alex."

"But I was mad at you. As a matter of fact, I was pissed like a muthaf . . . I was pissed to the highest."

"That was yesterday. The most important thing to me is today. That you're here now because I been wantin' to see you."

"And I been such a jerk."

"And I missed you."

"I missed you, too, Nikki."

We hugged, then walked into the study hand-in-hand. He took his coat off, then sat in the chair closest to the fireplace.

"You want something to drink?"

"What you got?"

"Pop, coffee, water, tea, beer."

"Beer?"

"Yeah. RudyAnn had a taste for one."

"Your sister?"

"Yeah."

"She was here?"

"Her and Mother."

"How'd it go?"

"I think RudyAnn and I are gonna be okay, because she's goin' away with me and Anna this weekend, so I know that's gonna do us a lot of good, but with Mother . . . " I sighed.

"You givin' her this house?"

"No. But I'm thinkin' about getting Isaac to remodel hers."

He looked puzzled. "I know she's your mother, but . . . "

"I just want to. Besides, she's been livin' there for a long time. Her house needs a lot of work. And I can't see myself havin' this one . . . "

"I thought you were gonna sell this place."

"Well, I've made other plans for it."

"Meanin'?"

"I don't wanna stay here anymore."

"So where are you goin', because I need to know . . . " He looked into my eyes. "What's gonna happen to us, Nikki?"

"I don't know. What do you want to happen?"

"I just wish that we could go back to where we were. I wish things hadn't ended for us the way they did. I wish . . . "

"We had taken our time and not rushed into the relationship." My remark seemed to hurt him instantly. "Because I never should've left Jeff for you, Alex. What I mean is if I was gonna leave him, I should've did it for me. For all of the stuff he did to me. Besides, I brought so much baggage with me that our relationship wouldn't have worked anyway. I was so messed up inside my drama would've eventually pushed you away. And look at all of the secrets I had. So if it hadn't been for him dyin' and me being responsible for his welfare, it would've been something else."

"True. But it's over now. Jeff's dead. And I know I may be movin' a bit too fast. But I'm standin' here with my heart in my hand. You shot me down once. Because I have never been so hurt or felt so betrayed before that I thought I would never forgive you. But we both know you were right. You did have drama and I shouldn't have forced your hand."

"You didn't."

"Yeah, I did. You were married and as much of a ass Jeff was to you, I should've never touched you until he was out of your life for good. And we were married. I made the move on you, remember. Because you would've kept on bein' my friend. But I had to have you. So I was just as wrong.

"But, Nikki, I love you. I always have and I always will. And I know I got some issues I need to work on too with my family. But what I'm tryin' to say is that you're a widow now. And I'm still single. And I know I'm zoomin' at you. And you may need some time. But can't we just try? We can take our time this time and . . . "

We stared at one another. He made a step. Then I made a step. We ended our dispute with a kiss that warmed me down to my bones. And as he always did whenever he touched me, he made my toes curl.

As Alex held me in his arms, me crying like crazy, I thought, *Jeff and Mother really did take me through some shit. And I'm still here. They tried to destroy me. But here I am. After all those years of walkin' around in total darkness. Hatin' myself and wantin' to die. Searchin' for some daylight. For some hope. But daylight ain't comin' here. It has arrived! And I'm gonna marry this man. I'm gonna be Mrs. Alexander Julian Knight. I'm finally gonna get something I truly want.*

I wiped my tears away as we let each other go. One of the *Custom Home* magazines slipped out of my hand. I laughed as I bent over to pick it up.

"What's so funny?"

"I know Mother is gonna be pissed when she finds out I'm givin' this house to LJ and Bethany for their weddin' present."

"So he finally popped the question?"

"We were talkin' this mornin' and he said, 'Oh, I forgot to tell you that Bethany and I got married last week at City Hall.' Can you believe that?" Alex smiled. "Oh, you know a sista was pissed, especially when he said, 'We didn't want to tell you because I knew you was gonna make a big deal out of it and I didn't want a big weddin'.'"

"Well."

"He could've at least invited me."

"So when is the baby due or have they had it already?"

"They have a few more weeks to go, but Bethany looks like she's gonna have it any day now."

"He teachin' yet?"

"He needs some more credits before he can graduate, but he was just hired as the assistant to the dean of a school in Chicago not far from here. He started last week, as a matter of fact. The day after he got married."

"That's good. So what made you decide to give them the house?"

"I really don't wanna sell it, because its value has almost tripled, but I don't wanna live here, either. It's too much space for one person. And it was all just for show anyway. I bought it because I could afford it. And wanted people, mainly Mother, to look at it and say, 'Look at what Nicole did.' I didn't ever need this much room.

"And besides, if I died tomorrow, it would still be his. I'm just glad I'll have the chance to see them enjoyin' it. You know, the kids playin' in the backyard. Runnin' from room to room. Havin' access to the beach, whenever. Havin' their own space. God, I can't wait to see the expression on LJ's face when I give him the keys, even though he says I need to quit tryin' to spoil him."

"You're just a great aunt."

"I am, ain't I? But this is gonna be the last major thing I'm gonna do for him. Because he is a man now and I'm gonna respect his request for me to let him handle his business."

"I hear you talkin'. Either way, I'm proud of you."

"Why?"

"Because you're so forgivin'. So generous and so beautiful. Man, I'm blessed to have you in my life."

"I'm blessed, too. But I'm gonna make some mistakes."

"I'm gonna make some mistakes."

"But I'm gonna try to learn from them."

"And I'm gonna try to learn from mine."

I pulled him to me. "And *I'm* gonna be your wife."

He wrapped his arms around me. "So, can we consummate that promise?"

"In my nephew's house? What kind of woman do you think I am?"

"At the moment, it don't matter. Because it's been a long time. And a brotha is feenin' like you wouldn't believe."

"Sorry." I pushed him away from me. "But you're gonna have to wait until after our weddin'."

"Well, consider us unofficially married, because I'm takin' you home." Alex swooped me up in his arms and carried me out the door.

"Help. Somebody help me!" I screamed, giggling like a schoolgirl all the way to the Land Cruiser.

32

As Alex drove us home, I couldn't help but think about how good it was going to feel, him washing my hair, massaging my body from head-to-toe with the oils he took special care in choosing, and holding me in his arms. He parked, then walked over to my side of the truck. He opened the door, lifted me out, and carried me inside, straight to the bathroom.

"I thought you were supposed to take me to the bedroom."

"Could you just be quiet?"

He put me down and walked over to the tub. He turned it on, then lit every linen-scented candle surrounding it. I squealed with delight as I watched him pour in my favorite milk bath and sprinkle rose petals into the water.

"Oh, so you just knew I was comin' home?"

"Or I was gonna do it caveman style and drag you here by your hair."

"Kinky. But ain't that called kidnappin'?"

He came and stood in front of me. He kissed down the front of my top, then started to unbutton it. "Could you just be quiet?"

Alex finished undressing me, then picked me up and put me in the water. I pulled him in with me. We splashed around hugging, kissing and caressing, then made love from room to room until the wee hours of the morning. God, I missed him so much that I cried in his arms. Several times.

After Jeff died, I slept better than I had in weeks. But cuddled next to Alex on the floor in the living room—I was so relaxed I didn't want to move. He picked me up to carry me to the bedroom. "What are you doin'?"

"Takin' care of my future wife." He put me in bed, kissed me, then said, "Sweet dreams, beautiful."

No sooner than I dozed off, it seemed like he woke me up again with a steaming plate of scrambled eggs loaded with Mexican sausage and topped with homemade salsa and grated cheese. I stared into his eyes as he fed me.

"I love you, Alexander Knight."

He kissed my lips. "I love you, too, Nikki-Nicole."

"Thanks for forgivin' me."

"Didn't I tell you I can't see livin' my life without you?"

"Yeah, but . . ."

"No buts. Everything that's happened is in the past. We both made some stupid mistakes, but now is what's most important."

"I still can't believe we're finally together. No one to run interference on our future plans. I feel freer now than I ever have before in my life." I grabbed him in a big hug, almost knocking what was left of my breakfast on the floor. "And it's all because of you. I don't know what my life would be like now if it wasn't for you—and Anna—and Isaac—and LJ. I can't leave them out. But have you ever just never had any hope whatsoever?"

"Yeah, I been there."

"That is a ugly feelin'. Especially when you can't find anything about yourself to love. Or like. But now, I feel so much better about me. Because I know in my heart I'm nothing like that person Mother and Jeff had made me think I was. And I can finally say, I love me."

He kissed my lips. "I love you, too."

"And I have so much to look forward to. I can't wait to tell RudyAnn you forgave me." I let him go and grabbed the telephone. She answered on the second ring. "Hey, big sis," I chirped.

"Nicole? Where you callin' from at seven in the mornin'?"
"What are you doin' up so early?"
"Couldn't sleep."
"What's wrong?"
"Well, I'm not as depressed as I was. I'm just so tired of livin' here with Mother and Lenny. You know she snapped on me when I got home about contortin' or consortin'- con-something with the devil."
"Meanin' me?"
"You, Anna, and Isaac."
"Ain't that the pot callin' the kettle black?"
She laughed. "You talked to LJ?"
"Not since yesterday."
"He told you he asked me to come live with them."
"Yeah."
"I can't do it, Nicole. How would it look, me movin' in with my child and lettin' him take care of me after all—"
"But he's forgiven you."
"They barely have enough room for themselves and all of those toys you keep buying. I know the people at *Toys R Us* love to see you comin'."
"I can't help it."
"See, that's what I'm supposed to be doin'."
"You will one day if you learn to be patient with yourself. So, we still on for the weekend?"
"Nicole . . ."
"I know you ain't tellin' me no. Ever since you agreed to come, I've been lookin' forward to us spendin' time together and . . ."
"I keep tellin' you I don't want you to spend no more of your money on me."
"Pay me back when you get your first job, if it bothers you so much. Oh, I just thought of a way you can earn some money."
"Is it legal?"
"Oh, no you didn't."
"I'm just jokin'."

"I know, but don't trip with me. I'm givin' my house on Sheridan Road to LJ and Bethany for a weddin' present." She got silent, then I heard her sniff and could tell she was crying.

"Nicole, my goodness. That's the most . . . the most wonderful thing. Do you know how many black men his age whose aunt or family member is able to give them a house like that?"

"So, you don't mind?"

"How could I mind—*why* would I mind?"

"Because I thought . . . "

"I don't want that house. What good would it do me if I can't afford to live in it?"

"You got a point."

"So, when are you gonna tell them?"

"Soon."

"By the way, where are you?"

"Home."

"This ain't your number."

"With Alex."

"That was quick."

"And guess what—we're gettin' married."

"Congrats to you."

"And guess what again?"

"What?"

"Guess who I want to be in my weddin'."

"Me?" she asked as if it was shocking news.

"Of course. So that's something else we gotta plan while we're gettin' our backs massaged."

"Can I ask you a favor then?"

"Go ahead?"

"Can I help you plan it?"

"Girl, please, if you want, you can coordinate the whole thing. Just don't try to dress me up in that color you got married in."

"It wasn't that bad."

"It was salmon."

She laughed. "It's so good to be talkin' to you."

"I agree, but I better get off the phone. Alex and I still have a lot of makin' up to do."

"I don't blame you because he is a good-lookin' guy."

"Girl, please! My baby is fine."

She laughed. "I'm so happy for you."

"You know what? I'm happy for me, too."

Being able to talk to my sister like a friend was something I had been looking forward to all my life. I lay back on my pillow so elated I cried.

"What is wrong with me?" I asked myself. "It seems like I cry for everything. But at least these are happy tears." But how often does the devil—as it is often stated in religious sects all over the world—come to rob you of your joy?

33

After a rejuvenating weekend of drinking apple martinis and chitchatting in the Jacuzzi, getting full body massages, indulging in herbal wraps and mineral baths, and pampering with facials, pedicures, and manicures, RudyAnn, Anna and I packed our bags, headed for home.

"I could do this at least once a month," RudyAnn said as she pulled my car out of the parking lot. "I've never been this relaxed or felt so good before in my life."

"All it takes is a steady job," Anna replied.

"And comin' to work every day and on time," I added.

"Oh, I'll be there," RudyAnn said, smiling, as she pulled onto the highway.

Before I would even consider giving LJ and Bethany their wedding present, there were several things I needed to do to get the house ready for them. I hired RudyAnn to be my assistant. She shocked me with how eager she was to learn the tricks of the trade and how well she followed my directives. Even Isaac was impressed with how we painted the interior of the house, bought and hung new blinds, and made all of the necessary repairs. And I owed him plenty thanks for his teachings.

Still sometimes as we worked, I had to keep looking at her, because it seemed too unreal. One day we couldn't stand to be next to each other for more than thirty seconds and the next we were kicking it like buddies from back in the day. Alex started joining us to help out, anxious to see the looks on LJ's and Bethany's faces as well as assisting us in getting it ready for their one-month anniversary.

DAYLIGHT COMING

Even more excited than him, RudyAnn had been staying in the house working around the clock to get away from Mother and Lennox, who both demanded to know where she was at all times.

She said, "I keep tellin' Lenny I want a divorce, but he still won't go nowhere. He's workin' my every nerve and Mother, too. Until some weeks ago, I never really thought about how evil she really is. And I can't be like her, Nicole."

"Then just stay here. Plus it'll give you some time to think about what you're gonna do, since you have such a long to-do list."

Her main priority was making LJ and Bethany's day as special as possible. With her earnings from me, she bought balloons, champagne, caviar, shrimp, lobster, and tuna steaks, without an inkling how to cook any of it. While she decorated, Anna, Alex, and I prepared the food—us women sipping on Amaretto Sours and eating tortilla chips with Alex's infamous homemade salsa.

Bethany's eyes filled with tears when she walked in the door and saw how the place was decorated like there was going to be a wedding. The boys ran straight to the table in the dining room, adorned with an ice sculpture of a heart surrounded by exotic flowers and fresh fruit. They *o-o-hed* and *ah-h-ed* as they swiped strawberries, grapes, and raspberries, popping the morsels in their tiny mouths.

She asked, "What are you up to, Nikki?" as we hugged and Anna took her coat.

"That's what I wanna know," LJ said, looking at me suspiciously.

"You'll see." RudyAnn and I said in unison as we both reached for him to give him a hug.

He grabbed both of us. "Don't tell me now I gotta worry about both of y'all schemin'."

"Who's schemin'?" I asked, pinching his cheek.

"How often does one come to dinner with an ice sculpture, champagne—your future uncle-in-law cookin' on the grill in the middle of winter?"

"Well, since you're so nosey, we have shrimp kabobs, tuna steaks, and steamed lobsters. But I made your mama return the caviar."

He shook his head and went over to Bethany. "Do you think we wanna hear this?"

She nodded with excitement. "You know I do, because I love surprises."

"Well," I said. Her mother, sister, two brothers with their wives, Isaac, and Anna's mother came out of the den. Bethany really started crying. "Why are you doin' this, Nikki?"

"Your first-month anniversary," I said. And we all shouted, "SURPRISE!"

All the while we were enjoying dinner, I wanted to give LJ and Bethany the keys to the house so bad I handed them to Alex. After dessert—Tiramisu for us and lemon ice cream from the Marble Slab for the boys—he finally gave the box back to me. As they were getting ready to leave, RudyAnn said, "Before you go, Nikki has one more surprise for you."

LJ sighed. "It better not cost more than ten dollars."

I held the black velvet box out to them. He passed it to Bethany. With excited hands she snatched it open. "What do these go to?"

"This house."

"What?" she screamed.

"It's yours."

LJ said, "Nikki, we can't take this house. It'll take my entire paycheck to heat it up in the winter and two paychecks to keep it cool in the summer."

Bethany hurried up and added, "I love this place, LJ. Can't you see the boys growin' up here? Havin' their own rooms. And the lake right outside our back door. Do you know how long we'll have to work and save to be able to afford something like this? I'll take another job if it's necessary." She was only working part-time at a lawyer's office as a receptionist while waiting to start college and deliver the load she was carrying.

"So, you don't like where we're livin'?"

"I love bein' anywhere with you, but Nikki is givin' us her dream house."

"And," I added, "Your mother helped me fix it up just for y'all, if that helps my case. Besides, you really don't need to know this, but I was gonna leave it to you in my will. So don't you want me to be around to enjoy you havin' it?"

He shook his head. "You really know how to put me on the spot, don't you? But I still love you. Troublemaker." He grabbed me. I grabbed RudyAnn. Together we hugged with us women crying like we were at a funeral. The doorbell chimed throughout the house.

"I'll get it," Alex said. "Just keep on enjoyin' yourself even though I did help a little."

Anna said, "I'm beginning to feel left out myself." She turned to her mother. "Can I get a hug?"

Alex laughed all the way to the door, but I could imagine how quick his smile disappeared. "Good evenin', Mrs. Borge," he replied.

"Is Rudalia here?"

RudyAnn said, "Yes, I am." We had invited her over, but Mother insisted, "I have better things to do."

She dropped the garbage bags she was carrying between her and Alex. "These belong to you, Rudalia. If this is where you're gonna be stayin', then your junk should be with you. And your husband, too."

RudyAnn stormed out the door behind her. "Mother, why do you have to always be so cruel?" Mother got into her car and left her where she stood.

"How could she interrupt such a joyous occasion?" RudyAnn said, as she came inside, slamming the door.

LJ said, "That's your mama." She could have at least told her only grandchild and his new bride congratulations or said hello to her great-grandsons.

Lennox knocked on the door maybe five minutes after she drove off. He begged RudyAnn to come outside so they could talk about their marriage even though she kept insisting, "It's over, Lenny. So you're just gonna have to go on the Southside with your people, because I can't do nothing for you."

A pitiful sight to see, he was begging so tough and sobbing so hard, he didn't notice any of us. LJ's oldest son tapped LJ on the leg.

"Why is that man cryin' like that, Daddy? Somebody died?"

"Somebody ought to," he replied. Bethany elbowed him.

"Lenny, you need to leave," RudyAnn told him for the fifth time.

"But I don't have nowhere to go. You know I can't go home to my mama."

"But you never had a problem goin' to my mama's house."

He peered at her as if he didn't know what to say. That's when he noticed LJ smoldering and the rest of us staring at him dumbfounded that he would be carrying on like he was.

LJ's oldest ran over to him with a napkin. "Here."

Lennox took it out of his hand, murmuring, "Thank you."

LJ said, "You ready, Bethany?"

"Well, ain't you gonna speak to him?"

"Hell no. Let's go."

"I thought you said you forgive him."

"I still ain't got to talk to his ass. Now let's go."

RudyAnn said, "Lenny, I been blessed to be forgiven by my son and my sister and I refuse to let you, Mother, or anyone else interfere—"

"But I'm your husband. So what are we gonna do?"

"*We* ain't doin' nothin'. I'm movin' on with my life. Nicole has offered to let me stay here for a while and I'm gonna be workin' with her until I can find a job with some benefits. Therefore, I can't be married to you no more, because I need to move on."

He turned even redder. "After all these years."

"Good-bye, Lenny." His head dropped and he drug himself back out the door. "Whew," RudyAnn exclaimed. "That felt good. But, just so you know, LJ, I'm only stayin' here until y'all get ready to move in."

"Then you're goin' where?"

"I don't know."

DAYLIGHT COMING

Bethany said, "You're stayin' right here with us. So pick up your bags and choose any room, except the master bedroom, because we're movin' in there tonight."

LJ said, "She's been wantin' it ever since she first saw it."

That ended our evening on a happier note than I expected, because after Mother coming and Lenny going, I had started to feel it was ruined. It was just like Mother to do what she had been accusing me of all my life—being evil. But I don't think she intended for the tables to spin out of whack the way they did.

34

Instead of sticking to what I swore I was going to do— "Stay away from Mother—" I decided to go with my second intent—surprise her by showing up with Isaac and a major plan to renovate her house. Even RudyAnn was against it.

"Nicole, if the roof was about to fall on her head, she'd never agree to it. Trust me, she would rather sleep on ice than to accept anything from you or me at this point. I know I keep sayin' this and you may not want to hear it, but Mother is evil."

"There's a little bit of evil in all of us."

"True, but let's just face it, when it comes to you—and I ain't sayin' this tryin' to hurt your feelings. I would love for us to be together as a family—but if she ain't bent by now, I would just give it up."

It was the best advice my big sister had ever given me, because the second Mother opened the door and saw Isaac and me, she said, "What do you want?"

I explained the purpose of the visit.

"I'm not so hard up that I have to take whatever scraps *you* have to offer. You want to impress somebody with your change, take it to the Salvation Army." She slammed the door.

Isaac drove us over to Starbucks hoping to cheer me up with a mocha frappuchino, because once again she had ripped out a piece of my heart. RudyAnn called my cell phone just as he sat my drink in front of me, having told me himself he thought it was a bad idea.

"You know what she said to me?" RudyAnn cried. "She wants me to choose between you and her. She actually said that to me. 'It's either me, your mother, or her.' How dare she after what she did?"

"What did she do?"

"Nicole, there are so many things you need to know. And I've been tryin' not to tell you, because I don't want you to hurt no more, but…"

"Things like what?"

"Regardin' your father."

"Well, tell me now."

"No, I want her to confess."

"To what?"

"What really happened to him? I was young, but I know what I know."

"Did he molest you?"

"No, he was as sweet as he could be. A whore, yes, but he was so sweet, but it's her fault he was killed. And I'm gonna make her confess." RudyAnn hung up on me.

"Isaac, you gotta take me back over to Mother's."

"Why, what's goin' on?"

"I don't know what RudyAnn was talkin' about, but I know it has something to do with my father's death. Why can't I just know peace, Isaac?" I started crying again.

He walked me back to his truck with his arm around my shoulder. "Don't start givin' up on your life already. I guess maybe there are some things you need to know and maybe your sister just didn't know how to tell you until now."

"Like what? What could Mother have to do with my father's death? I don't understand."

He sighed. "I don't know how to tell you myself because it's all been hearsay." He opened the truck door for me.

"You know, too? Could you just tell me what is goin' on now?"

"Talk to your sister and your mother first and then I will fill you in the best way I can. But I wasn't there, so remember whatever I tell you will all be secondhand information."

"Isaac, please, don't let me walk in that door not knowin' what's goin' on."

"Nikki, it's best that you hear your mother's side of the story first. But I promise you we'll talk about it. I just ain't never know how to tell you."

"Did she kill him?"

"No. That ain't it."

"You want me to sit out here and wait for you?" Isaac asked.

"You don't have to," I said as I got out of his Tahoe. Jeff's Benz, which I had given to RudyAnn, was parked in the driveway, so I knew I had a ride home. She and Mother were shouting at each other loud enough to be heard on the street.

"You don't know what you're talkin' about!" Mother screamed.

"I remember it as plain as day. It's your fault that he was murdered."

"My daddy?" I asked, coming in the door.

"Don't you know how to knock?" Mother snapped, rolling her eyes.

"This is just as much Nicole's house as it is yours or mine, considerin' it was her grandmother's."

"It was our grandmother's, RudyAnn, unless you're sayin' we ain't sisters."

"No, this was your daddy's family's house."

"Shut up, Rudalia."

"Not this time, Mother. Now tell Nicole the truth. Tell her how you were responsible for Miss Lenoir killin' Walter."

"What is she talkin' about, Mother?"

"Some of you is just rubbin' off on her, because that's what happens when you start interactin' with the unsaved."

"Cut the bullshit, Mother! Why can't you just admit that you called Walter cryin' sayin' it was an emergency, because he was livin' down the street with Miss Lenoir. Tell the truth for a change. You know for a fact that when he got here, you begged him to come home. But he told you, he would rather live in the sewer because you gypped him out of his inheritance. You talked his mother into signin' this house, her insurance, and everything else she owned over to you before she died. Your family didn't have no more than the next person. So Nicole, all of the heirlooms she claim was passed down from her family, actually came from Walter's family."

"Say what?"

"His mother was a teacher and his father worked for the railroad so they had plenty money. But when your grandfather died, your grandmother became very depressed so Mother took advantage of it, then tried to use the money to make Walter stay with her."

"Oh my, goodness."

"The day before your grandmother's funeral is when he found out. And he was so pissed, he packed his stuff and moved out to keep from killin' her. He was already seein' Miss Lenoir. He started seein' her a week after he and Mother got married. And Miss Lenoir was very jealous and possessive. But so was Mother, because they used to fight over him all the time. That's how Mother got that long cut on her arm that she claimed came from a car accident. She went to Miss Lenoir's house to make Walter come home. They got into a fight and Miss Lenoir cut her with a straight razor. They fought over him almost every week and with other women, too."

Mother threw her hand in RudyAnn's face. "You're just as much of a liar as Nicole is."

I said, "This ain't about me. This is about you, the queen being dethroned. All of these years you callin' me a compulsive liar and insistin' I get down on my hands and knees when you're the one who needs prayer."

RudyAnn turned to me. "I treated you just as bad she did, Nicole. And there ain't a excuse in the world I can give."

"She let you."

"I knew better as I got older, but I was so jealous of you."

"Why?"

"Because you've always been the prettiest."

"Please."

"You are beautiful! It's just that we treated you so bad that we didn't leave you with enough self-esteem to even take it into consideration. Plus you're smart and never been afraid of seekin' out what you wanted. But every time you tried something, if she didn't beat the hope out of you, I ridiculed you so bad you gave up on your dreams. Not to mention the horrible things Jeff did to you and we just let it happen. We didn't even try to help you. But I was so jealous of you that . . . " She hung her head. "That . . . " She wiped away her tears. "That I was glad to see you miserable."

"That ain't important now."

"You two are makin' me sick. So could you both get out of my house?" Mother said.

"Not before you tell Nicole the truth."

"I don't know what you're talkin' about."

"The fact that the day Walter refused to come back to you, you called Miss Lenoir's house ready to beg some more and her sister answered the phone, but wouldn't let you speak to him. So you called Miss Lenoir at the hospital where she worked, swearin' you saw Walter and another woman goin' in her house. You said to her, 'He's cheatin' on you with me. He's cheatin' on me with you. Now he has this other woman.' Knowin' he hadn't been with you since the night you got pregnant with Nicole. And he was drunk then."

Mother had turned bright red, so I knew RudyAnn was telling the truth. "By the time you finished tellin' Miss Lenoir how they were huggin' and kissin' all over each other and slipped in you were three months' pregnant, she left her job. Walter was in the bed naked, because that was how he slept when he was drunk. But she was so mad, she killed him. Stabbed him to death because of your lies!"

"That's the most preposterous thing I have ever heard come out of your mouth, Rudalia!"

RudyAnn looked at me with tears in her eyes. "When we heard the siren she made me go over there. I was seven years old and she made me go over there to find out what was goin' on. She said, 'Remember everything you hear. I want to know everything, Rudalia.'

"I snuck in through the back door. The house was full of people. Miss Lenoir was sittin' at the dinin' room table in handcuffs, cryin', her clothes soaked with blood. And I snuck in the bedroom. Blood was everywhere—on the walls, the furniture, the carpet. And there Walter was, cut up so bad it looked like he had been put in a meat grinder. Scared me so bad that I ran back home screamin' and she slapped me. The only time in my life she ever hit me and she made me go back to the house. 'I want to know every piece of details, Rudalia.'"

In spite of guilt plastered all over her face, Mother still stuck to, "I don't know what you're talkin' about."

She was a sadder sight than Lennox had been when he begged RudyAnn not to divorce him and Jeff had been throughout our entire marriage. And to think all of the years she walked around with her nose up in the air, treating people like they weren't shit when that pristine background she claimed to have had was a lie. She was born on the west side of Chicago, poor as hell. And she was never married to RudyAnn's father, because he already had a wife and three kids.

It took me a couple of days to snap out of the shock, but it did open my eyes to the fact that there wasn't anything for us to patch up. Although she birthed me, she couldn't find a solitary thing to like about me, because I wasn't conceived out of love, but out of her lust and deceit. I represented what she truly was: a lying, conniving, and vindictive woman.

I still tried to convince myself that she didn't intend for the woman to kill my father, but who's to say. She used to say some nasty stuff about him when she was beating the crap out of me. So she was still hanging on to loads of pinned-up anger—whether it was because he never wanted her and she made a spectacle out of herself trying to hold on to him; or he died and left her; or because she never had anyone else after he died. Therefore, Christianity became her excuse not to face who or what she really was.

With my wedding approaching and RudyAnn bent on making it the best day of my life, I decided I would focus on my future with Alex—not my past with Mother or Jeff. I told him the story. I also told Isaac, who already knew, but insisted, "It wasn't my place to tell you. So can you forgive me for not pryin'?"

He knew I would and I greeted him with a big hug the minute he walked in the door of LJ's house as we gathered to discuss Alex and my wedding plans. "Thanks so much for comin'."

"Why wouldn't I? You feelin' better?"

"One-hundred percent. And I've promised myself and Alex, and now I'm promisin' you, that I ain't spendin' another second worryin' about whether or not Mother will ever learn to love me."

Alex said, "If she ain't learned by now . . . "

Isaac replied, "That's true. But either way, Nikki Kingston . . . " Alex cleared his throat. "Excuse me. Either way, the future Misses Alexander Knight, you're just gonna have to make due with me, since we adopted each other a long time ago. And I'm spendin' all of this money on a damn tuxedo I ain't gonna wear again. "

"Well, who else do I have to give me away? I told you to rent one but you're hardheaded. Besides, it ain't my fault that you insist you can't wear something somebody else already wore."

LJ said, "Well, I was drafted as best man and *told*—not asked—that I was gonna be in the weddin'. At least you had a choice."

"Are you two complainin'?" Alex asked.

LJ looked down at his Nikes. Isaac walked over to Anna's mother, smiling and pretending not to hear the question. Anna said, "Ain't that just like Negroes?" She rubbed her stomach. "Girl, I'm hungry as hell. LJ, what you got to eat?"

RudyAnn said, "I can cook y'all some chicken."

"Don't nobody want no damn chicken, Rudalia!" Anna replied, laughing at RudyAnn's insinuation.

I thought, *Especially if you're cookin' it*. Because she was horrible in the kitchen. She had agreed to alternate making dinner with LJ and Bethany, therefore, she was trying. But *when you ain't got it, you just ain't got it*.

"Let my sister cook us some chicken if she wants to."

LJ cut his eyes at me. "I'll order pizza."

Anna said, throwing her arm around his shoulder, "Boy, you have a lot to learn, because grown folks don't eat pizza every day."

"They do if they want me to buy it."

Alex said, "Just get the grill hot. I'll treat since this occasion is centered around me and Nikki."

Anna said, "Well, I want steak then."

"I'll half y'all on it," RudyAnn replied.

I smiled. "Thanks, big sis, but you better wait and see the bill first."

The End

Next Release

Lonely Color Blue
(Janeen Cooper's Story)

I was lying on my queen-sized sleigh bed listening to some old tapes I had made when Teddy Pendergrass started singing, 'Lonely Color Blue'. A tear rolled down the side of my face and disappeared into my down-filled comforter, as he bellowed every word from his soul identical to the way Al Green had sang, 'I'm So Lonesome I Could Cry' minutes before him.

It was as if they knew exactly how I'd been feeling for the past seventeen years of my life. Even if every night Percy, my boyfriend of 12 years, did snuggle next to me, snoring in my face. Blue, lonely, and fighting a compelling urge to end my life as I had tried several times before—especially the first three years after my only child had been taken away from me.

But lately the need to put myself out of misery had returned, and my heart ached so much that it took a shot of anything we kept in our well-stocked bar to ease my pain. I knew Adam Sinclair was behind my son's abduction, but I had no proof. I also knew Adam wasn't so ruthless as to kill him. After all, Justin was his son, too.

Coming in Spring 2007

Born in Williamston, North Carolina, Sheila Peele-Miller has been married for over twenty years. She is the mother of four and the grandmother of two beautiful girls. In addition to writing, Sheila is a gifted artist. She enjoys writing about African American women and the struggles they face with family, friends, and conflicting relationships.

Sheila attended Pitt Community College and East Carolina University in Greenville, NC, where she majored in Commercial Art and Graphic Design. She currently resides in Chicago with her family and is working on her next novel, 'Lonely Color Blue.' Her first book, 'Painted Picture' was released in October 2004. The sequel to 'Painted Picture' is on its way. Sheila also writes poetry and short stories.

*** A Note from the Author***

Thank you for your support, patronage, and for taking time out of your schedule to read my latest creation. May God continue to bless you and your family and may all of your dreams, hopes, and wishes come true . . . *sheila pm*

Printed in the United States
55792LVS00004B/214-285